True Ghost Stories

Other Brad Steiger books
published by Para Research

Astral Projection

Kahuna Magic

TRUE GHOST STORIES

A division of Schiffer Publishing, Ltd.
77 Lower Valley Road
Atglen, PA 19310

International Standard Book Number: 0-914918-35-4

Typeset in 10 pt. Paladium on a Compugraphic 8400
Typesetting by Camilla Ayers, Barbara Kassabian

Manufactured in the United States of America.

Published by WHITFORD PRESS
A division of
Schiffer Publishing, Ltd.
77 Lower Valley Road
Atglen, PA 19310
Please write for a free catalog.
This book may be purchased from the publisher.
Please include $2.95 for shipping.
Try your bookstore first.

We are interested in hearing from authors
with book ideas on related subjects.

Contents

Introduction

Please consider this question:

Can a ghost turn a light switch?

Many rational, well-balanced people have reported, seen or heard ghosts and visual or auditory phenomena that are not caused by ordinary events. But it is not often that the house of a reputable doctor and psychiatrist is haunted.

Dr. S. Kahn lives in an old house near Croton, New York, originally built by a man who was killed by the Nazis during World War II. For some time an unseen presence had smashed doors shut, caused doorbells to ring when there was nobody outside, while the freshly-fallen snow showed no footprints. One night the Kahns had gone to bed early. They were alone in the house at the time. Suddenly, the lights in the bedroom went on by themselves. On inspection, Dr. Kahn found that the light switch had been turned on. They turned the lights off again and returned to bed. At this moment the heavy draperies covering one wall of the room began to move violently, even though there was no draft and all windows and the door were shut tightly. Drawing energy from living people, "ghosts," split-off parts of a personality who died under traumatic shock conditions, can sometimes cause physical phenomena to occur. Science calls them *poltergeists* or noisy ghosts. Usually, these are their primitive ways of getting attention to their presence in the house.

A woman in Kokomo, Indiana, writes:

My grandmother lived in a house dating back to 1834. I always spent four weeks of my summer vacation with her. One summer a few years ago I was walking down the front staircase, when I met a lovely young lady in an evening gown coming up the stairs. She was not shadowy or misty or transparent. I received the impression that if I reached out, I could touch her. The dress was of a filmy, pink material, belonging to the period of around 1850. Her hair was dark brown and her eyes also brown. There were tears in them, but when she saw me, she smiled and then passed me. I started to follow her, but when she reached the top of the stairs, she vanished.

When I told my grandmother, she did not believe me, so I let the matter rest. The following year my grandmother redecorated the house, using authentic old furniture, much of it from the attic. Picture my surprise when I saw hanging on the staircase wall a portrait of the lady I had met on the stairs!

She was not wearing the pink dress I had seen her in, but it was definitely the same woman. I discovered her identity through my grand aunt. The girl was a distant cousin of mine who had lived in the house for several years. She had fallen in love with a ne'er do well man, who died in a tavern brawl. When this happened, she threw herself to her death from those stairs. The family resemblence is very strong and I have often been told that I look very much like the portrait. I like to think this is the reason why she smiled at me. Incidentally, our names are the same. She was Elizabeth Mary and I am Mary Elizabeth, and we both have the same nickname, Libby.

When a person dies violently, a part of the personality may find itself tied to the spot where the tragedy took place. Such "ghosts" are reliving their final moments, unable to break free from their past emotional entanglements.

But there is a difference between the "earthbound," nearly psychotic *ghost*, and the free spirits who know their true status. Still, apparitions of the dead occur all over the world; the majority are not true ghosts, but what I have termed *stay behinds*, people who have passed across the veil, but for one reason or the other wish to communicate with the living.

There are thousands of verified accounts of such happenings in the files of reputable research societies, reports which cannot be explained by hallucinations or other means.

Take for instance the case of Margaret C. A few years ago, when she lived in New York State, she decided to spend Christmas with her sister and brother-in-law in Pennsylvania. The husband's mother had recently passed away, so it would have been a sad Christmas holiday for them.

Mrs. C. was given a room on the second floor of the old house, close to a passage which led to the downstairs portion of the house. Being tired from the journey, she went to bed around eleven, but found it difficult to fall asleep. Suddenly she clearly heard the sound of a piano, a very old piano, playing what sounded like church music. At first Mrs. C. thought someone had left a radio on, but a quick check found this not to be the case.

Over breakfast, Mrs. C. mentioned the experience to her sister. Without a word, her sister took her down the stairs where an old piano stood. It had been the property of her dead mother, but had not been played in many years, since no one else in the house knew how to play it. When the two ladies pried the rusty lid open they found that thick dust had settled on the keys. However, etched in the dust were the unmistakable imprints of human fingers, very thin, bony fingers! Prior to her passing, the deceased woman had been very thin indeed, and church music had been her favorite. Was the lady of the house still around, playing her beloved piano?

Mrs. Anna Arrington of Deposit, New York, writes:

> When I was a little girl, I once stayed home from school because of a cold. I was looking out the window when all of a sudden there was a strange woman standing next to me, a woman with big brown eyes. She came real close to my face before she vanished. I had never seen her before in my life.
>
> I almost fainted, and when Dad came home, I described her to him. He immediately recognized her as his aunt Maggie. At 6 p.m. that evening, a telegram came for Dad; his aunt Maggie had died exactly at the moment I saw her apparition in our house.

Mrs. Arrington's experience is far from rare. When ordinary communication is impossible, telepathic messages sometimes occur. Mrs. Arrington's natural psychic ability made her a good receiver for the last farewell of Dad's aunt.

Thus it appears that the old proverb "dead and gone" leaves much to be desired. The evidence for survival of human personality beyond physical death has been piling up in various research organizations for many years. There, it is not likely to inform the average person whose very life and outlook on existence might very well be affected.

It is therefore terribly important that writer/researchers like Brad Steiger come along and inform the general public through their books and lectures. What Brad Steiger presents is nothing less than the evidence for the existence of another life beyond this one. Most important, Steiger's work is couched in language and concepts everybody can understand.

Mr. Steiger deserves special thanks for his work in this area. It can be a lonely outpost indeed. It was to me, for many years, earlier in my career.

Ultimately, the more reserved members of the scientific community will have to learn the fact of life—or afterlife—from the likes of Brad Steiger.

Professor Hans Holzer, Ph.D.
Parapsychologist and Author
New York Institute of Technology
New York, New York

1

The Nature of Ghosts and Hauntings

"Key to the door of the Garden of Dreams," Giralda Forbes read aloud from the tag attached to the rusting key. "Just the kind of excitement that I am looking for," the girl said, removing the key from its hook. "Now all I have to do is find the door that it fits."

Giralda had been one of the few members of the family to be genuinely excited at the prospect of spending a summer in Italy in a somewhat decaying villa. The house and grounds retained an aloof grandeur, even though the roof leaked a bit, the lawns had gone to seed and the hedges had long ago grown into a wild tangle. However, it was an authentic Italian villa, and Giralda Forbes could not help falling under the romantic spell it cast.

Even after a month in residence, the Forbes family had not completely explored the house, and Giralda had begged off going on a family trip to Rome in order to have a chance to investigate all the shadowy corners of the sprawling mansion.

As she clutched the key, she was doubly glad that she had not gone with the family. She would have an adventure to tell them about when they returned. She would be the first to find the villa's "Garden of Dreams."

Giralda paused in the hallway and considered calling for Julia, the maid, to see if she had correctly interpreted the inscription on the key tag. Not the most gifted linguist, Giralda was nevertheless certain of her translation. She did not need Julia to read the inscription, and she doubted if the maid would be of any real assistance in locating the proper door. Besides, the key itself contained a clue. The word "garden" suggested that an enclave might be hidden in the garden or in the overgrown boxwood maze that occupied a large portion of the grounds near the house.

The broken down boxwood hedges proved to be greater barriers than Giralda had expected. She had to step over fallen branches and even break through some of them as she continued her search for the mysterious door.

Then, as she approached an old stone bench, she was overcome by a sudden rush of dizziness. Perhaps the day was too warm for such exploration...perhaps she had overexerted herself.

Giralda tried to move toward the stone bench so she could sit down, but the dizziness became so oppressive that she was forced to grasp the slim trunk of a tree for support and to close her eyes.

She had not stood there for more than a few moments when the vertigo passed as suddenly as it had come upon her. Giralda opened her eyes, blinked them rapidly in surprise. An old lady was now seated before her on the stone bench.

Giralda noticed at once the woman's eccentric manner of dress and her aged, though haughty, features. Rejecting a momentary fear of the strange woman, Giralda decided that her surprise visitor must be the family's landlady, whom Giralda had never met.

The aged woman's first words seemed to confirm Giralda's conclusion. In Italian she said, "I see that you've found the key."

Giralda felt uneasy and uncomfortable in the woman's presence. The cracking, aged voice had a strange quality that sounded as old as the woman's clothes looked.

"Yes," the girl answered finally. "It says that it is the key to the Garden of Dreams, and I am looking for the door."

"I did not think anyone would find the key," the old woman said. "Come, I will take you to the garden. It was once mine, you know."

The woman rose from the bench and took the key from Giralda. With a curt wave, the woman bade Giralda to follow her through a tangled maze to a spot that seemd the thickest.

Without hesitation the aged dowager reached among the branches and swept them aside to reveal an ancient wooden door in the side of a stone wall. The key fit the lock, and with a slow turn, the latch fell away.

The woman pushed open the door. It protested the disturbance with a sharp cry of rusted hinges. Beyond the door was a stone enclosure that Giralda estimated to be nearly fifteen square feet. The girl admired the symmetry of its planning; and, in spite of its rundown condition, she knew that it had once been a beautiful and obviously secret spot.

"Here love lived and died," the old woman said, her voice like the sound of a harpsichord struck in a deserted hall.

"Tell me about it," Giralda asked. "Who were the lovers?"

The woman told a story of two princes who had come from Cyprus to visit the province at the behest of the Duke. During a hunting trip, one of the princes had happened onto the estate. "It was his undoing," the woman concluded.

"Why?" Giralda wanted to know.

The woman leaned closer. "He was murdered," she said in a hoarse whisper.

Horrified, Giralda jumped back from the woman. She began moving toward the door.

The old woman cackled at the girl's obvious fright, then she became suddenly angry. "Do you know what it is to have your love betrayed?"

Giralda shook her head, convinced that the woman was not only eccentric, but also mad. She decided that it would be to her advantage to remain calm. "Was he murdered here, Madam?" she asked.

"No," the woman snapped. "In the house. Come, I will show you."

The dowager led the way through the maze of boxwood and entered the house by a side door. It was apparent that she was well-acquainted with the estate.

Once back in the house, Giralda looked around for the maid. She saw that the door to the basement was open and assumed the servant was doing some work downstairs. It was more than a little discomforting to Giralda to realize that her only assistance, in the event the old woman became violent, would be quite some distance away.

Yet the girl could not help following the woman. The strange old lady had a mysterious hold on her that was more compelling than the fearful images that crossed her mind.

Giralda was surprised when the woman continued to move in the direction of her own room. The girl blanched at the thought that a murder had been committed in the bedroom she occupied. She resolved to move from the room at once.

Entering Giralda's room, the old woman looked about and smiled. "This was once my room."

"And it happened here?" Giralda asked.

"No, not here," the woman replied, "but he spent his last night here."

She motioned for Giralda to help her move a small table from the wall next to the headboard of the bed. When this task had been accomplished, the woman pushed a nearly invisible bulge in the wallpaper, and an entire section of the wall folded back to reveal a steep, spiral staircase. The woman smiled in satisfaction, and directed Giralda to light a candle.

"Come," she bade the girl, and taking the candle, she proceeded up the stairway.

At the head of the staircase the spiraling channel seemed to stop abruptly at a wall. The old woman pressed another concealed button, and the paneling slid back to reveal a small studio that had been furnished with heavily stuffed pieces of furniture.

"This is the room," the ancient voice cackled.

"Was it here that he was murdered, Madam?"

The woman nodded, then, obviously becoming excited, shrilled in a high-pitched voice, "He made love to one woman while professing love to another!"

The ancient dowager crossed the room to stand beside a long chest that sat against one wall. "Here," she said. "His body is in here!"

"Who killed him?" Giralda whispered, horrified.

A strange light flared in the old woman's eyes. "I did!"

The jagged edge of fear pricked the base of Giralda's spine. Was it possible the old woman once had been capable of murder?

"The faithless one!" the woman spat. "After he had lain the night with the woman he betrayed, he came here to his own doom. Here we drank wine and here I stabbed him to death. No one ever discovered his body, and no one ever inquired about his disappearance. Only you know."

"Let us go down," Giralda said as calmly as she could. "I do not like your terrible story."

"First we must look in the chest," the woman insisted. She stopped to open the hinged top of the chest. "Come and see," she invited the girl.

"No," Giralda said resolutely. "I do not want to." She moved slowly to the door.

A surprised expression crossed the woman's face, then resignation and weariness took its place. She let the chest cover fall back.

Giralda heard the footsteps of the old woman behind her as she went down the spiral stairs, but the girl had decided exactly what she would do when she reached the bottom. She crossed her room to the bell pull and summoned the maid.

"Why did you do that?" the woman demanded.

"I'm feeling faint," Giralda told her. "I want to have a glass of water."

The old woman laughed. "You do not like me."

Giralda was suddenly enveloped by the same peculiar dizziness she had experienced in the garden near the stone bench. "I—I really must have some water," she said. Out of the corner of her eye, she saw the old woman hurry from the room.

In an instant, Julia appeared at the door. "A glass of water, please," Giralda said to the maid. "I'm feeling very faint. And show the old woman to the door."

Julia looked down the hall in bewilderment. "What old woman, Signorina?"

"There is no one in the hall?"

"No one," the maid assured Giralda.

Although she felt relieved, Giralda was perplexed. She did not receive an answer to the enigma until, a few days later, when Julia showed her the gallery of portraits of former residents of the villa. Among them hung a portrait of the old lady who had frightened Giralda. The woman in the portrait even wore the same costume as the woman Giralda had discovered sitting on the stone bench.

Julia smiled at the girl's obvious display of emotion when she was confronted with the painting. "Has she visited you, Signorina? They say her ghost still walks from time to time."

Giralda Forbe's own account of her ghostly confrontation appeared in *Everybody's* magazine and has since been reprinted in a number of publications as an authentic, face-to-face encounter with a ghost. Ungallant as it may seem, I think that the restless spirit of Miss Forbes' Italian murderess is made of the very pseudo-ectoplasmic stuff from which fictional ghosts have often materialized.

Real ghosts—and we shall see throughout this book that ghosts do indeed impinge upon the world of reality—do not engage in lengthy dialogues with those witnesses who perceive their ethereal presence. Real ghosts do (as did Miss Forbes' murderess) appear to be as solid and as material as a living being, but there have been few documented cases wherein there was any verbal interaction between the ghost and the percipient.

Also, as in Giralda Forbes' case, there may indeed be a strange sensation of chill, uneasiness or dizziness of which the percipient is aware before the image of the ghost materializes. But the extensive conversation which Miss Forbes claims to have shared with the ghost and the confession of murder which she heard from the earth-bound spirit, serve to place the whole report in the genre of imaginative fiction or, at best, a highly colored and greatly exaggerated account of an actual confrontation.

How, then, does a real ghost perform?

For one thing, a ghost acts more like an animated memory than a creature of independent intelligence. It is as if something has impressed a memory pattern upon a certain environment and the pattern, like a brief strip of film being fed into a projector keeps "remembering" the same bit of action night after night. The ghost-actor is as indifferent to the observers who see its performance as an actor on celluloid is to the audience in a theater. It would be as out of character for a ghost to take notice of someone and engage that percipient in conversation as it would be for an image on a strip of film to suddenly step off the screen and begin shaking hands with the moviegoers in the front rows.

Let us examine a classic case of a real ghost in action.

On a chilly autumn night in 1879, Dr. Augustus Jessop was concentrating only on the appreciation of his host's library. A dentist by profession and an antiquarian by avocation, Dr. Jessop had been invited to Mannington Hall, London, by Lord Orford, to spend the night in perusal of the many treasured volumes on the shelves of the family library.

At dinner the conversation had been light and animated. Nothing of a morbid or eerie nature had been discussed. When Lord Orford, his family, and the other guests had retired, Dr. Jessop had arranged full, bright illumination in the library and was busily taking notes from six of the rare volumes.

He first noticed the hand out of the corner of his eye. Resting about a foot from his left elbow was a large hand, very pale in color, with dark blue veins across its back.

Dr. Jessop raised his eyes to meet the penetrating gaze of a solidly built man who had come silently to share the desk with him.

The unannounced visitor had a lean, rugged profile and closely-cut, reddish-brown hair. He was dressed in a clergyman's black habit, and he sat in a posture of complete relaxation, his hands clasped lightly together. After a few awkward attempts at communication, Dr. Jessop realized that his anonymous companion was not staring at him at all; rather, the stranger seemed completely oblivious to Dr. Jessop's presence.

Dr. Jessop thought it a bit peculiar that he had not been introduced to the cleric earlier in the evening, but not for a moment did he suspect that his late evening visitor was anything other than a living person. It was when he was about to initiate another attempt at conversation that the silent clergyman vanished before his eyes.

Dr. Jessop was not one to be unnerved by such an occurrence. He concluded that he had witnessed what was commonly called a ghost, and with a shrug of his shoulders, he resumed his note-taking. The only reaction to the specter that he could later recall was regret that he had not had time to make a sketch of the phantom clergyman.

Only moments after Dr. Jessop had resumed his work he again noticed the large, white hands next to his own. The spectral cleric sat in precisely the same position as before, the expression on his face unaltered. The ghost sat, hands folded, in an attitude of contemplation.

It occurred to Dr. Jessop that he might be able to speak with the phantom. He was trying to frame just the sort of provocative question that might prompt a ghost to utter a reply, when the eerie impact of the situation suddenly struck him. The fear of the unknown that lurks within nearly everyone flooded Dr. Jessop's being. A nervous movement of his hands knocked a book to the desk, and at the sound the ghost instantly vanished.

Because of the reputation of the percipient, the story of the ghostly cleric in Mannington Hall was given wide circulation. Soon it became so exaggerated in the retelling by others that Dr. Jessop allowed the *London Athenaeum* to print an authorized account of the incident two months after the experience had taken place.

Dr. Jessop's character was above reproach, and it was well-attested that he was not the sort of man to engage in the recitation of fanciful stories. The doctor emphasized in the authorized telling of the incident that he had been in perfect health on the night of the visitation and had been in no way approaching weariness or fatigue. The ghost, he stressed, had not appeared wispy or cloaked in the traditional sheet. The figure had appeared completely lifelike, natural and solid enough to block the light from the fireplace.

The ghost Dr. Jessop witnessed was rather like a three-dimensional projection of a color slide. The phantom did not move, did not take notice of Dr. Jessop and certainly did not take him by the arm and lead him about on a tour of Mannington Hall. Again we might compare the specter to a memory pattern that had left a psychic residue powerful enough to make itself known to certain individuals when certain stimuli were present in the environment.

By now, perhaps, some readers will begin to protest my thesis about the impersonality factor involved in authentic appearances of ghosts. Some readers are thinking about the news stories of ghosts that smash furniture, throw objects through the air and pummel the hapless residents of a house. Others will recall some extremely personal experience when the image of a loved one appeared at the time of that person's physical death. Still others will remember when a wrist watch stopped, a picture fell from the wall or a dog began to howl—all at the precise moment of the owner's passing.

The time has come, then, to define our terms.

In the jargon of parapsychology—the branch of behavioral science that undertakes to examine such phenomena—a *ghost* is a stranger to the one who perceives it.

An *apparition* is well-known by the percipient and is instantly recognizable as the image of parent, sibling or friend. An apparition usually appears at some time of crisis—most often that of physical death—and usually appears only once.

A *vision* is the appearance of a religious figure, such as the Virgin Mary, an angel, or one of the saints.

A *poltergeist* is a projection of psychic energy that finds its center in the frustrated creativity of adolescence and emanates, therefore, from the living rather than from the dead. A poltergeist is a ghost only in common parlance. What links the two is the "spook-like" nature of the poltergeist which causes the invisible pseudoentity to prefer darkness for its violent exercises of tossing furniture, objects and people about the room. We shall include the poltergeist in this study because, as every investigator eventually discovers, hauntings may precipitate poltergeist activity, and the energy of the poltergeist may recharge dormant memories and set a ghost in motion.

Parapsychologists have long recognized four main classes of ghosts and apparitions.

There are the ghosts that habitually appear in a room, house or locale; the crisis-apparition, in which a recognized apparition is seen, heard or felt when the person represented by the apparition is undergoing a severe crisis—especially at the time of death; the post-mortem apparition, in which the recognized person represented by the phantom has been dead for a period of time; and experimental cases, in which a living agent has deliberately set about to project an apparition to a particular percipient.

Researcher G.N.M. Tyrrel saw the ghost or apparition as a "psychological marionette" projected by an agent in a time of crisis or great emotion. The projection of an apparition involves the same kind of mental machinery necessary to formulate an idea or to establish a pattern of thought.

To Tyrrell, this "idea-pattern" finds its sensory expression in the apparition, which has been produced by the dramatic idea of an agent. The apparition is an incomplete expression until it has found someone to receive its impression. Tyrrell held that this dynamic "idea-pattern" is both creative and purposeful for it manifests an urge toward a completion of its expression and is amazingly resourceful in adapting and adjusting means to ends.

Psychic investigator Edmund Gurney put forth the hypothesis that the collective sighting of a ghost is due to a sort of telepathic "infection." The percipient sees the phantom and, in turn, telepathically influences another person, and so on.

In his presidential address to the Society for Psychical Research in 1939, H.H. Price put forth his "psychic ether" theory of hauntings. Price hypothesized that a certain level of mind may be capable of creating a mental image which has a degree of persistence in the psychic ether. This mental image may also contain a degree of telepathic ability by which it can affect other minds.

Price's theory holds that the collective emotions and thought images of a person, who has lived in a house for some time, may have intensely "charged" the psychic ether of the place—especially if there had been such powerful emotions as fear, hatred or sorrow, supercharged by an act of violence. The original agent, Price theorized, has no direct part in the haunting. It is the charged psychic ether which, when presented with a percipient of a suitable telepathic affinity, collaborates in the production of the idea-pattern of a ghost.

A ghost, then, has nothing to do with the "supernatural." The appearance of a specter is an out of the ordinary occurrence, a paranormal happening if you prefer, but there is a "natural" cause for the manifestation of the ghost. Once science determines just how the energy released by intense emotions is able to permeate the matter of wood, stone, metal and gems and just how the furnishings of a room are able to absorb these vibrations, it will be as easy to "dehaunt" a house as it is to rid it of vermin.

Medical doctors have learned to deal with the unseen world of viruses; physicists have learned to work with such unseen lines of force as electricity; so shall it be, one day, with the "psychic germs" that infect haunted houses and the invisible field of force that dictates the mechanism of ghosts. I am confident that there will be a time in the future when the unexpected appearance of a ghost will cause no more alarm than the sudden appearance of a mouse in the pantry.

For some time now, certain psychic investigators have accomplished "cures" of houses that have been severely infected by "psychic germs." In one case, the researchers were called to an apartment where a young widow and her three children had nearly reached the limits of endurance in regard to a persistent haunting. Each night the apartment would be filled with ghastly sighs, groans and sobs. Mysterious whispers would seem to come from over one's shoulder. One of the children had claimed to have seen the ghost of a "sad looking woman" in his bedroom.

A bit of investigation disclosed that a disconsolate young woman had committed suicide in the apartment shortly before the widow and her children had moved in. The young woman had become addicted to drugs, and according to the medical examiner's theory, had attempted to accomplish a "cold turkey" narcotics cure in her apartment. As the doctor reconstructed the suicide, the young woman had purposely injected herself with a lethal dosage while in a period of pain and despondency.

The psychic researchers prescribed a complete remodeling of the apartment. On their suggestion, the landlord had the walls repainted, the plumbing replaced, and the metal window frames repainted with a good white lead paint. Even the electrical fixtures were replaced and the entire apartment was rewired. Once this had been accomplished, the ghostly disturbances never returned to frighten the widow and her children.

In the researcher's opinion, the walls, furnishings and fixtures of the apartment had absorbed the psychic vibrations of the suicide victim's last night of life and had soaked up the negative emanations that had led the young woman to take her own life.

Perhaps every old house, courtroom, hospital ward, apartment, railroad depot is "haunted." Any edifice which has been much used as a setting for human activity almost certainly has been saturated with memory traces of the entire gamut of emotions. But it may be this very multiplicity of mental images that works against the chances of a ghost popping up in every hotel room and depot lobby. An oversaturation of idea-patterns in the majority of homes and public places may have left only a kaleidoscopic mass of impressions which combine to produce the peculiar atmosphere one senses in so many places. It is only when an idea-pattern that has been super-charged with enormous psychic intensity finds the mental level of a percipient with the necessary degree of telepathic affinity that a *real* ghost can appear.

It is the *real* ghost, in all its many roles, faces and manifestations, that we shall meet in the chapters to follow.

2

Things Between
Heaven and Earth

The voice at the other end of the telephone line seemed to be nervously sincere, but I could not refrain from asking what appeared to be an obvious question: "Do you mean that you are actually afraid of this...this ghost?"

The man to whom I was speaking had been a tough and hardened combat paratrooper in World War II, and he was still a man with whom one would not wish to trifle in a physical confrontation. He took a deep breath, then sighed and delivered what was probably an unconscious paraphrasing of Hamlet's admonition to Horatio:

"All I'm going to say, Brad, is that there are a lot of things between Heaven and Earth that we simply do not understand, and the ghost of Lady Martha is certainly one of them!"

"But," I pressured slightly, "you have actually decided against having Irene Hughes and me visit the site of the haunting because you fear retaliation from this ghost?"

"We don't want you to come," he said frankly and directly. "Especially after what happened with your friend's tape recorder. Goodbye."

I held the buzzing receiver in my hand for a few moments, then returned it to the cradle. I was very disappointed, and I regretted having to call the famous medium Irene Hughes and tell her that what had sounded like a dandy haunting and a promising research trip had suddenly been cancelled by the percipients' fear of revenge from a touchy ghost.

As difficult as it may be for the skeptical reader to believe, there are sensible, well-educated, practical men and women who still fear the supernatural, the unknown.

Sophisticated moviegoers may enjoy being cinematically frightened and titillated by horror films and afterward engage in bold laughter and self-conscious analysis of the manner in which they were able to temporarily suspend reality and enter into the frightening illusion projected by the creators of the eerie motion picture. However, if you take these same sophisticated individuals, place them in an environment of moss-covered crypts, moldering mansions and mournful midnight sighs floating up circular stairwells, some peculiar atavistic mechanism transforms them into shuddering, haunted men and women.

Take for example, the hardnosed businessman who had just hung up on me.

A good friend of mine had called some days previously to inform me that he had found a dramatic instance of what seemed to be a classical haunting in his home town. According to the information he had gathered, the ghost of a strong-willed woman was haunting an entire office complex. The woman, whom everyone had respectfully called "Lady Martha" in life, was, according to certain percipients, even more imposing in death.

Lady Martha had been the kind of woman, who, opposed to smoking, would walk up to a total stranger on the street, slap a cigarette out of his mouth, and deliver a blistering lecture on the evils of nicotine. If cigarettes aroused her ire, beer and liquor drove her into an absolute frenzy of rage. Those who had known Lady Martha and her opinions said that her oratory on temperance and the wonderfulness of prohibition made Carrie Nation and her hatchet seem an ineffectual protestor.

Some time after Lady Martha's death, so the story was told to my friend, an executive in the office building which she had owned and in which she had maintained a top floor apartment shook a cigarette out of a pack on his desk. He hung the cigarette on his lower lip, reached for a match— but before he could light the tobacco, the cigarette *and* the pack on his desk had vanished.

A thorough search of the office could not turn up even one crumb of the executive's tobacco. Word began to spread that Lady Martha's "no smoking" rule still held firm in her office building. And, what is more, the lady herself was somehow still around to enforce it.

A clothing store located in the same building had been undergoing a series of peculiar happenings which seemed to reach a bizarre kind of climax one night after work when certain of the sales personnel decided to have a few relaxing beers in a basement storeroom. Since the salesmen were married and the saleswomen were young coeds from the local college, a decision was made to bolt the firedoor behind them so that someone would not happen upon their innocent after-work libation and misinterpret the scene to the men's wives.

As the beer was being distributed, one of the men jokingly commented that it was a good thing that Lady Martha was in her grave or she would be able to smell the booze in her basement.

According to all those in attendance on that occasion, the words had scarcely been uttered when the bolted door swung open with a violence that slammed it against the wall. Then, to their immediate astonishment and their subsequent fear, a shimmering replica of Lady Martha drifted into the storeroom and shook a scolding finger at each participant in the after hours beer bust.

When my friend, who is also a businessman in that same city, began to hear repeated accounts of such confrontations with the unknown in Lady Martha's office building, he called me and asked if he might arrange for psychic-sensitive Irene Hughes and myself to visit the scene of the manifestations. He knew that Mrs. Hughes and I were extremely interested in being present at psychically infected sites in order that we might test her ability to gain paranormal impressions of the origin of such phenomena.

I agreed with his assessment that he had uncovered a story with a most interesting investigative potential, and I asked him if he might tape record an interview with some of the percipients of the phenomena so that I might evaluate the material for myself before I made arrangements for Irene Hughes and myself to travel to his city.

My friend earnestly complied with my request, but it was that simple act of tape recording that led to the businessman's fearful squelching of our visit to the haunted office building of Lady Martha.

At first the businessmen had no objections to their taking time to give my friend an interview regarding the phenomena they had witnessed. They had no objections to my bringing Irene Hughes to the building for the express purpose of conducting a seance in that basement storeroom where Lady Martha's ghost had so dramatically and forcefully appeared. In fact, they remarked they would be honored to have so well-known and so well-respected a lady as Irene Hughes as a guest in their city.

But then, as a courtesy, my friend offered to play back the tape so that they would be able to hear their comments before he mailed the cassette to me. Unexpectedly, any time any of them mentioned Lady Martha's name the tape went blank, so that the tape was full of such lines as, "Yes, I remember the time that _____ stopped me in my office to lecture me about smoking. Boy, could _____ ever preach against man's enslavement to tobacco."

And that was that. The men blanched and looked warily about the room, as if expecting to see an angry, shimmering form manifesting itself in a darkened corner.

Before my friend left them that evening, the businessmen were no longer eager to have a psychic and a reporter of the strange and unusual visit their building. They had enough of the strange and unusual happening about them every day, thank you, and the little demonstration that evening had convinced them that Lady Martha did not wish to have any spook hunters prowling around her building.

More than one of the men expressed his concern that if things had been "funny" and "weird" up to then, think what it would be like if Lady Martha really got angry with them for bringing in outsiders.

"In other words, Brad," my friend explained over the telephone, "we have a situation in which a group of normally hard-nosed, tough-minded businessmen are actually afraid of a ghost. I'm sorry I blew it," he apologized. "I never should have played back the tape for them."

I told my friend that he could hardly be held responsible for the strange malfunctioning of his tape recorder, which had either presented us with a most peculiar audio coincidence or had provided us with a record of a dramatic kind of ghostly interference with a mechanical device. I did, however, ask for the home telephone number of the businessman who had been most eager for us to visit the haunted office building. I hoped that I might be able to appeal to him to persuade the others to change their minds and allow us to enter their offices for purposes of psychical research.

Although he seemed reluctant to speak with me, the businessman did accept my call. He remained unimpressed by my arguments, however, and stated bluntly that even if we were to travel the distance to his city, none of the men would speak with us and none would provide us access to the building. My last desperate ploy of attempting to shame a combat-scarred veteran of World War II by expressing my incredulity at the possibility of his being afraid of a ghost had only succeeded in his bringing our conversation to a rather abrupt close.

I must confess that this initial abortive attempt at a psychic safari with Irene Hughes proved to be an eye-opener for me. In my books, articles and personal appearances, I have spent a great many words attempting to demonstrate to skeptical reading, listening and viewing audiences that such things as telepathy, mind-over-matter, ghosts and prophecy do have a place in our world of reality. Now I had just had a representative of the conservative and practical world of business inform me that he did most certainly believe in a place of existence beyond our own. In fact, he believed in it to the point of fear.

A few weeks later, Irene received a letter from a woman in Wisconsin who feared for the health and safety of a close friend who was living in a haunted house.

Here, again, we had a classic case of a haunting that will surely sound as though it had all been devised by a writer of gothic romances.

First of all, the house harbored poltergeist phenomena. Everything from dolls to dishes might become instantly transformed into ghostly guided missiles that would often pelt the occupants of the house, but never seriously injure anyone.

The teenaged daughter would often find her room in disarray when she returned home from school, and she noted that this bit of mischief would occur most often after a morning when she had taken careful pains to straighten up her room before leaving home. On the other hand, if she were to leave her room in a mess, she would often find that some invisible "brownies" had set the bedroom in order for her—right down to the last curler and comb.

The phenomena seemed to be centered in the attic, and the family reported that they often heard the sounds of something heavy being dragged across the floor. Although the house was quite large, the entire family circle, which was composed of father, mother and three children, aged nineteen to six, slept in two rooms downstairs. No one slept upstairs.

On occasion, the mother told us, the teenaged daughter would adamantly announce that she was not to be driven from her room and she would often sleep alone upstairs for as long as two to three weeks. Then the sound of mumbled half-words about her ears and the stroking of invisible fingers against her cheeks and hair would at last drive her downstairs to join the rest of the family in the relative quiet of the two back bedrooms.

The other center of the haunting was located in the basement. The phenomena in the eerie area under the house consisted primarily of knockings, thumpings and the sound of footsteps running down the stairs and shuffling across the floor.

The most dramatic manifestation of the haunting was realized in the materialization of four skeletons, which after appearing in startling blood-red color, would slowly clothe themselves in the flesh of a man, two women and a young girl. Each of the images appeared in period dress of about the late 1900s.

While the members of the Wisconsin family watched in horror, a bizarre ethereal tableau unfolded before them. As the lovely, long-haired blonde girl sat idly playing with her dolls, the man in the ghostly drama strangled one of the women, while the other stood by with a pleased expression of immense satisfaction.

To all superficial assessments, it appeared as though the haunting might very well have been set into motion by a tragic playing out of the eternal triangle. At one time, so the eerie paranormal production number seemed to be telling its percipients, the man of the house had either strangled his wife, or his mistress, to please the other.

This time we received eager confirmation from the lady of the psychically infected house. She was not about to forbid our driving up to the small Wisconsin lumber town. In fact, she all but begged us to make the trip.

We had been in the home but a few minutes when I began to feel rather nauseated and decidedly uncomfortable.

I had heard and read other investigator's reports of being similarly affected by certain haunted sites, but I had never been so afflicted in several years of prowling about allegedly haunted premises. After all, my parental home had provided the family with a continuing phenomena of treading footsteps and opening and closing doors, so I had always felt quite at home in other houses with similar manifestations. But now I could no longer ignore that which was making me increasingly aware of one of the unavoidable requirements of the human condition: I needed to find a bathroom.

To cover my embarrassment, I suggested that while Irene and others of our party conduct a preliminary interview with the lady of the house, I should scout around a bit and see if I might not discover a "cold spot" of the haunting. After all, I pointed out, my tape recorder was running right at the lady's elbow, and the others were perfectly capable of opening the interview.

Interestingly enough, I did run into an obvious cold spot in the house as I searched for a bathroom, but its significance soon diminished in comparison with a subsequent development.

While I was in the bathroom, I could clearly hear the sound of what was ostensibly the youngest girl playing with her dolls. She was singing a kind of semi-tuneless little song, the kind of mumbled, melodic chant that seems to be universal with children, especially little girls, at play. From time to time, she would interrupt her humming song to call rather loudly for her mother. Then, when there was no response, she would return to her playing and her singing

As a father of two girls, I created a mental image of a little girl dressing her dolls, combing their hair, creating her own world of imagination with the aid of a semi-trance state partially induced by her play-time chant. I determined that the sound was coming from upstairs, almost directly above me. I had not yet learned that no member of the family, with the exception of that stubborn teenaged daughter, ever went upstairs alone.

When I rejoined the group, my discomfort had passed, and I was prepared once again to assume the role of a bold and fearless ghost hunter. I excused myself for interrupting the conversation in progress, announced that I had found a cold spot, then, with additional apologies for asking what may have been an already asked question, I inquired of the woman just how many children she had.

She replied that she had three: a son in his late teens, who did not always live with them at home; a teenaged daughter in high school; and a six-year old girl, her only child by her second, and present, husband.

"May we meet the children?" I wished to know.

"Oh," she apologized. "I sent them all over to friends' homes. I thought that you would rather work without the interruption of children."

Irene told her that was fine, that investigation undoubtedly would proceed much smoother without the presence of the children.

I was puzzled by logic that would dictate that she see to it that the older children were removed from underfoot, but retain the youngest child in the home, the child who would be most liable to pop up where she was not wanted. So I said: "I suppose the little girl will just stay upstairs and play with her dolls."

The woman blanched slightly and shifted uneasily in her chair. "My little girl is also at a friend's house."

I laughed, a bit louder than was necessary. "Then you'd better go upstairs and have a chat with her. She has come home to the company of her dolls."

"Upstairs?" the woman echoed. Her hand clasped her friend's arm for support. "You heard a little girl upstairs?"

I am not as dense as it may be beginning to appear to the astute reader. I was by now quite aware that this was one family who had a great deal of difficulty with their upstairs and that the woman sincerely believed her daughter to be at a friend's home. It was also obvious that the combination of these two factors had visibly unnerved the woman.

But my ears had heard too clearly the sounds of a little girl's song, of a little girl's call to her mother, of a little girl's play noises, for me to be convinced for even one moment that I had heard anything out of the ordinary, anything supernatural.

"Your little girl is upstairs," I said firmly, determined not to encourage any display of hysteria that might psychically feed whatever other ethereal organisms inhabited the house. "I heard her playing and singing."

"My little girl could. . .could not be upstairs," the woman answered softly. It was obvious that she was struggling to maintain control of her fear, trying not to permit her dread of the unknown to warp the sound of her voice. "She is afraid to go upstairs alone. Upstairs is where. . . ."

She seemed unable to complete her sentence and her trembling hands brought a coffee cup to her lips.

"Upstairs is where the most things happen in this house," her friend said, taking up the thread of the statement. "About the little girl. Did you hear it calling for its mother?"

"Yes," I acknowledged. "From time to time, she would pause in her play and call for mother."

"She and her husband," the friend went on, "often wake up at night or in the morning hearing that little girl calling for its mother. Whenever they check the kids, they find them all sound asleep."

It took a personal exploration of the upstairs, the attic, the basement and the yard to convince me that no little girl was playing somewhere in that home. If I truly heard what I believe that I heard in that Wisconsin home, then I either heard the sound of some lost and confused spirit-child, eternally calling for its mother, or I heard some ethereal kind of phonograph record, eternally reproducing the sounds of a former resident of that house whenever someone of the proper receptivity entered the environment.

However I might theorize about the haunting from the safety of a distance, the manifestations constituted a persistent living nightmare for the occupants of the home. The woman appeared to be suffering psychic battle fatigue from her constant confrontation with the paranormal incidents in her home. She would not walk in any area of the house other than the kitchen and the living room without someone at her side.

We explored the basement, wherein she had so often heard heavy footsteps, thuddings and scrapings.

We ventured up to the attic wherein the family had so often heard the sound of heavy objects being dragged across the dusty floor. As we opened the door, we caught sight of a wispy *something* retreating to a darkened corner of the cluttered storage area. (Had we seen a ghost, an ectoplasmic spirit or a floating bit of cobweb reflecting the sunlight?)

We visited each of the upstairs rooms and discovered two additional "cold spots."

Irene offered many psychic impressions as we walked from room to room. The woman gave immediate feedback to the psychic's comments, and in nearly all cases, she credited the seeress with direct "hits."

Suffice it to say that the case turned out to be even more complex than we had anticipated. There seemed to be factors working within the mother's own psyche that were psychically feeding the phenomena. And, while there was no immediate exorcism of spirit or entity and no instant erasure of memory pattern, I do think that Irene Hughes' counseling session with the woman proved to be of great value to the beleaguered housewife.

As I have indicated I generally favor the theory that a ghost is much more like an animated memory pattern than an entity of independent intelligence.

When I speak of ghosts, I am not referring to survival beyond the death experience at all.

In my definition, a ghost is not an earthbound spirit condemned to wander a certain environment until it finds peace, rather, it is a bit of ethereal drama that is for some unknown reason fixed in an atmosphere that has somehow trapped it in a pattern of re-runs that may last for centuries until the energy is dissipated.

Throughout man's recorded history and as contemporary as the morning newspaper, sober and respectable men and women have published accounts of their confrontation with ghosts. Innumerable people have witnessed ghostly phenomena, but only a few of the more courageous and unorthodox have had the bravery to study them and to begin to scrub away the stain of superstition that has clouded ghosts for so long. It is now becoming possible to admit that one believes in such phenomena without suffering the slings and arrows of outraged scientists.

The question, then, is not whether people see ghosts. There is sufficient evidence to convince anyone who has managed to pry open a previously closed mind the least little bit that people really do see ghosts. Psychic research societies and independent investigators have files that bulge with accounts of men and women who have seen, heard, smelled, even felt ghosts.

The question is: What is it that these men and women have experienced? What *is* a ghost?

I have given my opinion that even though a ghost may appear to be as solid and material as a living being, there can be no verbal or physical interaction between ghost and percipient, because it is only the image of the ghost that is there, not its spirit.

A ghost represents a once-living human being in the same manner that a photograph represents him. Both are images of that person that have been in some way impressed upon certain artifacts in the environment.

However, I must not be dogmatic with my theory. Dogma may well be the blight of learning and the curse of religion. It has always seemed to me that when one hears a learned gentleman insisting that something is so because someone *says* it is so, one can be reasonably certain that there remains a great deal of doubt about the matter under discussion. All of us, including our scientific High Priests, really know very little for certain about anything.

Since this is a book dealing with the phenomena of ghosts and haunted places, I shall probably do better by my readers if I readily concede that a ghost may be more than one kind of thing. A house may be haunted by the aforementioned concept of an animated memory pattern, but it may be disturbed by things that are entities in their own right.

Ghosts may be the spirits of those who left the earthly plane and found themselves irritated or discomforted by a task or tasks left undone.

Ghosts may be symbols of memory pictures projected by the percipient's own mind.

Ghosts may be entities from some other world—strange, other-dimensional night creatures that cross over from one plane of reality to another.

I freely admit that I am not competent to make any dogmatic assertions about the ghosts and the hauntings that I have witnessed in over twenty years of psychical investigation. I am a ghost-hunting, anomaly-seeking journalist, rather than a parapsychologist; but I am also the sort of reporter who cannot resist theorizing.

3

Uninvited Guests

An issue of the *Seattle Times* of a few years ago carried an interesting article by Don Duncan. The headline, "Nobody Believes in Ghosts—Not Even Nervous Hosts," is most revealing of Twentieth Century man's attitude toward the paranormal.

"I don't believe in ghosts," modern man says, "and even if I see one, I won't believe it unless it can be dissected in a laboratory, distilled in a test tube and blessed with the scientific seal of approval." The notion that man and his mind may be something other than physical things is currently not in vogue.

The Lake Washington family about which Duncan wrote is headed by a successful businessman, who neither drinks nor smokes. The man emphatically denies ever entertaining even the slightest belief in things supernatural. Then, six years ago, he and his wife and five children were confronted with a series of events which none of them found easy to fit into the scientifically approved scheme of the universe.

The manifestations began shortly after Mr. X, who insists on anonymity, moved his family into a practically new, split-level house in a fashionable suburb. The original owner of the house had moved out after only a few months of occupancy. A young couple had moved in and had signed a six-month lease. They, too, had vacated long before the lease expired. Mr. X had credited his ability to drive a hard bargain to the fact that he had acquired the house for $5,000 less than the F.H.A. appraisal.

"Almost immediately," Duncan writes, "'strange things' began happening. Dishes rattled in cupboards. Billiard balls clicked in the night. Mr. X's slot machines—he owns several for his own amusement—clanged mysteriously without the benefit of a human hand. Furniture rearranged itself in the dark."

As any "sensible" person would, Mr. X kept quiet about the manifestations. Using modern man's favorite scapegoat of "too much hard work and long hours," Mr. X was able to quiet a nagging awareness that things were not quite as they should be in his new home.

One afternoon as he was parking his car in the driveway, Mr. X was surprised to see an elderly couple dressed in "very old-fashioned" clothing at the living room window.

Mr. X entered the front door, announced his arrival to his wife, then asked her who was the "company" for dinner.

"What company?" Mrs. X wondered.

Mr. X told his wife about the elderly couple he had seen in the living room as he had parked the car in the driveway. It was obvious to both the man and his wife that no one was there. It was after that incident that Mr. X unburdened the whole story to his wife. The billiard balls that moved by themselves. The clanging of the slot machines. The moving furniture.

"I'm glad you've noticed it, too," Mrs. X sighed. "I thought I was going crazy."

"Just a few weeks earlier," Duncan writes, "Mrs. X. . .had been waxing the floors when, lo and behold, right before her eyes, two men—dressed in very old-fashioned clothing—walked out of the closet and down the hall and into the bedroom."

Their daughter, a college student, arrived home for a two-week vacation. Her mother and father left her at home before a roaring fire while they went out to have dinner in a downtown restaurant. When they returned, they found their daughter pale and shaken. "I'm leaving tomorrow!" the girl said.

Their daughter did not reveal the reason for her sudden departure until two years later.

While she had been sitting before the fire, watching the logs burn, ". . .a man walked out of the closet—right through the closed door—and went down the hall and into the bathroom. And that door was closed, too!"

The girl had run outside and stood on the lawn for two hours. Shivering with fear and cold, she at last convinced herself that she had been studying too hard and resolved to leave the next day so that she would not burden her parents with her problems of mental fatigue.

The weird phenomena increased their repertoire to include the swinging about of croquet mallets in the X's back yard. Mr. X watched the performance through a window on a sunny, windless day.

Mr. X invited a number of close friends—the kind who might scoff at such phenomena, but who would not laugh at the percipients—to come over one night and watch the "things" move the billiard balls around the table. Not at all shy about performing in front of company, "they" rolled the balls about the table in a lively manner. Mr. X's friends checked the table for wires or magnets, but they could find no evidence of any kind of rigging that would offer a "rational" explanation for the animated billiard balls.

"Sometimes you get the idea that 'they' are just pulling your leg and having fun," Mr. X told Duncan. "At other times, it seems 'they' are angry with you for some reason. My wife refuses to stay home at night."

Mr. X told the journalist of the time his wife screamed from the bedroom. He rushed to her side and followed her frightened stare to the smooth bedspread where he saw the indentation of a human body. Then, according to Mr. X, the indentation began to move, as if someone were sitting up.

The family has become somewhat adjusted to their uninvited guests. The two boys still at home with their parents speak of the "things" collectively as "Sam."

But, as Mr. X told reporter Duncan, ". . . it makes you downright nervous to try to get into the bathroom and find it locked.

"You hear the water running in the basin. You hear it shut off. Then the door swings open. Only there isn't anybody there."

Mr. X contacted the original owner of the house and was told that he got out "because the house was eerie. Strange things kept happening."

The young couple who had leased the house from him "could barely wait to get out the door."

In spite of living in such a psychically infected house, Mr. X remains true to his indoctrination. "I don't believe in spirits," he told Duncan. "No, I'm sure that I don't."

The impersonal nature of such a haunting is again to be noted. The ghosts that appeared in their old-fashioned clothing and disappeared into closets and bathrooms took no notice of the woman washing the floor or the girl sitting before the fireplace. As I said before, a filmstrip performer cannot react to his audience. He is bound by the commitment of life to celluloid to repeat eternally his performance whether the audience is bored or responsive.

The percipient who provides the proper stimulus to enable the memory-pattern of a ghost to manifest itself is never bored when the specter puts in an appearance. The percipients may, however, misinterpret the action as being directed at themselves or to be interacting with his presence.

The moving about of the billiard balls, for instance, indicates a high level of psychic activity, but it should not be interpreted as the ghosts performing for Mr. X and his friends by rolling the balls about on "cue."

On the other hand, certain of the manifestations, such as the moving about of furniture and the playing of the slot machines, seem very much like a bit of poltergeist activity interwoven with the haunting. There were two adolescent boys on the scene, and as has been previously noted, the poltergeist may be prompted into performing by a strong psychic residue in a house and, on the other side of the coin, the projection of a pubescent psyche may activate and intensify the memory-pattern of a ghost.

The George Glines family of Greenville, Mississippi, were hosts to their own private ghost for four years when they lived in Pensacola, Florida. The Glines family seemed to feel that the ghost emanated distinct feelings of friendliness toward them, even though there was never any physical interaction with the ghost.

Once again we do not have a highly improbable incident whereby a ghost awakens the head of the household in the pre-dawn hours and warns him of a fire that is blazing in the kitchen. Nor do we have a specter that occasionally materializes for droll conversation in the manner of the sophisticated ghosts Thorne Smith created in his *Topper* stories.

The ghost in the Glines home first came to light in 1962, when prospective son-in-law, James Boone, was an overnight guest.

The young man came downstairs in the morning looking pale and distraught. He told his hosts that he had awakened during the night with the eerie feeling that someone was standing in the room watching him. When he opened his eyes, he saw a man about six feet tall standing in the room.

Boone said that he at no time felt that the man was a burglar or that he intended to bring harm to any member of the household. "He just stood there watching," Boone explained.

When the young man reached to turn on the bed lamp, the man vanished.

George Glines had listened to Boone's account in silence. But when Boone paused in his narrative, Glines said: "Now let me tell you how he was dressed. He had on khaki pants and a plaid shirt, and his face was kind of hazy."

"That's exactly how he was dressed," Boone agreed.

"But how did you know, George?" Mrs. Gline demanded of her husband. "Do you know who this man is who prowls around our house?"

Glines admitted that he had seen the man before. "But he's not a man," he said, "I think we've got a ghost in the house!"

George Glines then told his family and James Boone that he had first seen the phantom two years before, when he had stayed home alone on the night of a hurricane. He had been lying on the couch in the living room with just one dim light on, when he had the feeling that someone was in the room staring at him. When he had looked up, he had seen a heavily built man about six feet tall wearing a plaid sports shirt.

Glines got up and moved toward the intruder. As he did, the man seemed to take a step backward and disappeared. Glines turned on the light, but the man was gone. He checked all the doors and windows, but they were all locked.

"I've never mentioned this before," Glines confessed, "because I didn't want to upset the rest of the family."

Mrs. Glines told John Childs, a staff writer for the *Delta-Democrat Times,* that her son, George, Jr., who was about two at that time, may also have seen the ghost.

Reminiscing about their four-year residence in the haunted house, Mrs. Glines remembered the time that she remonstrated with her son about playing on the stairs. George, Jr., looked at his mother and told her not to worry because his friend, Puki, would not let him fall.

When Mrs. Glines asked her son to describe this "Puki," George, Jr., told her that his friend wore work clothes and a bright, plaid shirt.

"I can't see his face very well, though," the boy frowned. "It isn't clear."

The Glines family reported that "Puki" gave supplementary evidence of his existence in the form of a knocking that would begin each night at about 11:00 P.M. The sound would come from a certain section of the living room wall, and, on several occasions, evening guests had also heard the mysterious thudding. At Glines' insistence, the landlord tore out the wall to determine if some natural causes might be producing the peculiar, nightly knocking. Nothing was found that could have created any kind of noise.

"As soon as the wall had been refinished," Mrs. Glines told reporter Childs, "the knocking began again and continued as long as we lived there."

Puki had one more ghostly accomplishment in addition to visual materialization and wall knocking. The khaki-clad ghost was also able to produce the sound of running footsteps. Members of the Glines family testified that the sound of the footsteps sounded so natural and so lifelike that one never became alarmed at hearing them—until he remembered that he was all alone!

The house burned in May 1964. Although the home was not totally destroyed, George, Jr. dutifully reported that ". . .Puki doesn't like the house all burned. But he said he might come back when it is all fixed up again."

Mrs. Glines told reporter Childs that they did not stay to find out whether or not Puki returned. The family had decided to move back to Greenville, Mississippi.

A word might be said at this point about the apparent communication between the ghost and the two-year-old boy. Although a telepathic linkage between the boy and the phantom cannot be completely ruled out, it would seem more likely that the ghost had materialized in the child's presence on numerous occasions and that the boy had thereby christened it "Puki" and made a playmate out of the specter, much as any child would with any other interesting or attractive inanimate, yet material, object.

In a magazine article of a few year ago, Joe Hyams, the journalist husband of actress Elke Sommer, revealed that several witnesses had observed a ghost in their home in Beverly Hills, California. On each occasion on which the ghost materialized, it was described as a "husky, broad-shouldered man, around 50 years old, wearing dark slacks, a white shirt and black tie. His hair was thinning at the top and he had a bulbous 'potato' nose."

In addition to frightening a number of friends who were staying overnight in the Hyams' home, the ghost indulged in such physical activity as turning the electric lights on and off; opening windows and doors; and reproducing sounds of moving chairs in the dining room. At the time at which Hymans wrote the article, he reported that termite inspectors, private detectives, electronics experts and thirty-six sensitives, mediums and psychic investigators had not been able to rid the house of the persistent ghost.

In one of his essays on ghosts, Dr. Nandor Fodor mentions that often the tradition of the "family ghost" may serve to fortify the intensity of the idea-pattern of the phantom. It is as if each succeeding generation serves to give the family spook another psychic charge of rejuvenation.

Rocky Hill Castle, an old Southern mansion, was built by Reverend Thomas Saunders near Courtland, Alabama, in 1828. Until recently, the castle still sheltered Rev. Saunders' descendants—and the family ghost.

Once, when he was queried by reporters as to the reason why the Saunders family remained on the old estate, Saunders replied simply that they "...just happen to love the place."

During the interview, Saunders told the journalists that they had, on certain occasions, heard the clanking of chains coming from the basement. Upon investigation, Saunders said, nothing was seen that could have produced the mysterious noises.

On other occasions, they had heard a persistent tapping coming from the basement. It had long been a joke in the Saunders family that the sounds were the knocking of the two dead brothers who built the castle.

Mrs. Saunders recalled the time that she had seemed to sense the presence of someone in the room with her. "Whenever I turned to look over my shoulder, I would see no one," she said.

The strong feeling that someone was still with her remained, until, finally, Mrs. Saunders dared the thing to "speak or go away and leave me alone."

"Whereupon, according to Mrs. Saunders, a voice whispered: "Sister, do not be doubting for I am truly here." Later that same day, Mrs. Saunders was descending the staircase when she was startled to see a woman attired in the swirling petticoats of the antebellum South standing at the foot of the stairs. As a number of nearby towns were celebrating centennial observances at the time, Mrs. Saunders assumed that a solicitor for funds for some historical project in connection with a pageant had slipped into the castle without bothering to knock. Mrs. Saunders recalls that she did not for one moment suppose that the smiling lady at the bottom of the staircase was anything other than a living person.

When Mrs. Saunders reached out her hand to welcome her unannounced visitor, the costumed lady vanished. It was as if the voice had materialized the body to demonstrate to Mrs. Saunders that it had been "truly there."

Mr. Saunders had been a patient sufferer through all the weird noises in his old family mansion, but he was skeptical about his wife's account of the disappearing lady in swirling petticoats. He had never seen the family ghost, and although he was forced to accept the unaccountable noises in the basement, he did not believe in materializing and dematerializing spooks.

A few days later, when Saunders was in the basement on an errand, he was offered dramatic evidence which changed his mind about the reality of ghosts. There, sitting on a trunk, was a Southern belle from the Alabama of long ago.

The family ghost, built up through generations of psychic reconstruction, can almost become an independent mental mechanism. Whether or not the ghost actually whispered to Mrs. Saunders, or whether, because of the heightened psychic sensitivity, she was able to "feel" the presence of the ghost prior to its actual materializaton makes for interesting speculation. Some eerie and highly dramatic tales have been told about "family haunts," but it is the very nature of their high drama that makes their authenticity suspect. Stories that have the ancestral haunt advising the head of the household in financial matters or revealing secret passageways or whispering messages of assurance seem most often to be cases of the percipeint "wishing" a ghost might behave in such a manner.

Perhaps it is again time to answer some objections to the contention that all hauntings are impersonal in nature. We are speaking in this book of *ghosts*, "psychological marionettes," projected "idea-patterns." This book in no way concerns itself with the alleged communications of discarnate personalities from the spirit world, who "return" for the express purpose of relaying messages of importance.

Such spirit communication has been attested to in both the religious and secular literature of man since the earliest days of his recorded history. I have personally recorded the stories of those who have claimed such contact from a deceased loved one—spontaneously and outside the draperies of a seance room—and certainly these people believe that they have been given sufficient proof of spirit survival. But the type of ghost that we are examining in this book has little to do with the survival question.

Our ghost is composed, perhaps, of equal parts of psychic residue, ethereal impression and animated idea. Our ghost is not a "soul" or a "personality," but rather the impressions which a soul left behind in an emotion-charged situation.

No discussion of "family ghosts" would be complete if it did not consider a few of England's famous ancestral haunts.

Servants at Sandringham, the country house of England's royal family, have been finding it difficult to sleep for many generations. According to those who have inhabited the servants' quarters, the rooms are haunted.

According to one maid several years in service of the royal family, the disturbances always begin on Christmas Eve. Once the ghost has dumped the Christmas cards on the floor and mussed up the beds, ". . . we can look forward to enduring the ghost's pranks for from six to eight weeks."

The housemaids have known for generations that the most haunted spot is that of the sergeant footman's corridor on the second floor. Maids refuse to go there alone, and they clean and dust that corridor in small groups.

The ancestral ghost is noted for reproducing the thudding of footsteps in the corridor, the opening of doors when no one is near them and the clicking on and off of light switches. Its most grisly accomplishment, according to one sergeant footman, whose lot it was to occupy the room, is to sound like ". . . a huge, grotesque lung, breathing in and out. No man can sleep under those conditions."

Most of England's ancestral ghosts have marvelous old legends of unrequited love or grim murder to account for their presence, but I have been unable to determine any particular background incident which could have put Sandringham's ghost in motion. However, Longleat, one of England's largest and most elegant Elizabethan mansions, has been virtually saturated with history, legend and tragedy since its completion in 1580. Of special ghostly prominence is the "haunted corridor" where in the 1730s, the Viscount Weymouth was said to have strangled his wife's lover.

Psychic sensitive Tom Corbett provided readers with an account of some behind-scenes activity of an eerie nature which took place during the filming of NBC television's *The Stately Ghosts of England* in an article for *Fate* magazine.

Such spirit communication has been attested to in both the religious and secular literature of man since the earliest days of his recorded history. I have personally recorded the stories of those who have claimed such contact from a deceased loved one—spontaneously and outside the draperies of a

According to Corbett, microphones went suddenly and inexplicably dead, film taken in the mansion "turned out muddy," (in spite of the fact that two sets of recently inspected cameras had been used) light cords were unplugged at crucial moments and a series of annoying minor accidents plagued the crew.

The chief cameraman, who had entered the nursery on the third floor in search of a prop, felt "something oppressive and cloying" envelope him. He left the nursery in extreme shock and later said that he thought he would have suffocated if he had not been able to wrench himself away. The chief cameraman was not a fellow to start at mysterious noises and weird shadows. He had been decorated twice for valorous service during the war.

On another occasion, two young journalists had come upon the scene to have a bit of sport with the "cranks" who were making a film about ghosts. To get them out of the way, Corbett suggested that they go up to the Bishop Ken library. There, Corbett told them, they could see two pictures painted by Adolph Hitler and one by Winston Churchill. The Marquess of Bath gave them her permission and the key, and the journalists went up to the third floor.

Corbett writes that the young men returned less "full of their own importance." After they had seen the beautiful collection of books in the library, they had locked the door and started down the haunted corridor.

"They had gone only about twenty feet when they both heard a key being turned in the door." Startled, one of the young men shouted that he had the key. "Nevertheless they hurriedly retraced their steps and saw, to their amazement, the handle being turned. They did not investigate this occurrence, knowing that they had just locked an empty room...."

Those who watched the NBC special that evening remembered that the cameraman did indeed get "something" on film.

A weirdly glowing light came out of one door in the haunted corridor, bobbed about, moved about ten yards down the corridor, then disappeared into another door on the same side of the corridor. This light appeared on the film "from no known source" for nearly half an hour. Mysteriously, the usable footage had dwindled to eleven minutes by the time technicians began to edit the film for television. Corbett muses that such is the nature of ghosts.

There is a brick mansion on the corner of New York Avenue and 18th Street, Washington, D.C., that harbors a ghost and a legend to go with it. Built in 1800 by Colonel John Taylor, the stately mansion, known as the

Octagon, was used temporarily as an executive residence by President James Madison when the British burned the White House during the War of 1812. Today the mansion is an historic shrine and the national headquarters of the American Institute of Architects.

Caretakers and maintenance men have long told eerie tales of moans, groans and shifting furniture. A gardener told a journalist that he had heard "groans of distress" follow him up the stairs. A former caretaker told of the sounds of invisible feet, which he had often heard walking up the stairs.

The "eye" of the haunting seems to be the stairwell. It is proper that this should be so, for, according to legend, one of the young women of the Taylor family either fell or leaped to her death down the elegant stairwell. A maintenance man admitted that each morning upon opening the mansion he found the rug turned back at the foot of the stairway. According to the legend, this was the spot at which the young woman had died over 150 years ago.

A hostess at the Octagon has said that she has seen no ghosts, but she has watched the chandelier in the stairwell sway as if a hand moved it. The hostess is at a loss for a rational explanation to explain the swinging chandelier. There is no draft in the house nor any kind of vibration that could set the ornate fixture to swaying.

Another maintenance man recalled that, a few years ago, every bell in the mansion would begin to ring at a certain hour every night. That particular disturbance has ceased, but according to some observers, there remains enough activity in the Octagon to qualify the mansion for the title of "The Capital's favorite haunted house."

4

The Glowing, Swirling "Something" in the Darkened Lane

"You know, Brad," Angie McWane told me in May of 1971, nearly a year after my midwestern psychic safari with medium Irene Hughes, "I can still see that sparkling, shimmering, swirling something that formed before us on that spooky lane leading to the old Sumter house."

She gave a tiny shudder of recollection, then went on, "Some nights I even awaken and imagine that I can see it forming right in my bedroom!"

The eerie sight certainly had been impressive, and I don't think any of us who witnessed it on that warm July evening will ever forget it. In Angie's words, we "can still see it," building up before us like a misty collection of errant moonbeams.

Had we seen a ghost?

I don't know; but whatever it was, we all saw it on two consecutive nights.

On the first night our psychic safari had just arrived in Iowa City, and Glenn McWane, our host in that city and a friend of mine who would be accompanying us, suggested that we drive out to take a look at a house that he had lined up for Irene's psychic inspection. It was midnight by then, the witching hour and all, but I am certain that our crew did not believe the "high-dark" twelve to be any more magical than the "high-noon" twelve.

Glenn was driving my station wagon, and he edged it cautiously into the lane. "We can only drive in just enough to get off the street," he explained.

We soon saw the reason why when the headlights picked up the image of a wooden gate bearing an inscription advising any trespassers to keep out or risk being prosecuted.

"I've arranged for the caretaker to be with us tomorrow," Glenn told us. "I've also asked a policeman to accompany us just to be certain a passing squad car doesn't pick us up as vandals."

"This looks like a jungle," Irene complained, referring to the heavy overgrowth of weeds and bushes and the thick, drooping branches of untrimmed tree that virtually blanketed the narrow lane. "Where's the house?"

"I don't think you will be able to see more than the edge of it through all these trees," Glenn said. "It's hard to believe that this was once one of Iowa City's loveliest estates. But time and vandals . . ."

"What's that?"

I don't remember who first saw it and cut off Glenn's explanation of how the ravages of time and disinterest had wiped away the old estate's beauty, but no one had to point out the sudden intruder upon the dark and quiet scene. It appeared, to me, to be a very large, glowing orb of wispy light.

"Turn out the headlights, Glenn," I said.

"Yeah," Glenn nodded, pushing in the light switch, reading my thoughts, "maybe they're reflecting off something."

The strange orb glowed as brightly in total darkness with the headlamps shut off. Whatever the thing was, it seemed to have an independent light source.

The moon was covered by clouds that night. The nearest street light was a vapor-light, completely cut off from the old estate by the thick wall of trees. Actually, it would have been difficult for a powerful searchlight to have penetrated the tangled greenery and heavy plant growth and reached the dark pocket in the lane where the eerie light was glowing.

"How far away is it?" someone asked from the backseat of the station wagon.

"I would say that it is in the lane opposite the front door of the house," Glenn replied. "And that's probably forty to fifty yards from where we are sitting right now."

Glenn turned the headlights back on, and it appeared, whether optical illusion or what, that the orb of light was moving toward the old house.

Everyone turned to look at Irene, who was seated in the middle of the backseat. In the dim glow of the dashboard lights, I noticed a rather strange expression on her face, and it had occurred to me that she had been extremely quiet during our excitement over sighting the weird light.

"Shall we go right now and investigate the . . . whatever it is?" someone wondered.

"No," Irene answered, breaking her silence. "Not tonight. I have a very bad feeling that it would not be good for us to walk down that lane right now."

There was a certain tone to her voice that indicated she meant exactly what she said. Her psychic impression told her that the time was not right to invade the darkened lane and approach the shimmering orb that seemed more and more to be drifting toward the deserted house.

"Let's leave...*now!*" Irene said suddenly.

No one argued with her.

It was nearly midnight again on the second night when we approached the eerie mansion that had been so recently violated by vandals and frequented by some nameless thing that had been witnessed by several neighbors, as well as by the police.

"I got my lead on this house from some cops," Glenn had explained.

"Before the house was vacated, two old sisters lived alone here. Nearly every night a glowing, ghostlike *something* would appear, and the sisters would sit calmly and converse with it. On several occasions, the police got calls from neighbors who had seen the thing. I don't know what these people thought the police should do about the spook-light, and I guess the police didn't know either. They would just sit in their squad cars outside the house and watch the two old ladies talking with the glowing ghost. After one of the sisters passed on and the other was taken to a nursing home, the ghost-light continued to make its appearance every now and then."

Earlier that day, in the company of the caretaker, we had walked around the house and allowed Irene to pick up psychic impressions about its past inhabitants. I'll present that material a bit later, but right now, I would like to relate details of our second spotting of the ghost in the lane.

On this night, we had the caretaker and a policeman with us in the station wagon. We opened the gate, drove cautiously down the lane. When we were adjacent to the old house, Glenn stopped the car.

"Let us just sit quietly for a few moments," Irene requested, "and permit me to gain some psychic impressions of the house by night."

As Irene sat in meditation, I glanced absently out the windshield.

I blinked my eyes rapidly. I wanted to be certain that I was really seeing something before I nudged the policeman who was sitting next to me.

Unless I was badly mistaken, there seemed to be a slight tendril of mist-like substance forming directly in front of the station wagon's hood. Only a few more seconds of observation were necessary to convince me that my eyes were not playing tricks on me. I nudged the policeman.

"I see it," he said before I could whisper any comment to him.

"What is it?"

"Dunno," he replied honestly.

"I've been watching it for a couple of minutes now," Glenn whispered in response to our overheard conversation. "It seemed to come from that clump of bushes over there, then stop directly in front of the car."

By now everyone was watching the glowing, mist-like thing, and we all sat in silence for a few moments, as we watched the orb growing larger and denser.

Glenn turned the headlights back on, and we could see that the substance was palpable enough not to be dissipated by the powerful headlamps.

Glenn shut the lights off again, and we decided to get out of the car for a closer inspection.

"Is it ectoplasm?"

"A will-o'-the-wisp?"

"Maybe it's just night fog."

The small group of people who had accompanied us offered their queries and conjectures, as we surrounded the swirling, glowing, mist-like thing.

It was a very warm evening, but as I extended my hand into the mist, I seemed to feel cold. Or was that only my imagination?

"Could it be just a puff of vapor squeezed out of the cooling ground?" I asked the policeman.

"But why isn't there more of it?" he answered with a question of his own. "I mean, there's that field over there, and it doesn't have any mist in it. Here's all these trees and bushes, and there isn't any mist among them. Why is it forming just in this spot right in front of the station wagon?"

But then the thing seemed to be weary of our conjectures and our examination, and it was suddenly gone.

Before we could speculate on this rapid disappearance, Irene whispered loudly from the other side of the station wagon: "There are some people coming through the bushes by the house!"

I did not hear the sounds of footsteps and crackling brush myself, but others in the group swore that they could hear the approach of two or more people coming toward us.

Then the footsteps stopped, and one of our group directed our attention to the reappearance of the glowing mist between two trees. But before anyone could approach it, the light winked out as rapidly as if it had been an extinguished candle flame.

I moved to Irene's side.

"I swear they looked real to me, more than spirit," she was saying to Glenn. "But, of course, spirit can sometimes appear just as real as . . ."

"Did you see anything, Glenn?" I asked my friend.

"A white, misty thing that moved," he told me. "Right over there." He stabbed the spot with a beam of his flashlight. "We had seen it before."

"We heard something walking through leaves and pushing aside the bushes," Irene said. "When I looked over there, I saw the forms of people moving toward us."

"I could only see this glowing glob," Glenn said almost apologetically.

"Perhaps Irene's greater sensitivity enabled her to see images where you could only see this glowing mist," I offered.

Irene suddenly put her hands to her ears.

"What's wrong?" Glenn and I chorused in sharp whispers.

"I hear someone screaming, screaming just terribly! She's calling for help!" Irene replied. "Oh," she said, feeling the pain in a momentary jab, "she's broken her leg."

"There! There in the bushes." Irene directed us. "See her head?"

"I see some of that glowing mist again," I told her.

"Yes," Irene agreed, "but look. I can see her very clearly."

"I see a clump of mist," Glenn said. "I guess Brad and I aren't tuned in enough to the vibrations around here."

"Well, there are plenty of vibrations around here to tune in to," Irene remarked. "Wow! This place is just drenched with psychic vibrations."

We were unable to chase down any of the clumps of glowing mist and observe any of them transform themselves into clear images of men and women. Had our extrasensory receptors been tuned as finely as Irene's, we might have been able to see the psychic pictures much more clearly.

It appeared as though the sound portion of the ethereal broadcast had been received well enough, as several members of our midnight expedition insisted they had heard the sounds of footsteps and brush being parted. However, other than on Irene's super-set, the video portion of the program had been very blurred.

All of us had seen the glowing, mist-like clumps, but none of us, other than the sensitive Mrs. Hughes, had been able to adjust the "fine tuning" within our psyches enough to enable us to pick up a clear picture of the images that had been preternaturally recorded on the grounds of the old estate.

Earlier that day, Irene had walked around the estate with Mr. Roberts, the caretaker, and she had offered her psychic impressions of the former inhabitants of the Sumter place. We were unable to enter the home, because of the condition of the floors after several groups of vandals had struck the house to strip it of its valuable antiques.

The Sumter sisters, as well as their parents, had been real packrats and had never thrown anything away. According to Glenn's policeman friend, who had inspected the empty home during an early report of a mysterious light moving through the house and had seen the place before the vandals had looted it, the Sumters had never even disposed of newspapers and magazines. The floors were stacked with nearly a century's worth of periodicals.

Here is a slightly edited transcript of Irene's psychic impressions of the old Sumter house in Iowa City:

Irene: I feel that they lived more in the upper rooms than in the lower. Is that correct?

Roberts: Yes, that's true.

Irene: I see an old woman dying in the house.

Roberts: Yes, that's correct.

Irene: The father had a mustache, wavy hair and was meticulous with his personal records.

Roberts: Yes, absolutely. That's him.

Irene: One of the daughters was named Elizabeth.

Roberts: Yes.

Irene: The two daughters were different in every way, complete opposites.

Roberts: That is very true.

Irene: One left while she was quite young and married a man in uniform.

Roberts: Correct.

Irene: I receive a psychic impression that there were two rows of trees that once lined the driveway.

Roberts: Yes, that is so.

Irene: I get the name Floyd.

Roberts: That means nothing to me in relation to the house.

Irene: I feel that a lawyer spent a good deal of time in this house.

Roberts: That may well be so.

Irene: He was a big, jovial man, who liked to play chess with the father.

Roberts: I can't say yes or no to that.

Irene: Did they have plans to enlarge the house that were never carried out?

Roberts: That's very possible.

Irene: I feel that there have been three brides in this house, although one only stayed for a little while.

Roberts: I. . .I think that would be true.

Irene: The father was very violent verbally.

Roberts: That would probably be a fair characterization.

Irene: He kept some speckled hunting dogs.

Roberts: They always had a good many hunting dogs.

Irene: They also had a parrot.

Roberts: I was reared next door, and I remember, or seem to remember, that they had some kind of unusual bird when I was a boy. It may have been a parrot.

Irene: One of the daughters enjoyed painting and sketching.

Roberts: That's very true.

Irene: In her later years she had to spend a great deal of time in a wheelchair.

Roberts: True.

Irene: The father liked to make things in a blacksmith shop.

Roberts: Yes, he kept a small shop in that shed out in back.

Irene: Really? Well, we haven't been out back yet, so I didn't see that.

Roberts: You wouldn't be able to tell it was a blacksmith shop, anyway. It just looks like a shed now.

Irene: They raised guinea hens, did they?

Roberts: Yes, yes, they did.

Irene: I get the names Bullard and Wilson.

Roberts: Those names don't mean anything special to me, but the Sumters were always entertaining and having big parties.

Irene: The family liked to sing.

Roberts: Oh, yes! When I was a boy, many was the evening that we could hear them gathered around the piano singing away for all they were worth.

Irene: One of the daughters became very childlike as she grew older.

Roberts: Yes, that is true.

Irene: Oh, and I see that one of their prized possessions was a cabinet with carved legs and glass doors.

Roberts: Yes, that is correct.

Irene: Did they keep a family cemetery on the grounds?

Roberts: Yes, they did. It was supposed to be moved away when this part of town was annexed to the city, but there were rumors that they hadn't really complied with this ordinance.

Irene: Did you go over some legal papers with one of the daughters just before her death?

Roberts: Yes, I did.

Irene: Was the name Claude important to this family?

Roberts: Yes, it certainly was.

At first Mr. Roberts had been very skeptical of the idea of a psychic tromping about the grounds of the Sumter estate, seeking to pick up impressions from the past inhabitants. He had been quite reluctant to take time for such obvious foolishness, and it had taken a good measure of Glenn

McWane's persuasive abilities to convince the caretaker that he should bother with us at all.

It was most interesting to watch Mr. Roberts' obvious change of attitude as his exchange with Irene Hughes brought him deeper and deeper into a mysterious territory, the boundaries of which he had never before dreamed of transgressing. He knew that there had been no way in which Mrs. Hughes could have gained any information about the house and its inhabitants.

All Glenn knew of the house was that some policemen had seen strange lights moving around inside. Neither Glenn nor myself had researched the Sumter house in any manner whatsoever, and it is doubtful that even the most exhaustive search of public records would have turned up the personal details that Irene Hughes had siphoned from the psychic atmosphere of the old house.

The caretaker was, in a word, impressed, and I asked him afterward how he would assess Irene Hughes' percentage of accuracy in her statements about the Sumter house.

He grinned, and his answer came quickly and easily. "I'd have to give her a 90 percent," he admitted, "and it would probably be higher if there was some way to check out every name she gave. Really, just about everything she said fit in. I don't know how, but she really knows what it's all about!"

In my opinion, Irene Hughes utilized a particular facet of her ESP, that is, psychometry, to pick up an enormous amount of details, names, and accurate data about the Sumter place.

When it comes to that "something" in the lane, however, I'll have to acquiesce to Irene's oft-stated dictum that "spirits may sometimes return." I did not surrender without quite a struggle, and I may yet rally and find a way to make my theorization applicable.

A most irritating and eerie postscript to this case occurred approximately one calendar year after our psychic safari to this home when Glenn McWane and I were conducting follow-up research on the sites which we had visited.

We pulled into the lane about midnight in the company of a number of other men and women. We took careful notice of a wire stretched across the lane. Someone, undoubtedly the caretaker, had strung a number of white and red strips of cloth from the line. We switched out the headlamps, prepared to await the "something" which had been sighted by Glenn and a university professor just a few nights before.

Although we did not see the thing crossing the lane in its traditional spot, a column of light about the size of a human being appeared off to the right of the automobile. When Glenn snapped the headlamps on, we were startled to see that a three-tine pitchfork had been stuck in the ground a few feet in front of the station wagon.

I must confess that my attention had been directed to a spot farther down the lane from the moment that we turned into the drive; therefore, I cannot swear that the pitchfork had *not* been there before the headlamps were extinguished.

Glenn, whose powers of observation are extremely acute, insists that the pitchfork was not there before he switched the headlamps back on bright. He is supported in this allegation by everyone else who was in the party that night. All of us had to admit that we had not seen the pitchfork before the headlamps were turned on again. Glenn argues that since the pitchfork had been driven into the ground just in back of the white and red strips of cloth — and since everyone had commented upon this colorful addition to the environment — we would certainly have noticed such an obtrusive element as a pitchfork directly behind them.

If that shimmering column of light truly planted that pitchfork before us, then I must admit that I cannot imagine a "memory pattern" being quite so animated.

5

Quiet Haunts

Historical artist John Alan Maxwell had his studio at 51 West Tenth Street in the heart of Manhattan. Maxwell had worked hard through a warm spring day in 1948, and he decided to relieve the tension that afternoon by taking a brief catnap. He checked the lock on the door, stripped off his clothing and, after tossing the slip cover from his couch, pulled a sheet over his naked body and instantly fell into a sound sleep.

Hours later, Maxwell awoke with a start. The late afternoon had passed into night, and the skylight above him was dusted with stars. As his awareness emerged from the grogginess of sleep, Maxwell had an eerie feeling that someone had entered the room. To his surprise, he saw a woman, taller than average and dressed in the style of a past era, standing over him. Behind her, a man dressed in similar period costume, stood near a filing cabinet.

The tall woman bent toward him, and Maxwell, rather than experiencing either fear or resentment of his intruders, became acutely aware that he was undressed. He pulled the sheets up around his neck to cover himself, but the woman did not seem to notice him. She continued to lean over the couch, running her hands just above the slip cover as if she were smoothing wrinkles from it.

Maxwell had briefly entertained the notion that his unannounced visitors might be some of his friends who had modeled for him in historical costumes, but as he tried to see the faces of the man and the woman and failed, the artist concluded that the strange intruders were unknown to him.

The woman turned to her male companion, then moved away from the couch toward the dark room at the opposite end of the studio. Maxwell was then awake and completely alert, and he decided that the mysterious couple must be burglars or, at the very least, unwanted trespassers. Springing to his feet, the artist lunged at the man who was leaning leisurely against the filing cabinet.

Maxwell's fist struck the edge of the cabinet and his courageous blow against his intruder left him with a bruised thumb and a vibrating filing cabinet. Both the man and the woman had vanished at Maxwell's sudden attack.

Mystified, the artist gathered the sheet from the couch around him and hurried to examine the rest of his apartment. All the rooms were empty. He snapped on the lights and checked the door. The lock had remained secure. The studio was forty feet from the roof and one hundred and fifty feet from the ground. Maxwell doubted that his visitors had come in through the windows. Puzzled, he sank to the sofa, the sheet still gathered around him.

If such an incident had been without precedent, Maxwell might have shrugged off his strange intruders as some bizarre kind of after-dream. But in addition to the apparent physical reality of their appearance, the artist knew that 51 West Tenth Street had a history of mysterious visits by oddly costumed men and women. The tradition of the building linked each of these ghostly appearances with John LaFarge, a former resident.

LaFarge, a well-known artist, who died in 1910, is most famous for his painting entitled *The Ascension* which hangs in the Church of the Ascension at the corner of Tenth Street and Fifth Avenue. LaFarge first primed this canvas with four coats of heavy white lead base, instead of zinc. The first mounting did not have the strength to hold the canvas in place, and the heavy painting fell to the floor. LaFarge ordered a new chassis built and supervised the second mounting himself.

According to LaFarge's grandson, novelist Oliver LaFarge, John LaFarge died at nearly the same time the painting fell a second time.

All of LaFarge's friends knew that artist to take great pride in his skill as an architect. Those who claimed to have seen LaFarge walking the rooms of 51 West Tenth Street agreed that the ghost of the artist was seeking the lost plans for the mounting of his painting in the hope that he might right the error in construction which allowed it to fall. To a man as devoted to his craft as LaFarge, such failure would weigh heavily on his mind.

In 1944, artist Feodor Rimsky and his wife lived in studio 22, LaFarge's old studio. One evening when they were returning home from the opera, Rimsky found the door of the studio open, even though he distinctly remembered having locked it earlier in the evening. As he pushed through the curtains that separated the main room from the studio, Rimsky became conscious of another presence in the room.

The entire thirty-six-foot length of the studio was illuminated by but a single bulb, but Rimsky had no difficulty in picking out the intruder. The man wore a tall, black hat and a billowing velvet coat. Rimsky protectively pushed his wife behind him, then rushed at the stranger. Before Rimsky could reach him, the intruder had vanished.

The painter and his wife were recent immigrants from Europe. They had no knowledge of the past history of 51 West Tenth Street. When Rimsky described the incident to a local historian, the man quickly pulled out a scrapbook containing pictures of the house's former occupants. Without hesitation, Rimsky picked out John LaFarge as his visitor. Only then did the painter learn that his mysterious visitor had died in 1910.

The ghost is said to have rustled in and out of studio 22 many times after the night it startled Rimsky and his wife. One night, when the Rimskys were entertaining friends in the studio, a guest named William Weber stared in terror across the room at something that was invisible to everyone else. Weber was often teased by his friends, who were skeptical of his reports of occasional psychic experiences. When Weber was asked to describe what he saw, he gave a vivid description of the man in the tall hat and the velvet cloak.

The face of the ghost was not seen until John Alan Maxwell's occupancy in 1948. Shortly after he had had the unsettling experiences with the male and female ghosts interrupting his nap, a lady visitor to the studio had a confrontation with the spirit of LaFarge which left her in screaming hysteria. She described the face as cadaverous, with the gray-white color of the bones of a skeleton. The woman mumbled about sunken, gleaming eyes for several minutes after Maxwell had managed to quiet her screams.

51 West Tenth Street was demolished in the 1950s to make way for an apartment house. With its familiar surroundings destroyed, and with them the walls which had absorbed the psychic vibrations necessary for its spectral life, the ghost disappeared.

The ghost of Tenth Street is typical of the most common type of haunting, the quiet ghost that simply appears and disappears in its familiar environment. Seldom is there any aural phenomena associated with the quiet haunt, nor are there the violent assortment of rappings, bangings, and thuddings which so many ghosts seem to include in their psychic repertoire. It is true that a percipient may be frightened by the sudden appearance of the ghost, but that reaction is a human response and not necessarily the intention of some malignant spirit.

Consider the testimony of those who have observed the "phantom monk" of Basildon, England.

A number of women who do cleaning at night at a factory near Holy Cross church have seen the ghost on several occasions. They usually finish work about 4:00 A.M., and it is as they are leaving the factory and walking past the old church that they often see the phantom. Nine of the cleaning women had seen the ghost when they reported the phenomenon to a journalist.

"It is definitely that of a monk, and it walks across the church road and disappears among the graves in the churchyard," one of the women said.

"One time I ran right through the spook on my bicycle," recalled Mrs. Rita Tobin. "I wasn't able to put on my brakes in time, and I passed right through him. I didn't feel any impact at all, but the air was cold and clammy. That was the second time that I've seen the ghost, and I hope the last!"

The women all mention that the monk wears a red cowl and has a chalk-white face that is "grim as death." Some have described the ghostly monk as transparent.

"He was just floating when I saw him," said Mrs. Catharine Kistruck. "His feet didn't seem to be touching the ground at all."

An interesting aside might be interjected at this point concerning ghosts that appear to "float" on air. In one interesting case, a ghost was noted, on each occasion of his appearance, to be walking about six inches off the floor. Investigation revealed that the floor of this particular ground-level room had been lowered six inches after the death of the individual whose idea-pattern the ghost represented. The same may hold true for the "phantom monk" of Basildon. The animated memory of the monk may be several centuries old, and the streets in front of Holy Cross church may have settled sufficiently in that time to make the ghost appear to float, as the memory-pattern treads the old ground that is no longer precisely where it had been a few centuries back.

The November 20, 1960, issue of *Grit* newspaper disclosed that the celebrated muralist, Maxo Vanka, once painted a mural under the scrutiny of a ghost. The incident occurred when Vanka was commissioned by the Croatian Catholic Church in Millvale, Pennsylvania, to create an extensive series of murals in time for a church celebration. The artist was given an impossible deadline of two months to complete the work, and he embarked at once on a day-and-night schedule.

One night, soon after he had begun his frantic effort to complete the murals on time, Vanka glanced down from his scaffolding to see a dark-robed figure standing in front of the altar. The artist had set up floodlights to illuminate his work, and he was able to see the man clearly. Vanka concluded that it was the pastor of the church, Reverend Albert Zagar, at his meditations, so he went back to work. When he glanced back at the altar a few moments later, Vanka was surprised to see that the priest had silently vanished.

On the next night, the artist was able to see that the man was not Father Zagar. The cleric was clearly spotlighted in the brilliance of Vanka's floodlamps, but the identity of the priest remained a mystery to the painter. Vanka might not have made much of a strange priest slipping silently into the church at night to pray before the altar if he had not been fully aware that only he and Father Zagar had keys to the church. Then, when Vanka's attention was directed elsewhere, the dark-robed figure vanished, as it had the night before.

Not wishing to appear petty, but genuinely annoyed at the irritation of being confronted by such an enigma when he had a tight deadline to meet, Vanka decided to complain to Father Zagar about the nocturnal visits of the priest.

The painter found Father Zagar asleep in the chair in the rectory. Gently rousing the clergyman from his sleep, Vanka stifled his impatience and put the matter before Father Zagar as calmly as he could.

The bemused cleric told Vanka that he had not lent the key to any other priest. "Perhaps you have seen our ghost," Father Zagar said. "Several people claim to have seen a black-robed figure in the church late at night."

Vanka told Father Zagar of his experiences and urged the priest to wait with him in the church on the following night. Father Zagar observed the nocturnal meditations of the phantom and so did numerous other witnesses for many nights in succession. On one occasion, the black-robed figure lit the altar candles. The candles continued to burn even after the ghost had disappeared. On another night, the phantom blew out the flame of the altar lamp that had been designed so that it could not be extinguished by air currents.

In this physical evidence of the haunting, we see a most interesting aspect of certain ghostly manifestations. The emotion-charged memory that constitutes a ghost seems to be able to draw upon the collective psychic energy of its percipients. Such a phenomenon has often been noted in the demonstrations produced in a seance circle.

One psychic researcher makes a point of warning those who find themselves confronted with a ghost in their house not to encourage the energy by table-tipping experiments or by dragging out the old ouija board. Such psychic vibrations usually only serve to accelerate the manifestations and to increase the range and scope of the accompanying phenomena.

The old country road near Mt. Pleasant, Iowa, is guarded by many tall oaks and box elders that, by night, appear to be long-armed giants crouching over the gravel path that permits intruders to enter their eerie realm.

By now, no one really remembers who first saw the ghost, but nearly everyone agrees that it was two truck drivers who had turned off the main highway at about midnight one night when there was a full moon. As they rounded the bend that approached the old bridge, the driver suddenly slammed on his brakes.

His partner, who had been dozing, nearly slammed forward against the dashboard, and he came fully awake with some ungentle words for the driver.

"Look ahead!" the driver silenced the man. "Look there in the full beam of the headlights!"

"Jumping Jehosaphat!" the other trucker shouted, as the full impact of the sight penetrated his consciousness. "Come on. We'd better cut her down. Maybe she's still alive!"

Both men began to open their doors, then looked back at each other as if to form a mutual link of courage. There was something more than a little scary about coming upon the swaying body of a hanged woman suspended from the girder of an old country bridge. But they had to do something—whether it was midnight on an eerie gravel road or not.

Their feet had no sooner touched the coarse road when the form of the hanged woman began to fade from their sight.

"Hey," the driver gasped. "What's goin' on?"

By the time that they had reached the bridge, the woman, noose and all, had completely vanished.

The two men stared at each other with open mouths, mouths no longer capable of articulating the fear and confusion that jammed their brains. Just moments before, they had both clearly seen the wretched figure of a hanged woman swaying above the worn wooden planks of the old bridge.

It was not long before a young couple coming home from a Saturday night dance witnessed the same grim apparition on the dark and eerie country road. Then other truckers and townspeople were seeing the form of the hanging woman in the light of the full moon.

"But it appears that we will have to be there on a night of a full moon," Glenn McWane told me. "The apparition has never been sighted at any other time."

"That should be no problem," I said, checking the schedule of our psychic safari. "Let's see, according to the calendar, the full moon begins on July 18. We can be there on the night of the nineteenth."

Glenn and I had that discussion in May of 1970. Now on July 19, with the moon full above us, but intermittently blocked by clouds, we sat in my station wagon with Irene Hughes and a number of others, just a few yards away from that haunted country bridge.

"Just a few minutes before midnight," someone whispered.

"Shhh," another voice ordered. "I think Irene is in light trance."

A cigarette lighter flared in the darkness, made a small circle of illumination around someone's face, then snapped out again.

"There's someone coming down the road," Irene said.

Two or three people agreed with the sensitive. I strained my eyes to focus in on what seemed to be a person approaching the bridge.

I felt an icy feather stroking my abdomen, as a denizen from the unknown appeared to be entering our world. Then, as my eyes narrowed, I was at once relieved and disappointed when I perceived that the ghostly visitor was nothing more than a traffic sign advising approaching motorists about the narrow bridge and its load limit.

"No, no," I was told by others more sensitive than I when I aired this discovery. "It's not the sign. It is off to the right of the sign!"

Irene said nothing. She seemed to be tuned into another dimension. A dimension which we could neither see nor hear. The medium sat in silence for a few more moments, then she spoke, slowly, precisely.

"I see a woman swinging in a circle. A circle of confusion. She is disturbed, confused. She feels betrayed. She feels like she wants to jump over the side of the bridge."

A woman in our party began to insist in loud whispers that she could see the woman poised on the side of the bridge, noose around her neck. The man seated next to her protested that he could see nothing.

A high, thin wail seemed to come from the direction of the bridge. Was it only the cry of some night-hunting bird, the distorted complaint of some farm animal, or the keen of a tormented soul? The frogs and crickets seemed undisturbed by any of the possibilities.

"I see a circle," Irene said, speaking once more. "I see a woman committing suicide from this bridge." (Again it should be noted that we had not told Irene what she might expect to see at this lonely country bridge.)

"Was it suicide or an accident?" someone asked.

"It was suicide," Irene said. "And there was another person involved."

"You know," she said. "This is most unusual. Usually when someone in spirit appears, they are dressed just as they were in life. You know, there is never anyone who comes to me wrapped in a sheet like so many people think they do. But that is just what I saw on the bridge. I saw what looked like somebody wrapped in a sheet!"

"A shroud?" I asked her.

"A shroud," she agreed. "And she tells me her name is Brown. O'Brown. Maybe it was O'Brien. She was a brunette. I really don't feel that she was a sick person. I feel that this act was just a sudden thing in her life. I feel that there was a husband, but that he was not close by."

Irene sat quietly for a few moments, apparently sifting through the psychic impressions bombarding her from the bridge.

"I'm hearing the name Helen," she said, resuming her reportage. "I feel that this woman was dating...was having a love affair with a doctor in the community. And I feel that you will find that there was a doctor who left the town rather quickly after this woman took her life. I don't feel that this woman was emotionally ill or anything like that. I feel that her life was okay and then, suddenly, this involvement with the doctor began."

"How many years ago was this?" reporter Joan Hurling asked the medium.

"I have the feeling that it may not have been more than fifteen or eighteen years ago," Irene answered.

"According to the information that I have," Glenn said, "that would seem to be exactly the time that the ghost began to appear."

Irene had tuned back into the entity allegedly connected with the eerie hanging scene. "I feel that she was an accomplished horsewoman, but on the day that she took her life, there was neither horse nor car in the area. She walked out here from town."

"What time of day was it when she took her life?" Glenn wondered.

"It was close to noontime or around two o'clock in the afternoon," the psychic replied. "It wasn't any later than that. I feel that it was a rather sunny day."

After a brief pause, Irene added: "She wore some kind of ribbon in her hair. She was in her early thirties or her late twenties. She seems to be a tall woman. She had a baby...two children.

"I keep hearing a name like Parker...Barker....

"Look! Can you see it? A form was very clear there for an instant.

"She did it on the righthand side, but always I've seen the figure walk first over to the lefthand side.

"She was married. Either her husband or someone very close to her came from Philadelphia.

"It may be that my eyes are playing tricks on me, but right on the righthand side...Oh, there's a tremendous glow! It's real fuzzy and glowing and it's blowing in the wind. Right on the righthand side now! It's exactly what I saw when we first came to the bridge and it walked over to the other side. Oh, I see her so clearly. She's wearing a yellow dress!"

Irene suddenly stopped talking. Then, after several seconds of silence, she said: "She keeps telling me, 'Honey, don't talk. Honey, don't tell them.' I can see her fingernails, very nice and long...."

"Why wouldn't she want something told?" I asked. "Is there some reason why she doesn't want anyone to know why she killed herself?"

"I think it is the doctor," Irene said. "I think she was involved with the town doctor who left so soon after her death."

By this time we had left the station wagon and were standing in the middle of the bridge. There were holes in the wooden planking, and we had to move our feet cautiously so that we would not twist an ankle.

"Oh!" Irene gasped, jerking her body to one side. "She was a very fast driver! I had an image of her driving along this road and I wanted to duck to the side."

"But she didn't drive a car that day," I reminded the psychic.

"No," Irene said, "but it's my impression that she drove over this bridge often, mostly from that direction back there. Again, I am getting the impression that some member of her family was from Philadelphia, but she came here from Kansas. I'm seeing a huge sunflower, and that is the sunflower state, isn't it?"

As discreetly as possible, a follow-up investigation was conducted in the area after our psychic safari had spent several hours of a full-moon night near the bridge with the tradition of the hanging lady.

Through one of our sources, we learned that there had been a young mother, originally from Kansas and fond of wearing bright yellow dresses, who had become romantically involved with a local doctor. The young woman had committed suicide in despair over their impossible love affair, and public opinion, or conscience, had forced the doctor to leave town. While some informants believed that the ghost of the hanging woman might well be the suicidal Kansan, others said that the young woman in question had not hanged herself and that they were unaware of the legend of the haunted bridge.

It appears then, that the spirit of the young woman in the bright yellow dress shall rest in peace, until one night of the full moon when someone turns the bend toward the old country bridge and sees. . . .

6

Ghosts with a Mission

In May, 1913, a small group of pilots and mechanics near a workshop hanger at Britain's Montrose Air Training Station signaled the arrival of a new "aeroplane" to the grounds. The man most interested in the craft was the pilot who would fly it for the first time, Lt. Desmond Arthur, a black-haired young Irishman.

"She's got nice lines," Arthur said to the senior mechanic standing next to him on the field.

"Nice to look at, aye," the mechanic said skeptically. "But I wonder what's under that fabric? Ten to one it isn't built to take any extra strain— or maybe even normal strain."

The others standing around the new aircraft scoffed at the mechanic's pessimism. The new models that had arrived at the station had been getting consistently better. Why should this one be any different?

"We'll find out now," Arthur said confidently, stepping into the cockpit. A mechanic spun the prop, then jumped away as the motor caught. Without hesitation, the young pilot taxied the plane into the wind, then picked up speed. The plane lifted from the ground.

The spectators watched carefully as the accomplished pilot took the plane to nearly four thousand feet before he leveled off and began to test the new model's maneuverability with a series of stunts.

In the middle of a twisting roll, the plane heeled over on its back, then shed a wing. The machine and the pilot dropped to the ground like a falling stone. By the time the men of the Montrose Station arrived, Desmond Arthur was dead.

The tragedy did not receive official comment until 1916 when authorities blamed the accident on misjudgment by the pilot. The official report based its findings on the immediate investigation by military authorities after the accident and their evaluation of the testimonies of witnesses to the crash. There were those who protested that the crash was due to faulty construction of the aircraft, but the investigators' assessment discounted such testimony.

A few weeks after the report was published, a mechanic at Montrose Station learned that the Desmond Arthur tragedy could not be dismissed so easily. While working on the inside bracing of an airplane, he noticed an officer in flight clothes approaching the craft. The mechanic continued work until the officer came very close and stood directly over him.

Becoming a bit uneasy at the officer's silence, the mechanic finally asked, without looking up, "Are you to fly this one, sir?"

When the officer did not reply, the mechanic slid out from under the brace, and looked up at the silent man.

The officer's face was contorted with rage; his lips moved furiously and he gestured as if he were shouting, but he made no sound. The mechanic fell away from the strange flier, the wrench he had been holding clattered to the floor. Before he could turn and flee, the officer disappeared. Terrified, the mechanic ran until he came to Flight Sergeant Wilkens.

"I've seen him," the man gasped, out of breath.

"Who's that?"

"The ghost! The Montrose ghost!" The mechanic recited his experience, and the description of the strange flier bothered Wilkens. It tallied exactly with several reports he had heard of a manifestation that had materialized before several of the officers on the staff.

The Montrose ghost first appeared in August 1916 to Second Lieutenant Ralph Peterson. Peterson had entered his room and found a fellow airman leaning against the wall. Surprised by the officer's presence, Peterson had just begun to question the man when the visitor "melted into the wall." When Peterson reported the incident, Colonel James Rutherford dismissed it as imagination and warned the junior officer of the hazards of alcohol.

A few days later, two officers, whose testimony the station commander could not question, saw the same strange flier. Major Jenkins and Captain Edward Milner, two senior officers who shared a room, had just retired. The bed lamp had not been off more than a few minutes when the sound of footsteps caused both officers to sit up in their beds. Before either of them could move, their door swung open and a young man in flying kit entered. He gestured wildly and seemed to be shouting at the two officers, neither of whom could testify that any sound issued from the angry visitor.

When one of the officers switched on the light, the figure faded before the astonished eyes of the two officers. They quickly had the building secured and ordered all exits guarded. Guards reported that no person had attempted to leave the building. After the officer had conducted a bed check, they were convinced that their visitor had not been a living man.

The next officer to see the restless ghost recognized its form. Lieutenant Edwards, the station adjutant and an officer in the regular army, swore that he had seen Desmond Arthur come into his room. Edwards had known Arthur well, and he, too, described a man who seemed to be shouting at the top of his lungs, yet made no sound.

The Montrose ghost added a bizarre note to the aviation news, but in 1916, aviators did not receive much good press. The high cost of World War I was bearing hard on the British, and it had become fashionable to take pot shots at the fledgling air corps and its personnel. It was in this spirit that the report on the Desmond Arthur crash had been compiled, and even though a few devoted airmen had fought to remove the blight from Arthur's otherwise clean record, their efforts had been overpowered by criticism of the corps. In addition to the great cost of the war, British air losses reached their peak in 1916, and Parliament appointed a committee to investigate the matter. The air corps cringed under the double obligation to reduce costs and increase efficiency at the same time.

But the ghost of Desmond Arthur seemed determined to bring about a change in the record the report had left of him. Once beyond the original witnesses of the phenomenon, the story gained momentum and soon the name of Desmond Arthur was widely known. The tale of the ghost of the airbase spread to the continent and even to the enemy. In one instance, a German soldier, shot down behind Allied lines, asked almost immediately for news of the Montrose ghost.

Meanwhile, the Parliamentary committee had found that to increase Britain's aviation efficiency would entail increased, not lowered, costs. Machines arriving in French bases were ill-equipped, seldom outfitted with essential parts, and the personnel arriving in the war zone often came prepared with only a few days' training.

It was at this point that the editor of Britain's leading aviation magazine, the *Aeroplane,* took up the cry for a reinvestigation of the Desmond Arthur case. "With training and machines in such bad shape now," wrote editor C.G. Gray, "imagine what it would have been in 1913."

With the aid of a friend, Commander Perrin, one of Britain's earliest fliers, Gray prodded the Air Ministry into a reinvestigation. In a few weeks, the Royal Air Club's Safety and Accident Investigation Committee announced that Desmond Arthur had not, after all, been guilty of an error in judgment.

With the help of influential men in Parliament, these findings were finally incorporated into the Parliamentary record on November 12, 1916.

About two months later, the Montrose ghost appeared for the last time. The phantom materialized first to Lieutenant Edwards, then to Major Jenkins and Captain Edward Milner. All three claim that the ghost smiled broadly at them. The Montrose ghost had vindicated his memory, and he has not been seen since that day in January 1917.

The ghost with a mission is usually a *crisis* or *postmortem* apparition. This ghost may be compared to an undelivered telegram that continues to appear until the party to which it was sent gets its message. The *crisis apparition* appears to either a relative or a close friend at the moment of the agent's physical death. (Crisis apparitions of those undergoing severe mental or physical stress may also be produced, that is, "ghosts of the living.")

A postmortem apparition appears long after the agent has passed from physical existence and continues to reappear until the percipient for whom it was intended is exposed to it. It seems to be very much like a telepathic communication that remains in a state of frustration until contact with the proper mind has been established.

In the case of Desmond Arthur, the young pilot must have sensed in the last seconds of life that he would be blamed for the failure of the new model airplane. There was no way that he could stop the plane from plummeting to earth and take time to discuss the matter with his friends and with those witnesses who had assembled to watch him test the new craft. There was no time to write a letter, no way to transmit a message. Psychic abilities function best when there is a *need* to utilize the hidden power of the mind. Such a need existed for primitives when they could not communicate intelligibly with their companions, and such a need exists today whenever a crisis situation exists in which normal sensory channels of communication are no longer able to serve us effectively. Desmond Arthur, only split seconds away from a fatal crash, found himself in such a situation of need.

The telepathically projected memory-pattern was probably intended for Desmond Arthur's friend, Lieutenant Edwards, and was no doubt activated by the discussion and mental activity which refocused psychic energy on the crash incident when the official report of the accident was released in 1916. Psychic phenomena are tremendously adaptable to the situation at hand, and Desmond Arthur's telepathic projection seems to have taken the form of an angry man, shouting his protest at an unjust decision.

Once the "message" has been received by the percipient for whom it was intended, the ghost is put to "rest." In other words, the communication has been completed and there is no further need for the dramatized memory-pattern, the "psychological marionette," of the ghost.

What happens when the percipient for whom a crisis apparition is intended has died or left the area? It would seem to me that it is in such situations that we have the traditional "restless" ghost that continues to haunt a locale. Perhaps the apparition will continue to appear, ostensibly "seeking" the proper percipient, until its energy is eventually dissipated.

In some cases the telepathic image is able to invade the subconscious of the percipient while asleep. In such instances, the percipient experiences a vivid "dream" about a loved one or friend in which certain instructions are relayed.

M. Pascal Cocozza had such a dream on the night of March 3, 1905. When he awakened the impressions were still deeply etched in his memory. His dead father had been speaking to him, scolding him because his privacy in death had been violated.

"You have neglected the care of my body," his father had said. "My grave has been disturbed and my bones cast into the snow where I bring folly among the wolves."

The dream was so clear in Cocozza's mind that he told his sister about it the next day. To their mutual amazement, she told Cocozza that she had experienced the identical dream.

Driven by curiosity, Cocozza defied an oncoming snowstorm to make his way to the cemetery of Castel di Sangro, a small village in the mountains east of Rome. There, among the gravestones, Cocozza found the remnants of a human skeleton. The presence of many wolf tracks gave still greater credence to his dream.

Appalled by what he saw, Pascal Cocozza filed a complaint against the caretaker of the cemetery, who along with three of his gravediggers, was subsequently brought in for questioning.

In the course of the caretaker's testimony, if was learned that the ten-year rental on the elder Cocozza's gravesite had elapsed. As was customary in such cases, the gravediggers had been told to remove the bones from the grave so that they might be placed in the cemetery charnel pit. By the time the men had completed the strenuous task of opening the grave's frozen ground and had removed all of the bones, dusk was falling. It had grown bitter cold and was snowing hard, so the three gravediggers decided to postpone the completion of their task.

During the night, wolves had come upon the bones and had scattered them about, possibly carrying off a few.

The gravediggers had no idea whose bones they were exhuming. The grave had been marked only by a cross. The identity of the remains was not revealed until an investigation of the cemetery records showed that the bones were indeed the remains of M. Cocozza, Sr.

Pascal Cocozza had not passed near the cemetery during the exhumation—the cemetery sits on top of a small mountain and is relatively inaccessible, even in a good weather. Other than the dream, Cocozza had no way of knowing that anything had been done to the grave of his father. It is of paramount intererst that the apparition came to two people at the same time, and conveyed to each the same message in an identical dream.

I do not wish to provoke an argument with the spiritistic interpretation of such an incident. Spiritualists would maintain that the case of M. Cocozza offers proof of survival.

That genuine instances in which the dead have communicated with the living have occurred, I do not doubt. Perhaps the case of the Cocozzas' dream of their father is one such instance, but might not a memory-pattern of the senior Cocozza, which contained the common mountaineer's fear of his bones being unearthed by wolves, have prompted a bit of clairvoyance on the part of Cocozza's children? This combination, blended, perhaps, with feelings of guilt at not having been more concerned about the state of the father's grave (subconsciously, they may have been aware that they had allowed the gravesite rental period to elapse) could have provoked a vivid dramatization that led Pascal Cocozza to investigate the validity of the dream experience.

A number of archeologists have credited their discoveries to having become *en rapport* with the spirit or memory of some ancient individual or culture. The story of the famous Assyriologist Dr. Herman Hilprecht and the ghost of the Babylonian priest that gave him the interpretation of the cuneiform inscriptions on the fragments found in the ruins of the Temple of Bel at Nippur is well-known and has been often repeated in collections of strange and unusual occurrences.

Another well-known case is that of the spirits of the three monks which, through a medium, directed the excavation of the ruins of Edgar Chapel at Glastonbury Abbey, the first seat of Christianity in Britain.

During excavations in northern Italy, Dr. Ervin Bonkalo experienced a vision of a lovely young girl with long black hair. The vision led him to the girl's grave. Dr. Bonkalo seems to have experienced telepathy from a two-thousand-year-old grave.

Some traditional ghosts may be post-mortem apparitions which linger in the environment awaiting a particular percipient who has long since died or moved. These ghosts—occasionally seen when someone of an approximate telepathic affinity enters the environment—may come to be considered either the ghostly *protector* of the house or its *monster,* depending upon both the demeanor and appearance of the ghost and the interpretation percipients place upon its automatic actions.

Volume 6, number 1 of *Tomorrow* magazine carried an article entitled "The House that Haunts a Ghost" by Louis M.A. Roy as told to Pauline Saltzman. Here was an interesting story of a ghost that has come to be looked upon as the benefactress of a home in Henniker, New Hampshire.

Mr. Roy told of the time, shortly after he and his mother moved into the house in 1938, that he had left the house to inspect the driveway to see how it had fared in the driving rain that had fallen for nearly the entire day. Although he did not know it, New England was about to lock horns with a hurricane. Roy found the road completely washed out and impassable.

On his way back to the house, he noticed the old garage beginning to sway in the wind. Fearing for his car, Roy quickly sought poles to prop up the sagging side. His task completed, he walked back to the house where his mother held open the side door.

"Who was that helping you with the garage?" she asked him.

Roy looked at his mother incredulously. "I was alone."

But his mother insisted that a "tall woman dressed in white" had helped him with the poles.

"Then what happened to her?" Roy asked. His mother explained that she had lost sight of her after looking away for a second.

Roy feels that a clue to the mysterious woman in white can be found in the records of the earliest owners of the house.

In 1720 a shipload of Scotch-Irish emigrants set sail for the New World in a little vessel called the *Wolf*. Their destination was Londonderry, New Hampshire, where many had friends and relatives waiting to greet them.

Just when the weary passengers, feeling that their long passage had been successfully completed, were practically in sight of the Boston Harbor, the *Wolf* was overtaken by a sinister-looking ship flying the Jolly Roger. Unarmed, the *Wolf* was helpless and had no choice but to heave to at the threatening shots from the frigate.

The pirate chief, called Captain Pedro by his crew, unceremoniously announced that every human on board the *Wolf* would die. In spite of his name, the pirate spoke flawless English; and, in spite of his threat, he changed his mind when he discovered that the captain's young wife had given birth to a daughter less than a week before. The pirate and the young mother struck a bargain. He agreed to let them go unharmed if she would name the girl Mary, after his mother.

Learning of the change in their fate, the passengers were overjoyed. But their joy turned to fear when Captain Pedro returned. However, he came bearing a gift—a bolt of greenish-blue brocade silk, which he wanted the girl to fashion into a gown to wear at her wedding.

Mary, the daughter of Mr. and Mrs. James Wilson, gained the nickname, "Ocean Born Mary," and her friends called her by it for her entire life. Her name, wrought by a pact with a pirate, and her wedding dress of the finest silk became legend even while Mary was growing into womanhood.

But while Mary matured in New Hampshire, Captain Pedro aged on the Seven Seas. Tired of his life of violence, the pirate dissolved his crew, retaining only the ship's carpenters, the Negro slaves, and one huge seaman-bodyguard. In the year 1760, Captain Pedro began building a stately Georgian house. He had kept close tabs on the girl he had christened and he knew that she had raised five sons and had been widowed. When Captain Pedro had completed his house, he summoned Mary, who went with her sons to care for the ex-pirate.

During the time that Mary stayed with Captain Pedro, the old pirate and his huge bodyguard made several mysterious night-time excursions, and the slaves whispered that they buried treasure somewhere on the grounds. After one of these nocturnal trips, the bodyguard disappeared and was never seen again. Pedro lived a few years longer, but one day, Mary found him with a sailor's cutlass driven completely through his back. Mary continued to take care of the stately house even after her sons had moved away. She died in 1814 at the age of ninety-four.

The house soon gained her name and, in fact, is still known as Ocean Born Mary's house. Mr. Roy believes it is Mary's spirit which protects the house, and certain incidents seem to bear him out.

Several people of the community of Henniker have claimed to have heard or seen a horse-drawn carriage pull up next to the house in the middle of the night, and they have watched, mystified, as a tall woman in white descends from the carriage and walks slowly to the house. One of the townspeople, who had witnessed the ghostly carriage, is so terrified that he cannot be persuaded to return to the house, even in the daytime.

Because of their mutual interest in preserving the old house, Mr. Roy feels that Ocean Born Mary has saved his life. He claims that he has had several serious accidents on the grounds, but each time, an event that might have been fatal to others has failed to claim his life. He believes that Ocean Born Mary will protect all who love her house.

In a famous case, which was first related by Daniel Defoe, the author of *Robinson Crusoe,* an apparition seems to have appeared for the express purpose of bidding friends farewell. The case is notable in many respects, particularly in regard to the natural appearance of the apparition. None of those who witnessed the appearance of the ghost realized that they were not seeing the agent in the flesh. The apparition was so solid and material that its dress was handled and touched and it appeared to take tea and nourishment. The length of conversation which some claimed to have had with the apparition may have become exaggerated through the retelling of the incident, but the psychic projection of Mrs. Veal remains a most intriguing case in the annals of paranormal research.

Mrs. Bargrave held the door open for her visitor as she entered. She and Mrs. Veal had been the best of friends from childhood, but Mrs. Veal had moved to Dover, England, several years before. The two women had not seen each other for almost two-and-a-half years. What a nice surprise to brighten up a Saturday afternoon. It was September 8, 1705.

"And what brings you to Canterbury?" Mrs. Bargrave asked her friend.

"Just visiting a few old friends," replied Mrs. Veal. "I'll be taking a rather long journey soon, and I wanted to see you all before I left."

Her answer struck Mrs. Bargrave as odd. Mrs. Veal had been plagued by fits, probably epileptic seizures, for many years, and she generally avoided travel whenever possible. As a matter of fact, she rarely went anywhere except in the company of her brother.

The two friends sat chatting about the past and, as two old ladies would, they talked about all of their troubles and of the comfort they had found in religion. When they had been younger and either of them had a problem, they would share it, search for a solution and console one another when necessary. They spoke briefly about Mrs. Veal's seizures, but Mrs. Bargrave did not pursue the topic for fear of upsetting Mrs. Veal and thus bringing about an attack.

Mrs. Veal appeared to be a little more emotional than Mrs. Bargrave remembered her, but she did not think too much of it. One thing that struck Mrs. Bargrave as peculiar, though, was Mrs. Veal's remark about how suffering here on earth is rewarded in heaven.

In an effort to direct the conversation along more cheerful lines, Mrs. Bargrave complimented her guest on her silk dress. Mrs. Veal stated that it was a new one and commented on the texture of the material. Admiringly, Mrs. Bargrave touched the dress and felt the smoothness of the silk.

And then Mrs. Veal made a very odd request. She asked Mrs. Bargrave to write down the details of her visit and tell them to her brother. To Mrs. Bargrave, it seemed rather silly to suppose that Mrs. Veal's brother would be even remotely interested in the conversation of two older women, but, as a favor to her friend, who seemed so insistent, she agreed.

After Mrs. Veal said goodby, Mrs. Bargrave happened to look at the clock. It was about a quarter to two. They had talked nearly two hours.

Mrs. Bargrave did not leave the house until the following Monday, when she went to the home of Captain Watson. She was curious to know whether or not Mrs. Veal had also stopped at his house on Saturday.

The Captain was not at home, but the family told her that they had seen nothing of Mrs. Veal. They were quite disappointed that she had not visited them if she had been in Canterbury. While they waited for the Captain, Mrs. Bargrave described her friend's visit in detail, mentioning among other things, the new silk dress Mrs. Veal had worn. Mrs. Bargrave was still talking about the visit when Captain Watson arrived home.

Before any of them had a chance to bring up the subject which was taxing their curiosity, Captain Watson informed them that he had some sad news. "I just received word that our old friend Mrs. Veal has passed away." He paused a moment and then continued, "She had a series of intermittent fits which lasted for about four hours. She finally passed away at noon, *last Friday.*"

It was true. Mrs. Veal had died about noon, Friday, September 7, twenty-four hours before she had visited with Mrs. Bargrave!

Had it not been for some of the things which Mrs. Bargrave had told the Watsons before the Captain had returned, they might have thought that Mrs. Bargrave was trying to create some sort of hoax. Perhaps most conclusive was the information Mrs. Veal had disclosed to Mrs. Bargrave concerning the legacy she planned to leave to a Mr. Breton. This had been a secret known only to Mrs. Veal and her brother, so the only place that Mrs. Bargrave could have possibly learned it was from Mrs. Veal herself on that most unusual Saturday afternoon.

7

Invisible Home Wreckers

A few summers ago I received a call from a policewoman in a southern city. The officer said she had read a book of mine on the phenomenon of poltergeist hauntings. She had thought the subject matter interesting, but at first reading it had seemed "a bit far out."

At the time of her call, however, she had been forced to make a reassessment of the book's contents. "We've got a poltergeist down here," she said, "and it is driving us crazy. What do we do with it?"

Briefly, she supplied me with the details. A young boy, who lived alone with his widowed mother, seemed to provide the energy center for the poltergeist. "It's just like you wrote in your book," the policewoman told me. "There have been raps on the wall and furniture moving across the floor for about three days now.

"I was there last night and a basket of laundry dumped itself on the preacher who had come to try to pacify the spook. A policeman stuck his head in the door to check on things and got hit over the head with a flying broom handle."

"The poltergeist usually exhausts his energy in two to five weeks," I said.

"Fine," came the reply, "but what do we do now?"

I suggested that a police youth worker counsel the boy and determine in what way he was being frustrated by the lack of a creative outlet.

"Perhaps he would like to paint or sing or write poetry," I said. "Creativity must find an outlet, and whether it takes the form of psychic manifestation or socially acceptable artistic expression is often only a matter of circumstances. Most of all," I stressed, "the boy should be made to feel loved and valued as an individual."

Poltergeist is German for "noisy ghost," although most researchers agree that the berserk bundle of energy is not a ghost at all, but a dramatic instance of uncontrolled psychokinesis (the direct action of mind upon matter). It is quite likely that the physical changes that accompany puberty have a great deal to do with an outbreak of poltergeist activity. Adolescence brings dramatic changes to one's physical structure. We can only speculate upon the traumatic changes that might be wrought in one's psyche.

To quote from one of my early journal entries: "The poltergeist often finds its energy center in the frustrated creativity of a brooding adolescent, who is denied acceptable avenues of expression. This brings up the question of just where man's limits of creativity might lie? It seems a bit startling to most people to suggest that man's mind may be capable of bursting free of its three-dimensional bonds and utilizing specialized talents that virtually know no limits. It may be within the power of man's psyche to materialize other voices, other personalities, and junior psyches. It may be within the power of man's transcendent self to skip blithely over, around, or through the accepted barriers of space and time and to bring back tangible evidence of this strange journey in the form of objects which could only have been obtained in their place of native origin. The poltergeist seems to offer measurable, weighable, demonstrable proof of this psychic capacity. The tragedy in the poltergeist phenomenon is that it illustrates a perverted or uncontrolled aspect of this incredible power."

In his *Between Two Worlds*, Dr. Nandor Fodor writes of the violence which accompanies such activity. The late psychoanalyst maintains that the poltergeist is "unquestionably sadistic." He theorizes that such projected aggression through "unknown biological factors" is the one way in which an adolescent can release hostility against his parents and other figures of authority and still maintain "conscious innocence." Such projected aggression can work considerable damage to a household, but it is seldom that anyone is seriously injured by the poltergeist. The most dangerous poltergeist, Dr. Fodor warns, is the incendiary variety. This poltergeist's aggressive tendencies can burn a house down through spontaneous outbreaks of fire.

In addition to the sadistic nature of the attacks directed at authority figures, Dr. Fodor also noted the manifestation of masochism in "stigmatic attacks, self-strangulation, blowing up of the body...writing appearing on the skin, or in the ghostly threats directed against the victim (and unconscious agent) of the ghost."

What strikes one in examining poltergeist reports is their great similarity, whether the setting be a London suburb, a frontier home in

Colorado of the 1860s, or a novelty store in Miami, Florida. Time, place, and societal influence have virtually no effect on the basic psychodynamics which somehow trigger the psychokinetic outbursts that make up the poltergeist.

"What was that noise?" exclaimed Mrs. Dennis Greenfield, startled to be awakened from sleep. Then she heard the noise again. The sounds seemed to be coming from the left.

"Wake up!" She poked her husband. "There's somebody up there!"

Dennis Greenfield sat up. He, too, heard the sounds. "Probably just air locks in the water pipes, dear. Go back to sleep."

The explanation seemed plausible enough for Mrs. Greenfield, who slept undisturbed for the rest of the night.

But the next evening the sounds returned, much louder than before, and they continued for several weeks. In the words of the Greenfields, "It sounded like gangs of furniture movers hard at work."

Each time, a search of the loft revealed nothing.

Then the noises ceased. For two and one-half years the Greenfield household was as quiet and normal as any other in the West Norwood suburb of London.

It was not until January 1950 that twenty-six-year-old Cecil Greenfield was awakened by a series of bumping noises on the landing. As he related the incident to a newspaperman, "I went out to investigate and saw a grey, shadowy figure coming up the stairs toward me. I shouted with fright—and the figure vanished."

A few nights later, when Dennis and his wife were returning home from the cinema, they encountered the ghost on the doorstep. In utter fear, they ran.

As time went on, the figure was seen more frequently. More unexplainable events were added to the program. Vegetables and cooking utensils would go flying around the kitchen. The radio would mysteriously turn itself on and off. Doors would open and shut without human aid; rooms would be lit without the aid of lamps. During one of its periods of more violent activity, the ghost snatched a child out of bed and hurled her across the room.

The strange goings-on had been witnessed by many. Some members of the local clergy tried to exorcise the spirit. Radio teams tried to record or track it. Psychic researchers were on the scene with infra-red cameras, hoping to get pictures of an entity in action. Yet, the disturbances continued.

After the rough-house play with their young daughter, the Greenfields feared for their lives. In desperation, they asked for police protection. Although ghost-chasing was a little out of their line, the police agreed to help in any way they could and a police sergeant was assigned to the case.

On a night in July 1951, the policeman was sleeping in an armchair at the foot of the stair. At 2:30 A.M. he was awakened by noises from above. As he moved to investigate, he noticed that the air in the house had taken on an eerie coolness, almost a chill.

With billy club and flashlight he crept up the stairs. The sounds led him to a back bedroom occupied by ten-year-old Patricia Greenfield. The policeman threw open the door and scanned the room with his flashlight.

The girl was curled up with her back to the headboard, horrified by the weird performance going on before her. The furniture was dancing. A cardboard box rose through the air like a helium-filled balloon. Drawers sailed across the room, as a wardrobe beat itself against the wall.

As soon as the officer switched on the lights, the antics stopped. The policeman naturally suspected some sort of trickery. He checked the furniture and other objects that had been in motion. He found no wires, no strings, not even a bearing on which the furnishings might have rolled.

The officer later told reporters that he was not strong enough to make the furniture move as it had; he did not see how the girl possibly could have animated the objects in her room.

The Greenfields moved out of the house and went to live with relatives in Surrey. Investigators moved into the afflicted house shortly thereafter, but they reported absolutely nothing out of the ordinary during the stay of over three weeks. Thinking that the ghost had finally decided to leave their house, the Greenfields reluctantly returned.

But on their first night, they were welcomed by a barrage of books and ornaments that left deep gouges in the walls. A box of jigsaw puzzles floated slowly toward the ceiling. A twelve-year-old boy, who was related to the Greenfields, said that he was dragged out of bed and across the floor by a force he was unable to resist.

The Greenfields kept up their struggle for another month, hoping that the intruder would leave. Finally, in desperation, they sold the house. As before, as soon as they left the premises, the hauntings stopped. According to the new owner, the spook has not been heard from since.

In the case of the Greenfields, it would appear that the girl, Patricia, provided the energy center for the poltergeist, and in turn, may have stimulated a memory-pattern which set a haunting in motion. The Dory-poltergeist gives us a more typical example of this particular manifestation of psychic energy.

On December 3, 1861, Mrs. Julia H. Dory of Idaho Springs, Colorado, worked with efficient speed to set her dinner on the table. She had a large family and three hired men to feed at the noon meal, and she knew they all would troop in the house in a few minutes. When they came she would be ready. In fact, she timed it nearly to the second, setting the last plate of steaming food on the table just before the hired men entered.

"It's on the table now," she said, leaving the kitchen to go and greet the other man.

"Thank ye, Mrs. Dory," one of them said.

"Maggie," she called into the house. "Bring the children to dinner." A muffled voice answered her. Then she turned back to the kitchen, with the hired men at her heels. After two steps into the room, she stopped short, her mouth wide open.

"It's gone!" she exclaimed.

The men who had followed, and nearly stumbled over her, first looked at her in surprise, then followed her gaze to the completely bare kitchen table.

"Look there!" one of the men shouted, pointing toward another door to the outside. The startled people saw the table cloth slipping under the door. It had stopped moving the minute the man had pointed it out.

Mrs. Dory hurried to the door and opened it. There was her dinner, spread on the cold December ground, set precisely as she had placed it on the table. No human being could be seen from the open door, and Mrs. Dory had not been gone from the kitchen for more than a few minutes. Dumbfounded, she collected the dishes and reset the table.

To Mrs. Dory, the disappearing dinner became just another perplexing piece in a completely illogical puzzle that had begun at ten o'clock that morning. She had been making a pie in the pantry, and her twelve-year-old adopted daughter, Maggie, had been washing clothes in the kitchen. The younger children demanded her attention for a minute. When she returned to the pie, she found a calico dress that Maggie had wrung out, immersed in her mixed custard.

Angrily, she called Maggie. "What is this dress doing in the custard?" she demanded.

Maggie looked at the dress in amazement. "I don't know," she said resolutely, "but I sure didn't put it there. I just washed it a few minutes ago."

Mrs. Dory finally dismissed the incident as some strange occurrence, but when Maggie turned to go back to her washing, she found that a basket of clothes she had just wrung dry had completely disappeared. Mrs. Dory and Maggie set out on an immediate search and found the clothes in a mud puddle behind the house.

After dinner, the hired men decided to stay around the house to see if they could catch the "prankster." Mrs. Dory wished that her husband would return home from the short trip he was on, so he could help solve the puzzle.

As the day wore on, the pranks became more frequent. The house was searched several times but to no avail. After a room had been searched, and locked tight, the men would return an hour later to find the room completely rearranged, with the contents scattered about and some pieces completely removed from the room.

In the evening, when Mrs. Dory prepared the children for bed, she could not find a single piece of clothing for any of them. The clothing was not found until more than a week later when Mrs. Dory's brother-in-law came home and opened his personal chest to which he had the only key. The children's clothing, still neatly folded, lay in the chest.

Mr. Dory returned early Sunday morning to find his house filled with baffled and frightened people. While his wife prepared a breakfast for him, he began ridiculing all those who mentioned anything remotely connected with the supernatural. He probably would have dismissed the entire story as a product of contagious imagination except that while he waited impatiently for his morning steak, the plate and table cloth his wife had set before him disappeared the moment his eyes left it. And while Mrs. Dory was saying. "I told you so," to her astonished husband, the steak she had begun broiling disappeared from the stove.

In the next few days, many people came to see the strange occurrences in the Dory house. The novelty of the situation had quickly worn off for the Dorys and had become frighteningly grim. Everything the Dorys sought to eat would disappear. They made one meal of potatoes alone, and these had to be cooked, unpeeled and watched every minute.

One of the hired men had braided a whip, and in order to foil the "prankster," had tied it in many intricate knots around a beam in the house. Proud of his resourcefulness, the man went to the kitchen to summon Mrs. Dory to see how he had made certain his whip would not disappear.

A few moments later, when they returned to the beam, the whip was gone. The knots which had taken the man nearly half an hour to tie, had apparently been undone in a few seconds. The whip later turned up in a five-gallon jar of buttermilk.

More than a little concerned, Mrs. Dory sent all the children to a neighbor's house more than a mile away, then requested that everyone leave the house. Mr. Dory himself checked the house for intruders, then slid the heavy bolt into the door. When the door was reopened, the Dorys found many articles from outside the house on the kitchen floor, including the contents of two ten-gallon containers of wood ashes that had been set aside for making soap.

Harried and weary of the strange phenomena, the Dorys had to admit that no natural explanation could be found for the mysterious occurrences. They appealed to a Roman Catholic priest, who agreed to help them.

First the cleric asked for some salt, which he ate, saying that it would prevent the "plague" from falling on him. Then the Dorys followed him around the house as he closed and locked all the windows. He drew three crosses above each window sill and three crosses above each door. Although none of the household was of the Roman Catholic faith, all prayed fervently that this man of God could stop the strange phenomena.

"Let no one enter the house while I am gone," he instructed the Dorys. The priest returned half an hour later, then led the family back into their home.

In the kitchen they found a heavy beam and a ladder, that must have come from the barn, lying on the floor in the shape of a cross. A rake and a hoe and several sets of knives and forks had been crossed. In other rooms, sticks of wood, toys, matches, and nearly anything that would move had also been crossed. When all the crossed items were counted the number exactly equaled the number of crosses the priest had drawn in the house. And with that, the strange activity ceased. It had begun at ten o'clock on Saturday and had stopped at ten o'clock on Monday.

Another interesting case is that of Alvin Laubheim, the owner of a Miami, Florida, company supplying novelties and souvenirs to variety stores, who had never believed in ghosts, until one started "busting up" his warehouse in January of 1967.

The prankster showed up on Thursday, January 12, and according to Laubheim, created such havoc that "one girl quit, and she hasn't even been back to pick up her pay."

Patrolman William G. Killin of the Miami Police Department entered the warehouse in time to be struck in the back by a flying object. Killin put in a call for reinforcements. The officers had not been there long when the invisible jokester tossed some small items to the floor.

Figuring that even a poltergeist should have some respect for the law, the sergeant drew his revolver and announced: "I'll shoot the first thing that moves."

"Things" started moving all over the warehouse. The sergeant looked in bewilderment about the place. Without further comment, he slid his revolver back in its holster.

The warehouse measures about fifty by thirty feet. Shelving, up to three feet in depth, runs around the room and there are bins for merchandise in the interior.

On Monday, January 16, the poltergeist amused itself by throwing baseballs around the warehouse.

"All night long it played baseball," Laubheim sighed wearily. "About $150 to $200 in merchandise was destroyed by those baseballs."

Susy Smith, a well-known psychic researcher, investigated the reports and afterward declared, "I've investigated numerous poltergeists, but this is the first time I've witnessed one at work."

Laubheim had a list of sixteen witnesses—not including his own workers or delivery people—who actually saw the poltergeist in action, tossing objects about the warehouse.

The appearance of a poltergeist in a place of business is rare. Home is usually where the haunt is.

And that was the case for Edgar Jones and his wife, who, when they were startled by a sound they had heard, ran into their dining room to see what had happened. There on a shelf and on the floor in front of it, lay what was left of fifteen miniature pitchers, which seemed to have exploded of their own volition.

That was the first appearance of the Baltimore Poltergeist.

Edgar Jones, a retired fireman, and his wife lived in a quiet residential section of Baltimore. They shared the house with their son-in-law, daughter and grandson Ted. Life in the Jones household had been quite pleasant and uneventful up until January 14, 1960, when the pitchers exploded.

In the days that followed, many unexplainable events took place. In the dining room, a ceramic flower pot left a shelf and hurled itself against a window, smashing the pane. A sugar bowl rose from the table and poured its contents into the candle holders on the chandelier.

In the kitchen some iced tea glasses mysteriously fell from a shelf and crashed to the floor. Bottles exploded. A plant jumped out of its holder onto the kitchen table.

Jones' daughter, Mrs. Theodore Pauls, had placed some small pottery pieces on the bed in the bedroom. They were found smashed.

Elsewhere in the house, the incidents continued. Pictures fell from the walls. A brass incense burner took a six-foot journey without any visible application of force. The poltergeist continued to make its debut a memorable occasion.

On Sunday, January 17, the ghost changed its tactics. Previously it had made its presence felt only in the morning, with an occational encore in the afternoon. On this particular Sunday, it struck at night.

A small table, which the Joneses had moved to a stairway landing to avoid having it damaged by the intermittent barrage of flying objects, fell down the stairs. A stack of kindling wood was scattered over the basement as if shattered by a dynamite charge. Mr. Jones had spotted a can of corn that had fallen off a shelf in the pantry. As he bent over to pick it up, a can of sauerkraut fell off the same shelf and rapped him on the head.

The next day, the activity ceased. The Joneses, thankful that their ordeal had ended, immediately set about the task of cleaning up the debris that had been left in the wake of their unwanted guest. They spent all that day and part of the next getting the mess cleaned up. But when they had finished—it was almost noon on Tuesday—the destructive spirit returned for another attack.

The dining room chandelier began swinging violently, as it had several times during the past session. The flower pot that had broken the window on Sunday managed to break itself by apparently exploding from within, blasting a film of dirt across the floor. Eight silver coasters flew from the top of a buffet and scattered themselves around the room.

In the living room, the Christmas tree floated into the air, then settled back down again.

In the basement a heavy floor lamp fell over with a resounding thud.

On Wednesday, January 20, the poltergeist escalated its siege. The Joneses and the Pauls had all they could do to just run from room to room to watch things break. And then as suddenly as they had started things quieted down.

On Thursday, Dr. Nandor Fodor arrived at the Jones' house to conduct an investigation of his own. He centered his attentions on young Ted Pauls after his diagnosis indicated that the boy's creative talent in the area of writing was being repressed. Confident that he had reached the crux of the case, Dr. Fodor returned to New York the next day.

The Jones household was allowed to spend the weekend in peace.

Then, on Monday, January 25, the bundle of psychokinetic energy was back at work, leading off with a nine-hour seige during which it broke almost every dish in the house. Mrs. Jones was at her wit's end. The continued bombardments had nearly driven her out of her mind. In desperation, she left to spend some time with her sister.

During the following week, the incidents seemed to taper off, with perhaps only one or two strange happenings a day. Then on February 9, the outbreaks came to a halt. The Joneses suspected a trick as before; they would get everything cleaned up and back in order and the ghost would return. They waited for several days, but no new incidents occurred. They were never again molested by the mysterious force which had sent so many of their personal possessions flying through the air and turned them into rubble.

Some investigators asserted that young Ted had created a hoax. Others thought that high frequency radio or sound waves were the cause of the destruction. Another popular theory was connected with tremors of underground faults. And somewhere in the speculation, came the age-old idea of the poltergeist.

All manner of modern technological equipment was utilized in an effort to substantiate these many and divergent theories, but nothing, including a seismograph or the high frequency radio receiver, was able to provide the skeptic with a rational explanation.

Imagine the terror of living in a house that keeps trying to burn itself down with mysterious outbursts of flame. As Dr. Fodor observed, the most dangerous type of poltergeist is the incendiary variety.

Mrs. Douglas MacDonald has her own theories concerning the cause of the mysterious fire that all but demolished her home in Glace Bay, Nova Scotia, but she generally does not mention them. "People would laugh at me," she says, "so I keep quiet, but I think there was something like witchcraft or an evil spirit behind this."

The MacDonalds have no children of their own, but through the years they have adopted several. Because of their high character and their success in rearing children, a three-month-old infant was placed in the MacDonalds' care by a child welfare agency. The child remained with them for five months until Mrs. MacDonald had made arrangements for it to be vaccinated. At that time, the child was removed from their custody, because its father objected to immunization for religious reasons.

Two weeks later, a fire was discovered on the second floor of the MacDonald home. Firemen were able to bring the blaze under control, but not before it had done extensive damage to the house.

At first it was thought that faulty electric wiring might have been the cause, but this theory was later disproved.

Two days after the fire, Mrs. MacDonald was in the house, trying to clean up some of the ashes and debris when she thought she smelled smoke. Immediately she called firemen who rushed to the home, but they were unable to find any sign of fire. Puzzled, Mrs. MacDonald resumed her cleaning.

Later that afternoon an insurance adjuster came to assess the damage. During his call, Mrs. MacDonald again thought that she smelled smoke. The adjuster agreed, and the two immediately set out to search the house. Together they discovered a fire smoldering upstairs. When they had put out the flames, the adjuster completed his survey of the damages and left.

Later that day another fire was discovered on the second floor of the house. This one was more extensive than the previous outbreak and did considerably more damage before it was brought under control. New pieces of furniture purchased to replace pieces destroyed by the first fire were also damaged.

Faulty wiring could not be blamed for the latest series of outbreaks, for the power had been cut off from the house after the first fire. There had to be some other explanation.

While the house was being rebuilt, the MacDonalds lived in temporary quarters some distance away. On May 16, Mrs. MacDonald and a daughter returned to their home to see how the remodeling was progressing. The moment they walked into the house, they smelled smoke. When they finally located the fire in the downstairs bathroom, the firemen were already on their way.

A half hour after the firemen had put out the small blaze, they were called back. This time it was a closet in Mr. MacDonald's bedroom. Two hours later the puzzled firemen were summoned to put out a fire which had broken out on the inside surface of a cupboard door. No logical explanation for the fires could be given.

Once more that day firemen were called to the MacDonald home, this time to extinguish flames that had broken out on the back porch. The firemen suspected arson, and they arranged for a police officer to be stationed at the home.

While Mrs. MacDonald, her daughter, a group of neighbors and the policemen were sitting in the house, they noticed a section of wallboard start to smoke and a red glow spread outward from its center. One of the neighbors quickly pulled the board down and snuffed out the flames. Once again, no reasonable explanation could be given for the fire.

Deeming it necessary for everyone's safety, the police officer ordered the house vacated until a proper investigation could be made and the mystery solved.

By then Mrs. MacDonald did not care if the house burned or not. The insurance money had been exhausted and so was she.

And then, as abruptly as they had started, the fires stopped. The poltergeist had spent its energy. The awesome power of the human mind to focus energy and ignite fires may be yet another unknown ability of the subconscious self. Perhaps one of the MacDonalds' children, or even one of the adults themselves, may have expressed their protest at having the baby taken from them in this extraordinary manifestation.

However, a poltergeist causing objects to fly around is much more common. Such was the case at the Szlanfucht home. "We had better call the police," said Walter Szlanfucht to his wife as they lay in bed. Walter had just returned from investigating a loud noise in the other room, where he found that an iron had mysteriously jumped off the sink onto a concrete floor.

The strange happenings had been going on for nearly three weeks. Seemingly without cause or warning, various objects would take to the air and fly through the house. The Szlanfuchts had put up with the inexplicable phenomena, but if things like irons started sailing around, someone could get hurt. Something had to be done to stop the incidents. They did, after all, have a nine-year-old son, and it was hard to judge what effect the phenomena might have on his young and impressionable mind.

The police were finally notified. Captain Hanley and Deputy Leonard Golba were sent to investigate the case. As the two officers were taking notes, recording the damage and carefully looking over broken furniture, the house began to creak as if it were being forced apart by the internal pressure.

Captain Hanley suggested that everyone leave the house. As Captain Hanley started for the door, a table began to follow him. Then it stopped, flipped over and landed on the floor. The officer went back and examined the piece of furniture. He found it to be a rather solid article, weighing perhaps twenty pounds, but he could give no plausible explanation why it acted as it had. There were no strings or gadgets attached to it.

Forgetting about the table momentarily, they once again started for the door. However, before they could get out of the room, a picture on the wall left its hook and fell to the floor. Another brief examination revealed that the wire by which the picture had hung was still intact on the back. It was as if someone had lifted it off the hook.

Once again they started to leave the house, Captain Hanley bringing up the rear of the party. As he stepped onto a small enclosed porch, a box of fairly heavy tools flew off the top of a stove. As Hanley approached the stove to investigate, it fell forward with an unnerving crash. As before, there were no wires or mechanisms attached to either the stove or the box of tools. No apparent reason could be found for their bizarre behavior.

A team from the physical science department of Notre Dame was called in to have a look at the house. They conceded that some strange things had indeed happened, but they gave no immediate comments as to what might have caused the incidents.

Meanwhile, more weird events occurred. Someone saw a small evergreen tree beside the front door bend over, touch the ground, then spring back into place again.

A neighbor standing in the front yard with Walter observed stones rising up from the driveway and hurling themselves against the side of the house. For a moment, the neighbor thought that he might be seeing things, until one of the stones broke a window and fragments of very real glass fell to the ground.

Unable to stand the continuous barrage of flying objects any longer, the Szlanfuchts left their home and went to stay with a relative for a few days. However, they could not shake their invisible tormentor so easily, for no sooner had they arrived at their relative's house when plates and ash trays began floating around in the air.

They reasoned that there was no justice in forcing the hex on the poor uncle, too, so the Szlanfuchts returned home. As if a feat of magic had been performed, the incidents stopped. The spirit seemed to have been purged.

Cases of poltergeists pelting innocent families with stones and pebbles comprise a large category of the evidence of this psychokinetic phenomena. Although people are seldom seriously injured by the stones, it must be more than disconcerting to find oneself the target of some invisible marksman.

"So what's the big mystery?" the reporter demanded impatiently of the weather-hardened farmer who stood before him. The reporter had made a hot dusty trip from Pumphrey, Australia, on what he thought must surely be a wild goose chase.

"You've heard it," the sixty-four-year-old head of the 2,500-acre Donaldson farm replied.

"You mean I've come all the way out here because somebody's been throwing stones?"

"That's not what I said," Donaldson snapped. "When it happens, it rains them—nobody could possibly throw that many at once."

"Hah," the reporter laughed.

At that instant, stones began pelting the ground around the two men. The shower of rock vibrated against the ground, and the reporter jumped back in surprise as one barely missed his head. Then, as suddenly as it had started, the shower of stones stopped.

The reporter looked dazedly at the ground.

"And now I suppose you're going to tell me somebody threw them at us," the Australian farmer said with a wry smile.

"They seemed to materialize in the sky," the reporter said, his face radiating new interest. "When did this begin?"

In March 1957, Mr. Donaldson and his son Brian had stepped from their house into a bright summer day with a flawless blue sky. But they had only taken a few steps when rocks began drumming the ground around them.

After exchanging amazed expressions, the two men hit upon what seemed the only possible solution.

"It must be some of the young aborigines," Brian Donaldson concluded. His father readily agreed, and the two set out to find the culprits. After searching the area, the two men again heard stones thudding upon the ground around them. This prompted a second investigation which proved no more productive than the first. Again the search ended in a stone shower, this one severe enough to drive the men to cover.

When the stone storm had passed, the men hurried to the house and found that Donaldson's daughter-in-law also had seen the falling stones.

"Are they real?" she asked Brian Donaldson.

"Just like ordinary rocks," he reassured her.

Donaldson needed no prompting. He called the police.

With customary thoroughness, the police overturned nearly every rock on the Donaldson farm. They were rewarded with more falling stones. They questioned all the workers on the Donaldson farm and found the first valuable information. Almost without exception, the natives explained that Cyril Penny, a young native stockman, had been cursed and that he caused the stones to fall on the Donaldson farm. Although the police were understandably reluctant to believe this tale of a hex, it remained the only lead they had produced. To test it, the officers directed Donaldson to send the stockman away from the farm on some pretext or other.

Cyril Penny spent Saturday, March 16, 1957, in Pumphrey on an errand for his employer. No stones fell from the sky while he remained in town, yet when he returned the mysterious stone showers resumed.

News of the falling stones spread quickly throughout the surrounding towns, and the Donaldson farm became the center of much activity. Newsmen, photographers, investigators, and curiosity seekers all wanted to see the falling stones. By Monday, June 18, the elder Donaldson had conversed with the *Sydney Morning Herald* by phone and described a cut in the head his son had received from one of the stones.

The stones themselves always seemed to materialize a few feet over the observer's head. The larger ones were nearly as big as a man's fist. Investigators found no finger prints on their dust-covered surfaces and, in fact, found nothing unusual about the stones at all.

The only possible explanation seemed to be a poltergeist. Psychic researchers reminded the local residents that similar strange incidents had occurred only a year before near Mayanup, a place southwest of Pumphrey. That mystery centered around a half-caste named Gilbert Smith. Not only did stones fall from the sky and within his hut, but newsmen observed a spoon, a bottle cover, and an apple floating from Smith's tent, even though the dwelling had been unoccupied at the time.

Although investigators and curiosity seekers found the falling stones interesting, the novelty soon wore off for the Donaldsons. The stones themselves disrupted work on the farm and the droves of people visiting the farm also interfered with production. In time, the falling stones spread to other areas, and workers who had moved in an effort to escape the stones found their exodus in vain. The stones had frightened them so much that they would not work. A deputation of natives asked Donaldson to dismiss Cyril Penny, but even after the stockman had left the farm the stones continued to fall.

Just when the Donaldsons had begun to seriously consider the idea of selling the farm, the stones ceased falling. Newsmen pressed for an explanation. They asked Cyril Penny; they asked all the experts; but no one could explain why the stones began falling or why they had as mysteriously stopped dropping from out of nowhere.

8

A Terrible Basement in Lincoln, Nebraska

April 20, 1970. I held the negatives up to the light, squinted as my eyes focused on the strange, reversed sight.

"Yes," I said into the receiver. "I can see it. It looks like a baby's face on the basement wall."

Dick Mezzy's voice crackled at me over the long-distance wire. "That's exactly what it is, Brad. I'm not going to give you any more details about the place now, but I hope that those negatives will intrigue you enough to direct your psychic safari to Lincoln for a few days."

Dick, who was at that time associated with the *Lincoln Journal and Star*, had become a local authority on the occult, the paranormal and the UFO phenomenon in his corner of Nebraska. An exuberant and talented young man, who was, incidentally, developing rather impressive psychic abilities of his own, Mezzy had become the Nebraska clearing house for reports of unidentified flying objects, haunted houses and things that go bump in the night. Since he had done some preliminary research on the house in question, which we shall call the Richard house, I knew that a recommendation from Dick Mezzy was an assurance that the home offered a number of psychic surprises.

Our safari checked into the Holiday Inn on the east edge of Lincoln about two o'clock on a blisteringly hot July afternoon. While we sought the air-conditioned shelter of our rooms, Glenn McWane called Dick and let him know that we had arrived in Lincoln. Mezzy told Glenn that he had confirmed our tour of the house with Mrs. Richard for that night.

"We'll have to be out of there before ten, though," Mezzy said. "That's when her husband will be coming home from his shift, and he would blow all gaskets if he found us there. He doesn't want anyone stirring up what is already there."

Glenn told the newsman that we quite understood the situation, as it was not an uncommon condition under which, from time to time, we were forced to carry out our ghost hunting.

Dick joined us for dinner that night, then left his sports car at the motel in order to commandeer my station wagon and drive us to the Richards' home.

"Now I've purposely not told you anything about the place," Dick said somewhat apologetically to Irene. "I hope I understood that that was the way you wanted it."

"That's exactly the way we want it," Irene replied. "I want to be totally free of any preconceived ideas or thoughts before I enter any of the houses on our psychic safari."

"Well, good, then," Mezzy said as we rounded a corner and began to slow down. "Here's the house. Sic'em, Irene!"

It was late twilight, and the air had not yet cooled from the day's extremely high temperatures. The Richard house seemed to crouch there before us like some panting beast, worn and tired from the summer heat. Although it was obviously an old house, it did not appear quite as ominous as some of the houses which we had visited on our safari. There was, though, a strange kind of presence, or vibration, that I think most of us seemed to feel as we walked through the screen door to be received by Mrs. Richard.

"Sorry we don't have air conditioning," Mrs. Richard apologized. "Terrible hot night. We have a lot of these in Nebraska."

We hastened to assure her that we were all Midwesterners and were as accustomed to heat and humidity as anyone could ever get. Mrs. Richard was obviously very nervous, and when Mezzy introduced her to Mrs. Hughes, the woman seemed to be torn between a desire to curtsy and a desire to run screaming from the house.

Melody, her daughter, blinked large, frightened fawn-like eyes at us, and acknowledged our greetings in soft, unintelligible mumbles. A slender girl in her mid-teens, Melody seemed at once eager to get on with things, yet visibly concerned over what might materialize.

"That lady's a psychic," I heard her tell her girlfriend. "She's gonna make that awful ghost go away."

"Most of the things have happened in the basement, is that right?" Mezzy said, sensing the need for a direction to the evening. I appreciated his assuming the role of guide in the Richard house, since he had met the woman and her daughter previously and had even counseled them about the phenomena that had continued to feed and grow in the environment of their home.

"Yes," Mrs. Richard admitted. "But we don't have to go down there, do we?"

"It would be better if we could be in the area where you have experienced the most disturbances," I explained.

The mother and daughter exchanged quick, worried glances. It appeared as though they might be saying to each other *"If we take these people down there and they stir up the haunting even more than it was before, what will become of us? It is well and good for these strangers. They will leave. But we have to stay here and suffer the consequences!"*

"I won't go down there even in the daytime unless...unless I have someone with me," Mrs. Richard said softly, as if she were concerned about someone overhearing her admission.

"We'll all be with you now," Irene said in her soft, soothing voice. "You have nothing to be afraid of. And we won't set anything loose on you before we leave."

The daughter emitted a strange little whimpering sound. Dick Mezzy stepped to her side and whispered something to her.

Since I had time to pay closer attention to Melody, it appeared as if she might nearly be in an altered state of consciousness, as though she were about to enter trance. Although I could not overhear Dick's conversation with the teenager, he seemed to be speaking to her in a kind of gruff, big brother fashion, which was totally applicable to the situation. I knew that I was making an extremely superficial assessment, but it seemed to me that Melody tottered somewhere in a borderland of reality that could lead to hysteria, involuntary mediumship or temporary possession.

"The door to the basement is back through the living room and kitchen," Mrs. Richard said, at last making up her mind to permit us access to what was ostensibly the seat of the haunting. Following her resolve, she even led the way down the stairs and into a back room of the damp, cluttered basement.

"Who draws the paintings on the wall?" Irene asked, indicating the bright artwork that littered the floor and in some instances had been applied directly to the wall.

"I do," Melody said, apparently quite proud of her artistic ability.

Irene turned back to the wall, then caught her breath in a sharp intake of air that became a startled gasp.

"What is it?" a number of us chorused in unison, at once solicitous of the medium's welfare and curious to know what she had glimpsed with the aid of her psychism.

"I saw the image of a man coming through that wall!" Irene said. "His hair was long and unkempt. He was unshaven with a thick beard."

Melody's eyes widened, and she once again uttered that strange kind of panting whimper. "I've seen him before. I've seen him before when I've been down here painting!"

"He has a very thin face and his hair is very shaggy," Irene said. "I had the impression that he was a wanderer. That he was unsettled. I felt as though he wanted to come home, and he considered this his home."

"I know who he is, too!" Melody said loudly. "He's that man who used to live here who blew his wife's head off with a shotgun!"

Dick Mezzy rolled his eyes upward in disappointment and controlled anger. "Melody," he said through gritted teeth, "I asked you not to give Mrs. Hughes any clues as to what happened here!"

"But I've seen that man she's described coming at me from out of that wall!" Melody protested in a loud voice, as if repetition and increased volume could vindicate her blunder.

"It's all right," Irene said. "Don't feel bad." Then, turning to Mrs. Richard, the psychic asked frankly: "You've seen him, too, haven't you?"

"Yes," the woman answered. Her face had grown pale, and her hands trembled, as she touched a handkerchief to the beads of sweat on her forehead. "Yes, I've seen something very similar to what you describe."

"I saw him coming through the wall over there," Irene said pointing to a back wall of the small room of the main basement area. "Do you feel that somebody might have died in this room? Do you feel that a man may have been stabbed to death?"

Mrs. Richard watched the back wall as if she feared that the ghost might appear at any moment. "You...you go ahead with your talking," she said, declining to answer the question Mrs. Hughes had posed for her.

"I see a man whom I feel was stabbed and it looks like his heart is stabbed and cut. It looks as if someone had carved a cross over his heart," the psychic said.

"There is a theory that a man, a murder victim, may have been found in that condition in this house," Mezzy said. "I can't find any proof of that. However, it does seem to be neighborhood legend...along with that shotgun murder—which did happen."

Irene turned to focus her attention on Melody. "You have sometimes been able to see the blood running from the wall."

"Yes!" the girl agreed. "Yes!"

"And you," Irene said, readdressing herself to the mother. "Didn't you once turn on a tap in the basement to do your washing and see blood running out of the faucet?"

Mrs. Richard looked very much as if she wanted desperately to leave the basement. "Yes," she admitted. "I have just completely stopped using the basement."

"You turned on the spout and it looked like blood coming out of the faucet," Irene repeated.

Mrs. Richard nodded. "That's one of the reasons why I simply will not go down in the basement alone, even in the daylight. I won't come down here anytime unless someone comes with me."

"And there is the form of a woman who bothers you," Irene said, zeroing in on the phenomena. "She is a fussy, argumentative woman who constantly talks and nags, and you wish that you could tell her to shut up!"

"I have told her," Mrs. Richard said, "but it hasn't seemed to do any good."

"Did you, about a week or two ago, awaken because there was a man shaking you and telling you to wake up?" Mrs. Hughes asked.

Mrs. Richard nodded. "Yes, I did. That's true."

"You awakened to see a man bending over you," Mrs. Hughes continued. "You knew at once that he was in spirit."

"But I didn't know who it was!" Mrs. Richard protested.

Mrs. Hughes stood for a few moments in silence. "I have the feeling that it was your father's brother. I see that the initial 'D' would belong to that man."

"That's right," Mrs. Richard said. "I mean, if it was my uncle, his name began with a 'D'."

"That next morning you got up and folded some bedclothes and old blankets, and you put them in a box," Irene told the woman. "You put them away because they reminded you of something and someone in your past, and you just didn't want to bother with them anymore. Is that right?"

Mrs. Richard nodded her head slowly, unbelievingly. "That's right, I did that."

Irene Hughes turned her attention back to the mysterious little room in which most of our party now stood.

"This is funny," she mused, "but up on that ledge I see what looks like a shell of something. I thought at first it looked like it might have been a watermelon. Was it a large gourd?"

"It was my pumpkin!" Melody volunteered. "I carved a jack-o'-lantern and put it on that ledge. And it just disappeared. I mean, it vanished. I never saw it again, and none of us could find it anywhere."

Irene considered this information for a moment. "A similar thing happened to a pair of your blue jeans, isn't that right, Melody? You were looking everywhere for these jeans, and when you found them, they were wadded up under your bed."

Melody nodded soberly. "That happens to me a lot," she said.

Irene moved closer to talk softly with Mrs. Richard and Melody. I had been inside the small room with Irene, Mrs. Richard, Melody, and Joan Hurling. Glenn and Dick Mezzy had been just outside the door of the back room.

"Hey, Brad," Glenn whispered. "We've got something weird going on with this door."

I frowned an unspoken question, and Glenn went on to explain. "Well, you've been too busy recording and making notes on the conversation inside the room to notice, but the door keeps closing on you people."

"What do you mean?" I asked, looking with fresh vision on the wooden door.

"First of all, " Mezzy said, "from the angle in which it is set, it should naturally swing open. See there? The floor slants a bit here, and the door jamb really isn't too cool a job. It would be an uphill fight against gravity for this door to close by itself."

"But," I said, supplying the cue line.

"But the door has been swinging closed," Glenn said.

"A couple times, just as I've tried to take a picture of you in the back room, the door has swung nearly shut and ruined my shot. Another time, I wedged my toe under the door to hold it, and the darn thing nearly bent at the top because there was so much pressure being exerted against it!"

"Okay," I grinned. "We're all out of the room now. Shut the door if that is what it wants so badly."

Glenn swung the door to the jamb, then found he had to lift it to make a tight fit. "Now the blame thing should be happy," Glenn said, "it's stuck closed good and tight."

The troublesome door firmly closed, we moved to join the others, who were walking toward the other end of the basement where the image of the baby's face had been set into the wall.

"Don't touch it!" Melody was shouting, as I joined Irene next to the strange effigy. "Don't touch it! It's evil. If you touch it, he'll come out of the wall. He'll come to kill again!"

Once again the resourceful Dick Mezzy was there to grasp the teenager's arm and pacify her. Melody's breathing had become very rapid. Her eyes were half-closed. She appeared about to enter a trance state.

"Listen to Mrs. Hughes!" Mezzy said sharply. "Listen to her! That baby's face can't hurt you!"

"Don't allow yourself to become hysterical," Irene said in her soft voice. "You'll only give strength to whatever negative forces might possibly be harbored somewhere in this house.

"Now, this face," she said, directing her attention to the strange impression in the wall. "First of all, I get the impression that no one in the family did this, did they?"

"No," Mrs. Richard said, "it was here when we moved in."

Irene paused, then continued: "There is no baby buried under here or anything like that, but I have the feeling that it was done to commemorate a family's first child. The parents were so proud that they did this as kind of a monument to their first baby.

"Nothing will happen to you if you touch this face," she said, directing her comments to the distraught Melody. "See?" she asked, as her fingers lightly stroked the baby's round cheeks. "This was a work of love. I think it is extremely interesting that people would do something like this.

"It's not a real baby's face," the psychic continued. "And that's not a real baby's skull under it, even though it looks so real. I would say that it was probably carved in the 1930s. Do you know how old the house is, Mrs. Richard?"

"Through research," our hostess answered, "we have found that the house is about eighty-five years old, maybe even older. There is a bit of confusion, but it seems the first record of this house goes back to 1880."

"I would say that it is older than that," Mrs. Hughes suggested.

"It could be," Mrs. Richard readily conceded. "The civic records back that far are a bit jumbled, and they may have got this place and the one down the street mixed up."

"Did you learn that the people who lived here and the people who lived down the street were relatives?" Mrs. Hughes asked.

"That's right," Mrs. Richard said. "They were."

"I feel," Mrs. Hughes went on, "that across from here and not very far away that the original owner of this house had some dealings in grain. I see large grain bins or elevators, and it looks like flour or meal or something is coming from them."

"There were some old grain mills and bins not too far from here," Dick Mezzy offered, "but I don't know how we could trace the connection today unless we could find just the right old-timer."

At this point, it was decided to return to the first floor of the home.

"How's the door?" I asked Glenn just before we started up the stairs.

"Shut as tight as a clam," he assured me.

Melody's bedroom was at the top and to the right of the basement stairs. Irene Hughes stopped suddenly in the middle of the teenager's bedroom, stringing our party in a line from Glenn and Dick Mezzy, still at the top of the basement stairs, to Joan Hurling, just entering the kitchen, the first room off Melody's bedroom.

The psychic paused, as if carefully sorting out the impressions that had begun to bubble up from her unconscious.

"Do you often feel that someone is peeking in that window at you?" she asked Melody.

"All the time!" Melody shuddered. "It's such an icky feeling!"

"What does he look like?" Irene wanted to know.

"I can never tell for sure," Melody said, her upper teeth worrying an edge of her lip.

Irene moved to a dresser. "There's a strange, almost electrical vibration near this piece of furniture."

"I have that same kind of feeling in that same spot," Mrs. Richard sighed. "And I've had several friends feel the same thing there."

"It feels like there is something moving underneath me!" Irene said loudly.

"I've felt it now for six years!" Mrs. Richard agreed, her handkerchief patting desperately at heavy beads of sweat.

Irene would soon share her feelings with us, and we would all be able to participate in an audible representation of the "thing" moving beneath the floor as well.

BAM! BAM! BAM!

"It's right under me!" Mrs. Hughes shouted. "It's like somebody pushing, banging up the floor! Did everyone feel it...hear it?"

One would have to have lost feeling below his knees and have gone suddenly deaf not to have felt and heard the powerful series of knocks.

"Do you want to look in the basement?" Irene asked, but Glenn and Dick Mezzy were already pounding down the stairs.

I knew where they were heading, and I walked back to the head of the stairs and shouted down: "Well?"

"The door to the back room is wide open," Glenn called up.

"We couldn't tame that door or whatever is in the room that easily," Dick added.

When the two men rejoined us, Dick said that he had felt a "force" push past him just seconds before the knocking had begun on the floor.

After the journalist had vocalized this admission, others who had been standing in line with the basement stairway said that they, too, had felt "something" rush by them.

"I'm getting another image of our man in the basement," Irene said. "He was seen in a mirror once, and the mirror was broken, because I see a new one being put in this room."

"That happened to me," Melody spoke up without hesitation, in spite of the tremor in her voice. "I saw the guy standing behind me when I was combing my hair and looking in the mirror. And he was so ugly that I just smashed the mirror. When my dad replaced the mirror, I had him put it where it wouldn't reflect that basement door."

"He's a tall man," Irene went on. "And in spite of his rather unkemp appearance, he is really not so ugly."

Mrs. Richard had been silent for several minutes, but Irene's continued description of the spectral interloper from the basement caused her to re-enter the conversation. "We see his shadow," she said quietly. "That shadow was the first thing that we had ever seen out of the ordinary in this house. I saw this man's shadow, his outline in this doorway . . . ."

"He was standing up straight," Melody interrupted her mother. "He wasn't leaning over."

"The first time," Mrs. Richard said, regaining the floor, "I thought it was my husband coming home from work. I kept calling his name, and he didn't answer me, and I thought he was doing something just to frighten me. I kept calling and calling his name, but he wouldn't answer. Then I thought someone had broken in."

"It was terrible," Melody added. "Every time we see that shadow is terrible. I know that it is that big ugly man trying to get us, trying to pull us with him into the grave!"

I could see that Irene was visibly upset by the girl's extreme emotionality. She reached out as if to touch Melody, but the teenager shrank back.

"Melody," Irene said, "I feel I have a message especially for you. You are a very distrustful girl. I feel that no matter how many girlfriends you may have, you don't trust any of them, and you push them away from you. It seems as though you want to push everyone away from you."

The attractive girl lowered her eyes, touched by the psychic's advice, yet apparently determined to resist absorbing any of her wisdom.

Irene continued her attempt to penetrate the psychic wall that the girl had erected around herself. "I feel that you are going to have to make some very important decisions about relationships very soon and that you really have to be very careful in these decisions and not become antagonistic. You are about to ruin a very beautiful friendship, and I feel that you have already had a parting with a very good friend."

"Jane Hanson," Melody supplied the name, the very utterance constituting her admission of guilt.

"Take a second look at yourself, would you please?" Irene told her. "You need to be cautious for your own personal happiness. I feel if you don't you will regret your actions very much within a year."

"You certainly have her right!" Mrs. Richard said, the eerie haunting momentarily forgotten in her concern for her daughter's future.

"But it was Jane's fault," Melody whined, shirking all responsibility. "It was all Jane's fault that we had that fight."

A bit sternly, Irene added the following postscript to her advice: "Within a year, you will need a doctor's care. You will regret it very much if you follow that young man to California. He doesn't intend to keep his promises to you. In October, you will have to make the final decision. Although I urge you to resist his offers, I fear that you will listen only to your emotions."

[According to a follow-up report, Melody left home in October to live with a young man who had promised to take the teenager to California to live with hippies. When last heard of, the girl had been left pregnant and addicted to heavy drugs by her unfaithful lover.]

Irene walked over to the kitchen sink. "There is another man who comes to you sometimes when you are doing dishes. Is that true, Mrs. Richard?"

"Yes, yes," the woman admitted. "It's a frightening presence to me. Whenever I feel him next to me, I run out the door. I can't stay anywhere in this house for too long a time when I am alone."

"I don't think you should be frightened of this spirit," Irene told her. "I think that this man belongs to you. He is someone who has passed over and wants to come through to you. Because you do not understand these things, you have only fear when you sense his presence."

"I'm not sure what the presence is," Mrs. Richard said, shaking her head vigorously, "but I know that it is frightening!"

"This is not the man in the basement," Irene emphasized. "This feels like a very different person. This feels more like your father."

"My father has been dead since 1959," Mrs. Richard told the psychic. "There have been times when I have felt his presence just before a crisis in the family."

"Before we entered this house tonight, Mrs. Richard," Irene said, "I said that someone had died of cancer in this house, and I felt sick for a few moments after we came in your door."

"My mother died of cancer in 1967," she answered. "She was here in May and died in July."

"When I feel her dying of cancer," Mrs. Hughes commented, "I see a large pecan tree."

"If it truly is my mother you feel," Mrs. Richard said, "she loved pecans!"

By now we had been in and out of every room in the house with the exception of the small utility room opposite the door through which we had entered the Richard home.

"I feel a fast heartbeat!" Irene said the moment she stepped into the room. "This was the room of the man who was stabbed in the basement."

"It is in this room that we see the moving light some nights," Mrs. Richard said. "We have never been able to explain it as being caused by any kind of reflection or any light source that we can account for. It moves across the room from the picture on the wall, to the window, to that light fixture over there."

"This was once a bedroom," Irene said. "He used to sit and read beneath that picture for a while, then he would become restless and walk over to the window and stand looking out. After more lonely hours in his room, he would shut off the light and go to bed."

"This was a bedroom when we moved in," Mrs. Richard said.

"I really feel that this man was a construction worker or some kind of trained laborer," Irene said. "And I feel that he was stabbed either in this house or somewhere else and robbed for his money. It may have been that he was brought to the basement and to that back room while someone went to notify the authorities.

"But now I feel that his spirit considers this house his home and that is why he keeps returning here," the psychic continued. "That is why you have seen his image coming out of the wall. That is why you have seen his shadow in the doorway as if he were coming home from work. And the blood pouring from the faucets is a reminder of the terrible way in which he was murdered. But please understand, he means no one any harm."

After Irene had offered a prayer and a meditation for the restless entity's peace of spirit, we left the house to enter a garage in the Richards' backyard. It was here, according to most reports, that a maddened husband had put a violent end to his wife with the blast from a shotgun. Since the medium had already picked up most of the impressions relating to the murder while she was in the house, she again asked for peace for the entities.

It would be ridiculous for us to say that we had "cured" a haunting or that we had effectively put a restless spirit or two to rest. It seemed apparent to us that the house did serve as a receptacle for paranormal phenomena. There was the door that would not stay either open or closed; there was the ghost of the unkempt man that had appeared in the back room of the basement and in the girl's bedroom; there was the "blood" that had flowed from the faucet in the basement; there was the thumping, thudding evidence of some kind of preternatural force in the teenager's bedroom.

The Richard house, in our opinion, was a kind of "psychic supermarket" with an extraordinarily wide range of phenomena co-existing within its walls. Irene left the Richards with brief instructions as to how they might employ psychic self-defense against any unwanted spectral visitors, and she gave the mother and daughter private consultations designed to fortify them against the fear and hysteria that had begun to warp their perspective toward life in the old house.

"How do you feel about Mrs. Hughes and her ability to tune in on the manifestations in your home?" I asked Mrs. Richard just before we left their home. We had been keeping one eye on the clock so that we could be out of the house before her unknowing and unsympathetic husband returned from work.

"The impressions she picked up of the things that happened in this house were just exactly correct," she admitted. "The man in the basement, the shadows, the ghost that shook me awake, the bood in the faucet—all those things were correct.

"Now, of course," she added, "I don't know about all those names she mentioned. This is an old house and some of those families might have lived here long before us. But she came very close to all the names that I know used to live here."

I would probably have to yield somewhat to the spiritistic hypothesis in this home, but there were certainly strong elements of poltergeistic-psychokinetic haunting involved. The disturbed teenager, so often a vital ingredient to poltergeist manifestations, was present, but then so were the possibilities of virulent memory patterns having been impressed upon the environment by two murders. The mother and her daughter felt a definite interaction with at least two spirit entities, and Irene seemed to sense them and described them exactly as the woman had seen them.

As we left the Richard house with its gamut of psychical phenomena, Glenn turned to shake his head at the platinum-haired, smiling lady in the backseat of the station wagon.

"Irene," he said, "I don't know how you do it. It was really remarkable the way you managed to tune in on all those things in that house. But there was one thing you couldn't do."

"Oh," Irene frowned, seeming to do a mental inventory of the house before she went on: "What was that, Glenn?"

"Even you couldn't make that spooky door in the basement behave!"

9

Olof Jonsson and the Phenomena of the Seance Room

By the time the haunted family in Varnersborg contacted Olof Jonsson, they had been visited by the eerie manifestations for fourteeen nights in succession. The phenomena seemed to center around the large table where they ate their evening meals. Knocks would thud so heavily on its surface that eating utensils and tableware would be sent flying to the floor. Then after the violent knockings, a flickering blob of light would materialize in a corner of the dining room.

"We've thought of appealing to Pastor Lund," the head of the family, Oscar Petersen, told Olof, "but we know that the Lutheran church is not especially receptive to tales of ghosts and requests for exorcism. Berit, my wife, has suggested that we contact Father Larsen, but . . ."

"Why not let me see what I am able to accomplish before you consult the clergy," Olof interrupted. "Sometimes if the entity is particularly malignant, prayers, incense, and holy water only serve to irritate it and bring about even more violent displays. Then, too, it seems that religious denominations and their dogmas have little meaning on the other side of the veil."

Petersen agreed to suffer one more night of the phenomena until Olof could visit his home on the following evening.

"I hated to leave the man and his family to face the unknown another night, but it was impossible for me to cancel plans and attend to them at once," Olof told me.

"Although I am continually being called a medium, I am not really a Spiritualist in the full sense of the term," said Jonsson, who, in February, 1971, participated in the famous Moon to Earth ESP experiment. "I have no spirit guides, and while I accept the possibility of entities contacting us from beyond the grave, I really believe that the phenomenon which we call a 'ghost' is most often a sort of radiation of the human personality which retains the memories of the physically deceased person.

"I also believe that many times that which is contacted at seances is actually this radiation rather than the actual surviving entity. It is my opinion that, in most instances, the actual Soul of a person has gone on to a different spiritual realm, or dimension, and the 'ghost' is but an astral form left behind."

When Olof arrived at the Petersen residence, he made certain to time his appearance so that he might witness the full event of the manifestation.

"Go on about your meal and your usual routine, as if I were not here," Olof told the Petersens. "Let me observe just what it is that visits you."

The family did as they were told and sat down around the large and heavy table to begin their evening meal.

The first knock was so violent that it sent a metal platter of fish to the floor, scattering its contents across the carpet.

The second thud sounded next to Mrs. Petersen's plate and caused her to jerk back in reflex action.

Olof stood calmly off to one side of the table, indicating by a gesture of his upraised hand that the family should remain seated.

"There are usually three heavy knocks before the minor rappings begin," Petersen told the psychic.

The words were scarcely out of his mouth when a pitcher of water shattered and drenched a bowl of hot vegetables and the three Petersen children. The youngest child began to cry, and Mrs. Petersen left her chair to comfort him. As she did so, her chair was tipped over, and the floor sounded with heavy footsteps which seemed to withdraw to a corner of the room.

"And now comes the light," Petersen sighed. "The phenomenon will have run its course."

"Not tonight," Olof corrected him, as he watched the flickering globe of light materialize in the corner opposite the one in which he had positioned himself. "I shall concentrate on sending psychic energy to the light so that we might better see what it is that is molesting you."

With Olof directing his mental energy toward the pulsating globule of light, the nebulous pocket of radiation began to take on form.

"My God, Berit," Petersen shouted at his wife, "get the children out of here!"

The mother gathered her children under her arms and ushered them quickly out of the dining room. The light had begun to take on the shape of an elderly woman whose face was an ugly mask of hatred. The image was not an appropriate one for small children to carry with them to their beds.

"It...it appears to be Sigrid," Petersen said. "But why...?"

Olof had slipped into a light trance. "She is angry, very angry that you have the table," Olof told the man. "And she says that you have cheated her and lied to her."

Petersen slumped into a chair. He had become very pale. He opened his mouth, made a few inarticulate sounds, then seemed to think better of it and chose to remain silent.

"She says that you have stolen from her daughter, that you have..."

"But can this really be Sigrid's ghost returned from beyond the grave?" Petersen wanted to know. "Surely she would know that these things are not so."

As Olof returned to a level of mind more attuned to the material plane, the image of the old woman began to lose its definition and became an abstract arrangement of flickering lights.

"This would seem to be a memory pattern of hatred that has been directed at you by someone in the last moments before death," the psychic explained. "It is of such strength that it can produce those telekinetic effects on your table."

"It...it isn't really a ghost, then?" Petersen asked, still confused.

"It *is* a ghost," Olof clarified, "but it is not really this Sigrid to whom you refer. What we saw was her astral form, which had been set free with a residue of her memories and her emotions. This astral form is acting very much like a puppet, only it is doing the bidding of a puppeteer who is no longer living."

"Sigrid was an older friend of my mother's," Petersen offered. "She was like an aunt to me, even though we were not really related. Sigrid had married late in life, and then her husband died and left her with an infant daughter. The daughter and I were childhood playmates, and it was Sigrid's hope that we would marry. Neither the young lady nor I felt romantically inclined toward one another, but we remained good friends."

Petersen paused to light his pipe, then once he had the tobacco burning, he set the pipe in an ashtray, as if the smoke nauseated him.

"Could it be that Sigrid was still alive that day and misunderstood our conversation?" he asked the empty space before him.

"I became Sigrid's attorney as soon as I had my law degree," Petersen said, turning to face Olof. "She was always a headstrong woman, and in her later years she became mentally confused, suspicious of everyone to the point of paranoia. On her deathbed, she charged me once again with my responsibilities as her executor, and she made a special point of reminding me that her daughter was to receive certain items of personal property, such as this magnificent old table here."

Petersen picked up the pipe and another match, then decided better of it and resumed speaking: "Sigrid went faster than anticipated toward the end and her daughter was unable to get to her bedside before she lapsed into a final coma. The doctor said something to me about what a grand old woman Sigrid had been, and I agreed, stating that at least I would have the old table and certain antiques by which to remember her.

"You see," Petersen hastened to add before Olof could think the worst, "Sigrid's daughter and I had had an earlier conversation in which she stated that she did not want the expense of hauling the heavy piece of furniture to her home in Stockholm. She told me that she did not really care about antiques anyway, and since I had always admired the pieces, I should keep them for myself as a remembrance of her mother. I protested, then consented if she would allow me to deduct a certain sum from my legal fees in return. Now it appears that Sigrid must have somehow been able to hear me utter those words to the doctor, and she has cursed me for a thief!"

Olof assured the man that there was no need to become upset. "The kind of ghost that is troubling you is very much like a persistent messenger boy who will not be put off from delivering the message that has been entrusted to him," he explained. "Just as the ghost was formed by the dying brain of a human being, so can it be dissipated by a living brain."

Olof meditated for a few moments, then entered another level of consciousness which permitted him to direct psychic energy toward the flickering lights in the corner. Within seconds, the "ghost" had disappeared.

"That was not just the ordinary brain of an ordinary human being that accomplished that feat," Petersen remarked in awe at Jonsson's psychic prowess.

Olof shrugged and smiled. "But remember, I did not destroy the soul of Sigrid, I merely dispersed the telepathic-telekinetic energy which she directed toward you in her last moments of confused hatred. Your 'ghost' has been exorcised."

After listening to Olof Jonsson recount this story, it occurred to me to ask why so much of the phenomena of the seance room seems to center around a tilting table, a rapping table, or a floating table. Olof replied with an interesting digression on what he termed the "table dance."

The table dance has an ancient history. Through the ages people in Scandinavia have used this phenomenon for amusement and possible edification on dark, winter nights. For the most part, they have entertained themselves by posing questions that are answered with knocks, or a leg-jerk for yes or no. Occasionally the answers have been optimistic and positive;

other times they have been extremely misleading and uninformative. In many instances the "answer" has depended upon the skillfulness of the inquirers and their ability to interpret the response of the table.

If strong powers have been at work among those seated around the table, the table can manage to behave like a ghost and glide across the floor, occasionally even standing on its end and pounding the floor so violently that neighbors grow uneasy. It is not unheard of that table legs have been broken off and damage has been done to other furniture in the room.

It is a very common misconception that it is necessary to use a round table without nails or screws in order for the phenomenon of table dancing to be effective. I have been present when heavy oak tables, yards long, have shown a capacity to move which one would not believe of such massive pieces of furniture.

Skeptical persons who attend table dances for the first time like to accuse one or more participants seated around the table of having purposely brought on the movement with their hands or feet. If the phenomenon has not been deliberately faked, however hard the skeptics try they will not find any fraud in the table dance. On the contrary, soon they will realize that there are other powers at work which no one can consciously develop.

Now and then, if the conditions are suitable, the table dance may set in motion other phenomena in the room. Pictures may slip from their hooks; vases may crash to the floor; and a great many other things may happen. Yes, now and then it has happened that someone in the group has felt movements as if hands were brushing their faces and breasts. Puffs of wind, like waves of intense cold moving through the room, are not rare; a great deal of noise and light can also manifest themselves.

Photographer and psychic researcher Sven Turck described many particularly conspicuous manifestations which occurred at seances in his studio on Vesterbo Street in Copenhagen, Denmark. Big, heavy tables lifted themselves to the ceiling, in spite of several persons "on board" as passengers.

One medium who sat in our group at Sven Turck's was named Michelson. He was able to bring about veritable flights up to the ceiling, and on some occasions his clothes were torn from his body without anyone comprehending how such actions could come about. During a number of seances, a long, thick rope would wind itself repeatedly around Michelson, as if it were a boa constrictor. Michelson grew to become deathly frightened by this rope, which he thought meant to strangle him.

During one seance, Turck's dog found its way into the laboratory. The animal jumped up exactly as if it saw something in front of it, barked angrily, then looked horribly frightened and crept away with its tail between its legs.

Such phenomena eventually got on the nerves of the mediums as well as the participants in these particularly dramatic seances—especially when the phenomena continued in Turck's private dwelling and in the homes of us mediums. At last it got to the point where the photographer and his family had to abandon their place and settle in the country. From Sven Turck's experience, the psychic researcher should realize that he must be cautious in his traffic with the "powers" that lie behind the phenomena of the seance room.

What are these powers? It is not enough to speak of the role of the subconscious or the unconscious muscular movements of the participants in such instances of widespread phenomena. The camera, film and flash attachment can register the very moment when the psychically influenced objects begin to move. But the origin of the power itself lies far beyond the photographer's lens.

Danish author-researcher Poul Thorsen witnessed a number of psychokinetic seance room demonstrations accomplished with Olof Jonsson acting as the medium. In Thorsen's opinion: "Engineer Jonsson's telekinetic demonstrations are always brought about through a conscious, concentrated effort of willpower, and are totally free of the cooperation of spirit guides and the like. When certain objects, as for example a flask standing on a table, moves as a result of...a concentration of will...we are facing a common telekinetic phenomenon. We are also facing a telekinetic phenomenon when a slip of paper, which I, myself, had inserted in the neck of a milk bottle, flies out of the bottle with a noise.... When clairvoyance is also added to telekinesis, we have an interesting combination of psychic and physical phenomena...."

In his book, *Man's Unknown Powers,* Thorsen described a seance during which he and five other people, none of whom had ever before met Jonsson, were present.

Among many other phenomena that evening I shall mention one, when someone present—and this was repeated several times—took a card out of the deck without anyone's looking at the card. After that we all sat down around a circular table, which on the medium's command should give the color and value of the card through knockings. In some instances the medium sat with the others beside the table; in others, he stood behind them.

Each time the table tapped out, with very powerful blows, the correct value of the card, and one time so violently that the leg of the table went to pieces.

All these experiments, therefore, showed a combination of telekinesis and clairvoyance. This medium showed, as he himself said, "by means of his subconscious," which one of all the unknown cards it was; and through the act of mental power, he raised the table to knock out the value of the card. The medium accomplished everything without the pre-engaged assistance of any invisible being.

Nor was I aware of any "invisible beings" at the seance that I attended in the home of a Chicago-area schoolteacher in which Ruth Zimmerman and Olof Jonsson served as the mediums. However, the table did become quite lively and, unfortunately, dealt the soft-spoken and gentle Mrs. Zimmerman a severe blow in the abdomen, as it rocked violently on its side. The low blow seemed to end the table dance for that night, but Mrs. Zimmerman did attract a number of glowing, firefly-sized lights around her face, and there were a few raps on the table's surface.

Ruth Zimmerman is one of Olof Jonsson's favorite "batteries." That is to say, the two mediums are *harmonious,* to use Olof's pet term, and they work well together. Ruth is a medium of no small ability herself, but she is one of those rare individuals who can subordinate her ego to another's during a seance and genuinely cooperate to produce a fruitful session. Modestly, Ruth maintains that her own abilities are still in the development stage, and she insists that she is contented to work in the shadow of a master such as Olof Jonsson.

"Ruth is very good," Olof says of his friend. "She gives excellent readings and has produced ectoplasm and a wide variety of manifestations during seances. One day I know that she will become very famous as a medium."

On one occasion, I had the opportunity to interview Mrs. Ingrid Bergstrom who had participated in a dramatic seance with Jonsson.

Ingrid Bergstrom: You want to hear about seances? I will tell you about a seance no one will believe. Betty attended it just before she married Olof, and she became so frightened that afterward I asked her if she would still go through with this wedding.

Betty Jonsson: I was so frightened that I was actually crying.

"Well, tell me about it. Where was it held?"

Mrs. Bergstrom: It was held at Verdandi's, in our spooky room. That's where they used to have the slot machines in the days when the clubs could have gambling. And there's still quite an atmosphere in there, I tell you. We used it as a storeroom for tables and silverware and things we weren't using.

Well, anyway, we had the lights dimmed, but not completely off. Betty held Olof's right hand and I held his left hand, and we had our feet on his feet so that he could not move. I think we sat for half an hour before something happened.

Mrs. Jonsson: You were singing a little bit, remember?

Mrs. Bergstrom: Yes, and then we heard footsteps, like dancing. Like someone dancing a waltz. Then the steps came from all over. A cloth came off a table without disturbing a tray of glasses sitting on it and came whisking by my face. I had an awful, cold feeling.

Mrs. Jonsson: Then a glass came flying through the air.

Mrs. Bergstrom: And for anybody to have reached those glasses, he would have had to go stepping over stacked-up chairs and tables. But that glass just came floating off a tray.

Mrs. Jonsson: Brad, you could hear things flying through the room; you could hear footsteps running around. I had always enjoyed attending seances, but this was the first time that I had ever been afraid. I mean, I had one of Olof's arms, and Ingrid had the other, and we both covered his feet with our own, and since we were the only three people in the room, who was throwing things all over the place?

Mrs. Bergstrom: The heavy table at which we were sitting came up and another table that was sitting on top of another across the room just came up by itself and crashed to the floor.

Mrs. Jonsson: Ingrid, tell Brad about the seance we held at your place last Valentine's Day.

Mrs. Bergstom: Ja, my cousin from Detroit and her husband wanted to meet Betty and Olof. My cousin's husband had made up his mind that he was not going to believe anything that happened that night, and he still says that if he had not seen those things with his own eyes, he never would have believed it. Now he says, he sits at his job and wonders about the meaning of it all.

We had dinner and afterward we placed our hands on the dining room table. It is made of teak and it is very big. It weighs, perhaps, over two hundred pounds. All of a sudden it began to rise and bang itself to the floor. After a while the young couple, who were having a party below us, knocked on the door and asked if I were trying to tell them that they were disturbing us. Oh, no, I told them, it is just my table. Olof Jonsson is here and we are making the table walk by itself.

Now, Betty, I am not going to send you a bill, but one of the table legs is broken. Who would have thought such a heavy wood could shatter? But it raised itself so high and slammed itself down so hard so many times, just as if it were angry.

I remember once moving out of its way, because it was coming after me. And it nearly got my cousin's husband into a corner. He, too, wondered if it were mad at him.

"How were you placed at the table? Were you standing or sitting? Did you have your hands on the table?"

Mrs. Bergstrom: We sat at first with our hands lightly touching the table. When it started to move, I looked to see if anybody was trying to move it with their hands, but then everybody had their hands above the table.

"Where was Olof?"

Mrs. Bergstrom: He was standing away from the table. He had been sitting for just a little while at the very beginning of the seance, but he soon rose to stand in a corner of the room.

When the table began to jump, everyone moved away. That heavy table jumped like a horse. Everybody backed away from it. It was like a living thing.

10

An Essence of Evil—Houses That Hate and Kill

A young couple of my acquaintance rented an old house in a medium-sized Midwestern city before moving into their new split-level home. For several consecutive nights after they moved into the old house, their two-year-old daughter would awaken with screams of terror.

The young mother would carefully check her daughter and try to determine what had caused the child such anxiety. After a week, the child refused to sleep in her room, and her parents were forced to move her into their bedroom for the four months they remained in the house.

"There *was* something about that room," the father said. "At night when I was getting ready for bed, I used to glance toward that door like I expected someone to come walking out."

The mother told me that she had once felt something brush across her ankles when she was in the room. She described the sensation as similar to having a cat brush up against one's legs. Although such a sensation might be described as being somewhat pleasant under ordinary circumstances, she said that the feeling filled her ". . . with absolute loathing, as if some repulsive creature had reached out and touched me."

It was not until after they had moved into their new home that they learned that an elderly recluse had once hanged himself in the old house. Several tenants before them had complained of something odd being centered in the suicide room.

A close friend of mine, who used to travel a great deal in connection with his work, told me of the time that he checked into a motel in eastern

Michigan and spent a night of terror in the presence of something "evil...something so palpably evil that I felt that at any minute I could reach out and touch it, or worse, that it could reach out and touch me!"

My friend spent the night with every light in the room turned on. Sleep was out of the question, and he sat in an armchair until dawn. It, whatever "it" might have been, seemed to be massed near the closet and gave my friend the uncomfortable feeling that he was being watched. "It was like spending the night engaged in an all night staring contest," he said.

This book has already put forth the hypothesis that a house can act as a reservoir of emotions from past occupants, that a room can become a psychically charged storage battery. Nearly everyone has had the experience of walking into a "happy" house, a "depressing" room or a room that seemed quite ordinary in every respect until it seemed suddenly to erupt with distinct impressions of unease or distaste.

Sensitive people, those possessed of the proper telepathic affinity with the implanted memory-patterns, may enter a certain room and receive an influence from those who have lived there before. They may experience the emotions, share the impulses, and, if the impressions are strong enough, even catch "glimpses" of the former inhabitants.

As yet, our vocabulary is inadequate to define precisely what factors must be present before such a thing happens. For the present, we must theorize that a psychic impregnation is made somehow on the room by the physical organism in a state of emotional intensity. Therefore, a certain room could be so "charged" that even years later these same impulses could be received and experienced by a sensitive person.

Psychic researchers W. and E. Denton hypothesize that intense emotional states such as a great sorrow, a great fear or a great hatred increase the "radiation" of these influences and make their primary and secondary results more effective. An extreme emotional experience, such as that of murder, which took place in a paroxysm of hatred and terror, would be expected to create the deepest psychic impression and have the strongest power to evoke similar emotions in a percipient. It may then be put forward that some houses, due to the highly charged emotional level of certain deeds of violence or enmity perpetrated within their walls, have become repositories of hatred and reservoirs of evil.

In my article, "Houses that Harbor Hatred," which appeared in the February, 1965, issue of *Exploring the Unknown*, I wrote:

> Fear, sorrow, and hatred, unfortunately, seem to be stronger emotions than happiness and contentment. While a sensitive person may feel warm and secure in a "happy" room, it seems seldom that he has ever gained any clear impression of what made a particular room joyful. Or is it the dark side of our personality that is most easily reached by psychic

impressions? Fear, Edgar Allan Poe believed, was the most primitive of emotions and the easiest to evoke in a fellow human. It should be a bit sobering to note that what we leave behind may be our worst impression.

When William Adams' family moved into the gray frame house on Detroit's Martin Street, only the children and the dog seemed to sense that something loathsome and evil had made its abode in the back bedroom.

The room was so tiny that it offered space only for a bed. No room could have appeared more innocent and less haunted. Because it was a quiet room at the back of the house, Adams began sleeping there when he came home from the midnight shift at the Cadillac plant.

Even though he had worked the midnight shift for several years, Adams had never quite adjusted to sleeping in the daytime, especially when the children were up. The tiny back bedroom seemed an ideal place for undisturbed sleep.

But Adams had not planned on the terrible dreams—so real he was limp with fear. He would awaken and find himself sitting on the edge of the bed, screaming until his throat was raw. In one particularly graphic dream, Adams saw himself opening the door to the tiny bedroom's closet and discovering a horribly mutilated body.

Adams told his wife that if the morbid nightmares did not cease robbing him of so much sleep, he felt he was "ready to see a psychiatrist." He resumed sleeping in the master bedroom, and at once, the bad dreams stopped. It was then that Adams began to associate the nightmares with the back bedroom.

Adams' grandmother came to visit the family in August of 1962. Both Bill Adams and his wife had assumed that his reaction to the back bedroom had been caused by some personal association, so they did not hesitate in assigning the small back room to Grandmother Adams for the duration of her stay.

Grandmother's sojourn with the Adamses was brief. That next morning she came to the breakfast table with a complaint of "terrible sounds" in the room. All night long the woman had thought that someone was trying to break into the room to do her personal harm. She refused to sleep in the room again. Within a few more nights, Grandmother Adams had become so uneasy in the house that she cut short her visit and returned to Georgia.

Bill and Lillian Adams began to wonder if there really was something peculiar about the back bedroom. They noticed that their small terrier could not be made to enter the room. Their five children also avoided the room.

In October, the Adamses were expecting a visit from Sam Patterson, a hometown friend. They knew Patterson to be a practical, no-nonsense person. Bill and Lillian decided to make him their final test.

They would tell Patterson nothing of their previous unpleasant experiences with the room. They would say nothing that could color his imagination or influence his thinking about the tiny back bedroom. If Patterson could spend a night in the room without suffering any ill effects or reporting anything unusual, they would conclude that they had allowed their imaginations to get the better of them.

Patterson said later that there had been no reason for him to suspect anything about the room. The Adamses had mentioned nothing of their experiences. On the first night, he had been in bed for only a few minutes when he felt something turn him over. Then he saw "it" standing outside the bedroom door.

At first Patterson thought that he saw Lillian, but then he saw that it was a woman with long hair. She had her back to him and was looking into the kitchen. She wore a short fur coat and a blue dress.

Patterson screamed as loud as he could and ran toward the thing. At the moment he approached it, every light in the house went out.

Patterson stumbled about in the darkness until, a moment later, the lights came back on again. He met Lillian in the kitchen. She had been setting her freshly shampooed hair in curlers. Bill had left for the midnight shift at the plant.

Patterson was about to describe what he had seen in the back bedroom when he was interrupted by a terrible wailing—a mournful half-human, half-animal sound.

And then there can an awful smell "...that made both of us sick. It was coming from the room where we heard the moaning."

An eerie moaning and a nauseating stench were not to be the limit of the ghost's manifestations for that evening. While Lillian Adams and Patterson watched, a heavy trap door in the floor of the utility room raised itself several inches before it slammed back into place again. Lillian knew that only a set of flimsy steps and a partially scooped out basement lay beneath that door.

The beleaguered man and woman at last managed to free themselves from the spell of terror that had seized them, and they called the police. When the officers left, they reported that they had been unable to find a natural explanation for any of the phenomena which Lillian Adams and Patterson had witnessed.

When Bill Adams returned from work and heard the story which his wife and friend had to tell him, he decided to take action against the "thing" that had taken over their back room.

After all, he was not the kind of man who would believe in such a thing as a ghost. He was a grown man with a family. He could not convince himself that there was anything to the whole business. He had to try again and see what would happen.

At 7:30 that night, Adams lay down on the small bed in the back bedroom. He had lain there for quite some time when he thought he heard Lillian come into the room. Adams had left his wife and Patterson sitting silently in the front room with a small table lamp providing their only light.

Without turning to face the sound, but assuming that it was Lillian, Bill Adams whispered to his wife to leave the room. He told her that they had to get the thing settled once and for all. It probably would not show itself, he suggested, if there were two of them in the room.

Bill Adams turned over to look into a face that was inches away from his own. He later described the visage as the most horrible thing that he had ever seen. The eyes stared past him and the mouth moved to talk, but only a hissing sound and a terrible stench came out.

Adams ran out of the bedroom in a state of hysteria. He screamed wildly and tore his hair. Patterson attempted to grab him and hold him down.

At last Lillian and Patterson managed to throw a blanket over Bill and wrestle him to the floor. It was not until they had Bill nearly calmed down that the three of them noticed the fetid, nauseating stench that had once again permeated the house.

An hour later, the house on Main Street was vacated. Bill Adams had admitted defeat. The "thing" could keep the back bedroom and the entire house to itself. The next morning, the Adamses moved in with Lillian's parents in a suburb of Detroit.

On Sunday, November 4, 1962, the *Detroit Free Press* broke the story of the ghost that had driven the family from their home. By then, the Adamses had rented another house and had moved all of their furniture from the house on Martin Street during a series of daytime visits.

As a kind of eerie postscript to the haunting, Mrs. Adams' brother, Leo Sanocki, and her sister, Virginia, entered the deserted house one night to see for themselves if there were really any truth to Lillian's and Bill's weird story of an ugly hag that possessed the back bedroom.

While Virginia waited in the kitchen, Leo went into the back bedroom to lie down on the bed. It was their plan that Leo should lie there in the dark for ten minutes.

Her brother had only been in the bedroom for a few minutes when Virginia heard an "awful groan" come from the room. She said later that if the noise had been made by her brother, she had never heard him make such a sound before.

Then Leo came rushing into the kitchen ". . .with the most horrible look on his face, like he was scared out of his mind." Virginia asked her brother what he had seen, but Leo refused to tell her.

Certain dwellings can become so infected by negative "psychic germs" that they become sick houses, loathsome repositories of hatred that can instill terror into those who attempt to dwell within their walls. In some instances, the blanket of evil can become so thick that it can smother and kill.

The priest spoke softly in Latin and Mr. and Mrs. Frank Pell looked on. Grim determination marked Pell's face. Mrs. Pell wore a haggard, tragic expression. Father Etherington crossed himself, the rite finished, then he turned to the couple.

"The ceremony to purge the house has been completed," he announced. Then a worried look came to his features. "But the ceremony is no guarantee that the spirits will not return."

At that instant a tapping came to the ceiling, and Mrs. Pell looked up in fear before falling into the arms of her husband. The tapping continued for a while, then stopped abruptly.

Father Etherington looked quickly at Frank Pell. "Why don't you take your family and leave this unholy house." When Pell did not reply, the priest continued, "You've already buried one child here—what can you help by staying?"

Frank Pell looked to his wife, then to the priest. "No," he said resolutely. "We will not be driven from our house by a pack of . . . pack of spirits."

The priest shook his head. "I hope God will grant you peace from them. I must go."

"Thank you for coming, Father," Mrs. Pell said.

"We can't let them defeat us," Frank Pell said, as the priest left the room. "We can't." As if in retort, the unexplainable tapping began on the ceiling again.

In May of 1955, when the Pells acquired the key to the house on Coxwell Road, Ladywell, in Birmingham, England, the home seemed to have been built just for them, the precise reality of their dreams. They thought it a stroke of great good fortune that they had acquired the house, and they never doubted that they would be happy and secure in their new home.

But pleasant as it looked on the outside, and neatly furnished as it was within, the house carried with it an air of foreboding. Hoping to dispel it, the Pells called upon Father Francis Etherington to bless the house.

On the first weekend they spent in their new home, the Pells were awakened by a slamming door.

Both Mr. and Mrs. Pell sat upright, Mrs. Pell reaching automatically to protect the baby that slept between them. They listened in the darkness and a door slammed again.

Frank Pell told his wife that a door must be caught in the wind. To himself, he wondered if the wind could turn the knob on a latch door, open and close it.

He slipped out of bed to investigate the noises. Although a man of uncommon courage with a war record to prove it, Frank Pell admitted that the strange sounds not only bewildered him, but made him feel decidedly uneasy.

As he stood in the kitchen, he heard a scraping sound like the noise of a scrambling animal. When he looked at the ceiling no animal caught his eye. For a moment all remained silent, then a loud clunk sounded in the room.

Again, it seemed to come from the ceiling. After that, the house was silent, and Frank Pell returned to bed.

As time passed, the Pells were visited nightly by an array of strange sounds. The greatest concentration occurred about midnight, and no matter how the doors had been secured, they banged to and fro as if they had a will of their own. Eerie whispers of half-words and snatches of nearly understandable phrases echoed in the air around them.

Both Frank Pell and his wife knew that such things could have no natural explanation, and they lay awake at night, listening and wondering. The Pells' dream house had begun transforming itself into a nightmare.

The paranormal activity had concentrated itself in a bedroom directly over the kitchen. Loud, unexplainable bumps and thumps sounded, mostly at night, but also occasionally during the day. A tapping noise came to the ceiling of the kitchen every night at 10:20, and in the bedroom the temperature seemed to change every hour.

Once while cleaning the bedroom, Mrs. Pell felt a cold draft and what she described as "icy, intangible fingers" running over her body, but she resolutely told herself that if she refused to fear such manifestations they could do her no harm.

Frank Pell reasoned in nearly the same manner. Even though the sense of evil had clearly presented itself to the Pells, both were sure that fear of it would only give it greater power over them. Pell told himself that only those who feared supernatural forces could be harmed by them. It seemed a reasonable assumption.

Then one hot June morning, the Pells awakened to find that the baby girl who slept between them had died.

Although the girl had been in perfect health and no mark of violence appeared on her body, doctors pronounced that the child had died of suffocation. The night of the child's death had been hot and the Pells had used no bed covers. With no marks on the child it seemed unlikely that either parent could have rolled upon the infant and smothered her.

Shortly after the burial, the Pells were startled by a question from one of their sons. "Did the baby go with the little white dog?" he asked.

"What little white dog?" he asked.

"The one that comes and sits on my bed at night," the boy said instantly.

"When did the dog come last?" Frank Pell asked quickly. He knew that no dogs had ever entered the house.

"The night the baby left us," the boy replied. "He was sitting on the baby's face."

Mrs. Pell became hysterical, and Frank Pell could not calm her. The thought that their daughter had died from supernatural strangulation horrified her.

Although the Pells summoned Father Etherington to exorcise the spirits of the house, the bumping and banging continued with even greater regularity.

On one of the first days in July, the evil focused itself to a horrible point. Downstairs, Frank Pell had begun shaving while Mrs. Pell worked at some household task on the second floor. Although he experienced distinct feelings of unease, Frank Pell did not become conscious of the foreboding whispers which floated through the air until they had surrounded him with greater volume than he had ever heard. They encircled him and closed in upon him, until the suggestion of evil became so strong that he feared for his wife.

Dropping his razor, Pell rushed to the stairs where a frightening scene awaited him. His wife stood on the landing, transfixed with terror. Her limbs had stiffened, and her hands clutched frantically at her side. The veins along her neck had swollen and were darkly visible. She had her head thrown back. Her eyes bulged with terror, and her mouth gaped in a scream Frank Pell could not hear.

He had to get to her. However, when he moved up the stairs he ran directly into an invisible force that would not let him pass. It seemed to shroud him like an invisible net, holding him fast, while his hands flailed the air and his feet worked futilely.

Then a hand found the banister, and with it as a lever, Pell summoned all his strength to throw his body into the palpable wall of evil. He broke through with a lunge. Instantly, the sounds of his wife's screams filled the house. The next moment he stood at her side, as she sobbed into his shoulder. She, too, had been gripped by the whispering evil and seized by its terror.

The Pells could take no more. Without bothering to pack, they took their children and left the house. Later, two friends of the Pells went to the house to collect their belongings. They, too, heard the strange whispers and thumping sounds, and once they had finished packing, would never enter the house again.

My wife Francie is the author of *Reflections from An Angel's Eye*, the fourth book in our Star People series; the co-author of *The Star People* and *Discover Your Own Past Lives*; and the channel and the co-founder of Starbirth, Inc. An internationally known teacher of metaphysics, she is featured in Irving Wallace's *The People's Almanac: The Book of Predictions* and many other books as the only psychic-sensitive who has submitted her interaction with angelic intelligences, along with the channelled teachings she received, to the PSE, the psychological stress evaluator. The results of the PSE are accepted as evidence in courts across the nation; and Forrest Erickson, one of the nation's foremost PSE examiners, has declared Francie to be telling the truth in each instance in which he has tested her.

Francie has interacted with three beings, whom she labels as angelic, ever since she was a child. To Francie, death is but a part of the Divine Plan, a scheme of things which was devised by our Creator, the Source of All Things. This is the vision she was shown in that regard:

> In the beginning, the Source devised a plan that would permit it to grow, to expand, and to experience life in a myriad of dimensions. It sent forth life essences and caused countless beings to exist in many levels of reality. Each being, in its own level, is to gather the fruits acquired from existence and thereby raise its vibrations so that it might evolve ever upward to the Source.
>
> In the physical realm, humankind is to gather the fruits of its experiences—love, wisdom, and knowledge—in order to elevate its vibrations and to cause it to proceed forward on its own path to the Source.
>
> The final result of this remarkable plan is that the lifeforms created by the Source will one day return bearing many fruits, thus making them far more complex than when they were sent forth. The lifeforms will gather many energies—the fruits of their experiences—which they, themselves, caused to exist. These new energies will permit the Source to expand and to experience life in a myriad of dimensions.

Francie has been shown that, at the moment of death, a three-fold process takes place between the Soul, the Spirit-Within, and the Flesh. The Soul vibrates at a very high energy rate, filled with the wisdom that has been gathered during many lifetimes. Death occurs because the Soul has perceived that it is unable to gain additional vibrations or experiences in that particular life expression. When that assessment has been made, it withdraws, severing the connective silver-umbilical-cord that links it with the Spirit dwelling within the fleshly body. The Spirit vibrates on its own for a moment in time and has two possibilities available to it.

According to Francie:

It will either harmonize with the high vibrations of the Soul, or it will be forced to remain separate, soulless, unable to join the Soul in the spiritual world. The decision is one of self-judgment, depending on vibrational awareness. With the removal of the Soul's purposeful contact, the fleshly body begins slowly to decompose in its inevitable return to pure energy.

Those spirits who do not join their Souls have now lost their fleshly bodies, and they find themselves trapped between the dimensions of the physical and the spiritual. In this void, this limbo, the spirit often becomes disoriented, frightened—or enraged, mad with fear.

In this place of nothingness—sometimes called the astral world—the spirit does not have the ability to gain from experience, as it did when it occupied flesh in the physical domain. Many of those spirits entrapped here try desperately to inhabit an earthly body once again, so that they might control flesh as they once did. In their anguish, they see the inhabitation of a fleshly frame as their only hope of escaping the hellish domain of limbo.

One day in time, a new plan will no doubt be devised by the Source to aid these spirits in limbo, for they are the lost, the demonic, who shriek, curse and sob long into the night. Those spirits who now exist in limbo did not perceive what life is truly all about. Throughout their lives, they remained as if stillborn, thereby gaining little, or no, awareness.

In the region of the lost, all manner of spirits can be found. Some are merely bewildered, unknowing as to what has occurred when the moment of death was upon them. Others are furious, filled with anger at themselves and whatever power it is that holds them in this hellish domain. Yet other spirits are the malevolent embodiment of evil, who have continued their ways beyond death.

For those of you who naturally have the psychic door ajar to varying degrees, you should learn to control the operation of that door. You should learn to close it completely until you have chosen the moment you desire to make contact. This is a form of mind control, and many naturally psychic children have now entered adulthood without the control necessary for total clarity in vision and for protection.

In learning total control of your psychic door much can be gained, for you will also learn how to open it wide whenever you are meditating. With total mind control you will be more able to tune in to the benevolent spiritual beings and the angelic ones, rather than to be affected by the lost spirits in the domain between the two worlds.

If you feel you have made contact with one of the entrapped spirits, you must exercise mind control, utilizing your will to its fullest capacity to close off such contact. Cease listening to the voice you hear and pay heed to it no more in this manner.

It is easy to identify whether a spirit contact, or an inner voice, is for good or for evil. Remember the phrase, "By their fruits you shall know them." And another, "If they speak of good and of God then they are from

God. Satan does not divide against himself, or he shall perish." The same holds true for identifying your contact.

When in communication with an enlightened being from the spiritual world, you feel as if you are being bathed in love of the highest kind. No fear or apprehensions are present. However, if you should come in contact with the chaotic vibrations of an entrapped spirit, you will feel a prickly sensation that seems to crawl all over your being; and a mounting terror will begin to slowly overtake you—depending on your own personal awareness as well as the degree of evil present in that spirit.

If you have identified that your contact is evil, say a prayer of love, sending the vibrations to the spirit, and imagine that you are slamming a door, cutting off the spirit. Speak no more to it, nor listen again. It will venture forth for another who will listen and do its bidding.

Contact with the entrapped spirits should never be performed by a person of weak will or faltering spirit, for possessions of varying forms can easily take place. Most of you have heard of people who have unknowingly had contact with those in limbo, who consequently were goaded or tricked by those spirits into committing foul deeds, only to be left alone to pay the consequences.

Whenever people become drugged to the extent of losing control of themselves, whether through the use of alcohol or other narcotics, they make themselves available for contact with the domain of the lost; for remember, all is vibration and both the drugged and the limbic spirits would then be operating in a similar low frequency, in tune with each other.

In like manner, when anyone, whether he is drugged or going about his daily functions, operates with the low vibrations that emanate from the negative thinking that comes from hatred, avarice, contempt or apathy for a fellow human, then that person has made himself available for contact with the entrapped spirits; for he is operating on the same vibrational awareness. Many people already have made such contact with the entrapped spirits without knowing it. Such contact will only serve to lower their understanding, compound their feelings of negativity, and never permit them to know what life is truly all about.

To prevent contact with the entrapped spirits of darkness you must practice loving all living things unconditionally and seek to make contact with your Higher Self, your Soul. When you vibrate with the highest form of love, contact with your Soul is quite easy, for both of you are vibrating on a similar frequency.

The strength of love, with its accompanying vibrations, lessens when it is given conditionally, when its existence is contingent upon other factors. Operate on the vibration of the highest form available, unconditional love. The attitude achieved from practicing this form of open love will more easily permit contact with your Soul so that you might receive the wealth of wisdom and knowledge it has stored within it from the previous lifetimes it has lived. You will also be made to know of the Divine Plan and your purpose in being.

Prayers do help—prayers are vibrations of the highest order, as are the vibrations that come from unconditional love. All things, all events, all thoughts, and all of life are vibrations of one type or another, of a higher or lesser order. Earth, a polarized world of positive and negative energies, of plus and minus, was created in the physical dimension for the purpose of gaining through the experiencing of various thoughts and actions which have their own vibrational frequencies.

Prayers serve to affect those things prayed about by assisting on many levels, often beyond the scope of our reality. The energy from a prayer creatively affects that which we pray for, whether we are able to see that effect or not. Also, the energy that emanates from a prayer exists *ever more*, and its energy becomes a part of Earth's electromagnetic vibrations. Know that there are creative and destructive prayers and creative and destructive energies, which will exist forever in Earth's vibrations. These are polarized as positive and negative, north and south, physical and spiritual.

People who vibrate with creativity tune in, either knowingly or unknowingly, to similarly existing vibrations of thoughts and prayers that exist in our atmosphere. They will then act upon these thoughts, performing many acts of mercy and an abundance of good deeds. The same is true of chaotic thoughts and destructive prayers, for they also have become a part of our atmosphere on Earth. Destructive thoughts have caused many evil actions to be performed by unknowing persons who, operating on the same low vibration, tuned in on such thoughts and carried them out.

We are held responsible for the destructive thoughts that may influence another to act upon them just as we are responsible for the creative thoughts which are also acted upon. Both help to make up our personal vibrations and are attached to us through the electromagnetic energy that governs all of matter.

The spirit of Ida came through to Francie when it felt no other person would help her. In Francie's own words:

> One evening while performing a particular type of meditation with my four children, Ida came through, blocking our contact with the spiritual realm. She begged that we hear her out before sending her away.
>
> I could feel no malevolent evil presence in her vibration, just a frantic bewilderment, a pathetic loneliness. We permitted her into our circle, but with a good measure of caution, knowing full well how to be rid of her if she trespassed the area we had given her or if she overstayed her welcome.

Ida told us that she had died in a fire in Illinois. The apartment in which she had lived had been ravaged by the flames and had collapsed on her. Many had died; but in Ida's particular case, the death of her flesh came at the exact time her Soul was in the process of withdrawing its energy, since there existed no further gaining to be had in the lifetime of Ida. Ida's spirit within was totally unprepared for death. Throughout most of her life she had been an agnostic, and her indifference to any belief construct created a firm wall through which little could penetrate. Ida lived her life gaining very little from it, rarely partaking of the vibrations of love, wisdom, or knowledge, but merely existing.

There was so much potential within Ida that her Soul chose to remain, hoping, waiting for the day when she might spiritually awaken. It knew full well that if Ida would ever make soul-contact and realize what lay beyond, she would become a most energetic worker, gathering many fruits from positive experiences. She would have served to awaken others, assisting in the lives of those around her in fulfillment of the Divine Plan.

Yet, too much time had passed, and the Soul realized that Ida would not read or understand the many signposts that pointed the way to the law of equal return, that she would never come to know the balanced justice of Karma. The Soul knew that she would, therefore, never know the reason for her being, for her existing on Earth, of her particular role in the Divine Plan.

With no other recourse available to it, the Soul withdrew its energy, and this act coincided with the exact time the flesh of Ida was to be consumed in the flames that destroyed her home. Without the contact of her soul, and no longer enveloped by the flesh that held her to the physical world, Ida's spirit became lost in limbo, unable to make the transition to the spiritual realm. Her spirit vibrated at the low frequency that comes only with little or no awareness, and it could not transcend to the spiritual world to join with her Soul. Caught in the dimension between the spiritual and the physical, it remained lost and bewildered for many, many years.

Ida's mournful contact alternately grew louder and softer, coming in and out at a steady rate, as though she were rhythmically touching upon the physical world. She explained that she was frequently fearful and that she would imagine herself at home, rocking in her favorite chair to calm herself. This intermittent contact with the physical world helped to soothe her on many levels, for the vibrations of the physical, even if felt for only seconds at a time, comforted her, helping her to forget her great loneliness in the loss of her Soul and her body.

The children and I spoke often with Ida, counseling her and sending her the loving, high vibrations of prayers, until she at last transcended to an area where we could no longer be of help.

11

Human Doubles and Ghosts of the Living

Mrs. Boulton sat down across the breakfast table from her husband, who was already deeply engrossed in the morning newspaper. "I dreamt of my house again last night," she said.

"That's nice, dear," her husband said mechanically. Mrs. Boulton had had a recurring dream of a house for the past several years.

"It seemed so real this time," Mrs. Boulton continued. "It seemed as if I were so much nearer to it than ever before."

Mrs. Boulton was soon to find out just how near she was. For many years she had been frequently dreaming of an elegant old mansion, and each time that her dreams took her there, she would meticulously walk the house, inspecting each item of furniture, the windows, the curtains, to make certain that each was in its place and that everying was in good condition. Over the years, Mrs. Boulton had come to know her "dream house" as well as she did her own.

Mrs. Boulton's husband was a man of many interests, but he was particularly fond of history—and he loved and studied the mysteries and folklore of the Scottish Highlands. When he learned that Lady Beresford, owner of Ballachulish House in the Appin district, was planning to go south to spend the summer, Boulton immediately wrote her in hope of renting the famous old house during her absence.

Although neither Boulton nor any member of his family had ever been in the house, he was well aware of its romantic and violent position in Scottish history. Lady Beresford answered Boulton's query with a letter approving his proposal to rent Ballachulish and they worked out the details of the arrangement through correspondence.

Toward the end of the negotiations, Boulton visited Lady Beresford at Ballachulish. Thinking of the many stories and legends he had heard about the famous old place, he asked her if the ghosts in Ballachulish were as plentiful as ever.

"As a matter of fact," Lady Beresford answered, "there is only one at the present time. I hope that you won't be too disappointed."

"Not at all," Boulton chuckled, wondering which famous ghost walked the halls. "And who might this spirit be?"

"I really couldn't say," Lady Beresford said. "She's really much too docile to be of the Glencoe Massacre or any of the Highland wars. It seems to be the ghost of a sweet little lady, who makes her rounds like a nightwatchman."

Boulton returned to his wife completely exhilarated by the prospect of spending a summer in such an historic location. Mrs. Boulton was pleased to see her husband so excited, and she, too, was eager to obtain her first tour of Ballachulish.

Lady Beresford had agreed to wait until the Boultons had taken up residence before she left for the continent. She would show them about the place and allow them to become accustomed to the mansion before she would leave them on their own.

As it turned out, Mrs. Boulton did not require the services of Lady Beresford to make an adjustment to life at Ballachulish. "This is *my* house," she told her husband as they approached the historic mansion. "This is my house!"

Warning his wife not to be silly, Boulton rang the doorbell. When Lady Beresford arrived to welcome them, her eyes widened in strange disbelief as she saw Mrs. Boulton.

"It was kind of you to wait," Mrs. Boulton smiled at the astonished Lady Beresford, "but a tour won't be necessary. I've walked through these halls for many years now, and I know where to find everything. This has been the house of my dreams!"

Lady Beresford nodded her head slowly in agreement. "And now I know who the little lady is who has been keeping such a close watch on the house. I recognized you as the 'ghost' of Ballachulish the moment I set eyes on you."

It was all a bit too much for Boulton, who stood by in amazement, as the two women traded stories about Mrs. Boulton's nocturnal projection.

"But it is true," Mrs. Boulton told her husband. "Come, I'll take you on a tour of Ballachulish."

Before Mrs. Boulton entered a room, she would describe its floor plan and give an exact descripton of the furniture to be found within. In each case, she was absolutely correct.

It seemed once that she had made a mistake when she told of a staircase that had seemingly never been where she described it. Lady Beresford quickly removed Mrs. Boulton's doubts when she told her that the staircase had been walled up to block the draft it caused in the upstairs corridors.

The Boultons spent a most pleasant summer at Ballachulish. Upon returning to their own home, Mrs. Boulton never again dreamt of touring the historic mansion, and Lady Beresford never again saw the ghost of the sweet little lady that she had come to know so well over the years.

Mrs. Boulton had produced her own "ghost," a phenomenon which is known as astral projection or out-of-body experience. Psychic researcher W.H. Myers has written that cases of astral projection present perhaps not the most useful, "but the most extraordinary achievement of the human will. What can lie further outside any known capacity than the power to cause a semblance of oneself to appear at a distance? What can be more a central action—more manifestly the outcome of whatsoever is deepest and most unitary in man's whole being?" Myers contends that of all vital phenomena, out-of-body experience is the most significant. ". . .self-projection is the one definite act which it seems as though a man might perform equally well before and after bodily death."

A closely related phenomenon would be that of autoscopic hallucinations in which one is presented with a projection of one's own body image. One sees oneself, as it were, without a mirror.

In an issue of *Fate*, Dr. Edward Podolsky related a number of cases wherein various people have reported seeing their own ghosts. Typical of the experiences recorded in the article, "Have You Seen Your Double?" is the case of a man who returned home with a migraine headache after a hard day at the office. As he sat down to dinner, he saw opposite him an exact replica of himself. His mirror-image double repeated every movement he made during the entire course of the meal.

A young woman told Dr. Podolsky that she and her double had reached out to touch one another and that she had actually felt the touch of her double's fingers on her cheek.

Dr. Podolsky theorizes that such phenomena may be due to the results of ". . .some irritating process in the brain, particularly of the parieto-temporal-occipital [visual] area." Another theory sees in autoscopy the projection of "memory pictures." Dr. Podolsky observes that certain pictures may be stored in the memory and when conditions of stress or other unusual psychological situations arise, these memories may be ". . .projected outside the body as very real images."

Another unusual phenomenon which must fit somewhere in between a "ghost of the living" and a poltergeist is the *Vardogr* of the Norwegians. The Vardogr is a kind of spiritual projection which its possessor unconsciously employs to announce his physical arrival.

In 1917, Weirs Jensen, editor of the *Norwegian Journal of Psychical Research*, conducted an examination and evaluation of Vardogr reports. Jensen found that the stories were all alike ". . .the possessor of a Vardogr announces his arrival. His steps are heard on the staircase. He is heard to unlock the outside door, kick off his overshoes, put his walking stick in place. . . ." The percipients open the door to admit their expected friend or loved one ". . .and find the entry empty. The Vardogr has, as usual, played a trick on them. Eight or ten minutes later, the whole performance is repeated—but now the reality and the man arrive."

In an earlier work I related my experiences as a teenager when I was tricked on several occasions by the Vardogr of my parents.

As I would be sitting upstairs in my room reading, I would be certain that I heard my parents returning from town. I would hear the door open and close, the sound of feet shuffling—all the normal sounds that a man and a woman would make upon entering their home. When I would call down my goodnight and receive no answer, I would find that the house was empty and that I was alone.

Often, while I was still calling to my parents to answer my goodnights, I would see their car lights coming down the lane of our farm home and realize that I had been fooled and frightened once again by the Vardogr.

My sister often had similar experiences with the Vardogr, especially after I left home to attend college and she found herself alone in the evenings, awaiting my parents' return. We have compared notes on a number of occasions and have agreed with Weirs Jensen, who reported that, as a rule, the Vardogr announces itself by imitating the sounds made by inanimate objects, such as the sound of a key in the lock, the placing of overshoes and coats in their proper places, the stamping of shoes on the floor.

Another observation we have both made is that the sounds are so natural that one does not suspect for even one moment that the noises are being made by any other than the individual one expects. Because of the naturalness of the sounds, the percipient is not frightened by the footsteps and other sounds on arrival. Often, of course, there comes an eerie and uncomfortable moment when one realizes he is alone and that the sounds have been made by some invisible agent.

My mother is first-generation American of Danish descent, and my father is a second-generation American of Norwegian descent, but I must point out that neither of my parents' families had any particular knowledge of this uniquely Scandinavian phenomenon. There was certainly no Vardogr tradition passed down from father to son and built into some kind of charming folk-legend.

Indeed, when I had my first experience with the Vardogr as a teenager, I was not even familiar with the term, and it was not until long after I had begun a serious study of psychic research that I was able to identify the phenomenon which I had experienced so often as a youngster.

When my sister and I used to discuss our eerie experiences with the phenomenon, we simply referred to it as the "weird noise." I can never recall either of us using the term "ghost" to describe what we heard, and certainly neither of us ever thought of our house as being haunted.

Once I asked a Lutheran pastor of Norwegian descent if he were familiar with the Vardogr phenomenon, and he replied that he was not. When I described what I meant in terms of the sounds of arrival before the actual person arrives, he smiled and nodded his head emphatically. He had experienced such things all of his life, but he had never thought them particularly "spooky," and he certainly did not realize that such happenings were noteworthy enough to have a name of their own.

Weirs Jensen's research led him to observe that the Scottish people also experience the projection of a spiritual forerunner. This has led me to speculate on what peculiarities of psychic makeup the Norwegian would share with the Scot.

Jump back several centuries and one finds the fierce Viking warrior and the equally fierce Highland clansman—both lusty, crude, rough and barbaric. Today one often finds both people taciturn and frugal. The highlands of Scotland and the fjords of Norway look beautiful on picture postcards and the tourists' slides, but they offer the inhabitants a hard and sparse existence, tempered only by the mercy of the sea with her harvests of fish. Perhaps it is the introspective nature of the Norwegian and the Scot that has given them a spiritual forerunner, which on occasion, breaks loose from the normal barriers of time and space and is as free as their untamed ancestors.

A former student of mine, whose mother was of Norwegian descent and whose father was of Scottish descent, has related a number of her experiences with the Vardogr. It would seem that her double-barreled inheritance has given her husband more than one occasion to wonder if she might be playing tricks on him. Several times he has called her name when he was certain she was moving about in the kitchen. Upon investigation, he always finds the kitchen empty. He has learned, however, to wait just a few minutes so that he might be there at the door to help her with the groceries when she arrives in reality.

It was not until the summer of 1967 that I learned that I may possess a Vardogr of my own.

I had been gone for two weeks making television and radio appearances in conjunction with the promotion of my books, and I was eager to get home. I knew that it would be nearly 2:30 A.M. before I could pull up in my own driveway, but I was determined to continue driving and not to add another day to my trip.

When I arrived home shortly before 2:30, I was surprised to see the lights on and my wife awake and waiting for me. It seems that about five minutes before I actually walked in the door, my wife had been alerted by the sounds of the front door opening, suitcases being set down and the shuffling of footsteps.

She had come down the stairway to greet her husband and welcome him home only to find a dark and empty hallway. She was sitting on the living room sofa trying to puzzle out the strange sounds which she had heard when she saw my car pull up in front of the house. Within a few moments, the same sounds were repeated, only this time I had arrived with them.

My wife was nearly as eager to tell me about the visitation of the Vardogr as she was to fill me in on the activities of the children while I had been away. The sounds, she said, had been so natural and lifelike that she had not shown any hesitation in running down the stairway to greet me. I suppose that one's walk is nearly as distinctive as his fingerprints, and my wife had been certain that she had recognized the sounds of my footsteps.

"Just think," she smiled, "after all the writing and research which you've done on the Vardogr, it appears that you may have one of your own."

The house was set next to a large, green yard, and the very grass itself seemed to be shimmering in the heat of July afternoon in Moline, Illinois.

Irene Hughes was walking a bit ahead of us, so Tom Holloway, reporter for the Davenport (Iowa) *Times-Democrat* drew next to me and whispered: "This is the commune I was telling you about where the weird things have been happening. Apparitions, sounds, and so forth. I'm not to say anything more about it. I want to see what Irene will pick up."

Holloway is a journalist who maintains an openminded interest in psychic phenomena. In fact, his interest in the development of his own "psi" abilities had led him to the point where he will admit to being "just a little psychic" himself.

"I've known of this house for some time now," he said a bit louder now that Irene and Joan Hurling, a journalist from Kankakee, Illinois, had reached the steps of the house and were a considerable distance from us. "When I heard that you folks were looking for midwestern haunted houses, I thought this could produce some psychic paydirt for you."

Holloway laughed. "You know, once I got to know these kids, I really got to like them. And they, especially the young artist, are really eager to have Irene attempt to discover the cause for the disturbances they've been experiencing."

We reached the steps and joined Irene and Joan. I asked Irene if she were picking up any impressions about the home before we entered. She only smiled, and I knew better than to attempt to rush her attunement with the house's vibrations.

The door pushed open and two young men with shoulder-length hair walked out, flashed us the peace sign, and smiled as they continued down the street. Their bib overalls were colorfully stitched with multicolored patches. One young man was barefooted; the other wore heavy workshoes.

Holloway indicated that we should enter and walk up the flight of stairs immediately to our left.

Within a few moments, the introductions had been made, and we found ourselves up in the stuffy, stifling attic, because "something" that did not want the young people up there had once chased them down in the midst of a party that our artist host had given during one winter night. Perhaps the attic would have been a wonderful place for a party in much cooler weather, but on that July afternoon, the heat made even the simple, but necessary, act of breathing a bit of a chore.

Jim, our host, was a tall, thin young man with long hair and a pencil-line mustache. A shorter man, equally as thin but a good deal younger, was never far from his side. A quiet, deeply tanned, lovely young woman sat on a mattressbed with her bare feet tucked under her and looked at us with friendly eyes and a calm smile. We were told that Jim's wife was at work.

The session that afternoon at the commune in Moline was most remarkable for the incredible wealth of personal information which Irene Hughes divulged about both the young man and the manifestation that had been haunting the house. The session was also remarkable in that Irene's psychic impressions could largely be verified instantaneously by Jim, thereby removing the burden of subsequent verification from our shoulders.

Because of the impressive manner in which this transcript reveals how a topnotch psychic can work when she really gets tuned-in on the vibratory waves of the subject or a place, I have decided to reproduce the script in its entirety, even though much of it pertains to personal matters in the life of our artist-host, Jim. It will be seen, however, that such information had to be learned before Mrs. Hughes could effectively put this particular ghost to rest.

The transcript begins in the attic:

Irene: I have the feeling that you found a dog by the house when you moved here.

Jim: Yes, next door there was a big one. A St. Bernard. Weighed about two hundred pounds.

Irene: Did a couple live up here before you and your wife?

Jim: Yes.

Irene: Was there violence with that couple? Did they fight a lot physically? Did they fight so much that the woman actually left?

Jim: Yes, that's true. [Sensing the discomfort of those assembled in the stifling attic. . .] We moved up here last winter, because it's nicer. The heat comes up and counteracts the cold from the roof. We were listening to records up here when the thing, whatever it was, materialized. Something just didn't want us up here.

Irene: It came to me that you had incense and candlelight. Did you have long incense sticks?

Jim: Yes.

Irene: Did you smoke a long pipe?

Jim: Yes.

Irene: I saw red ribbons, too, and I wondered why you would have red ribbons in your hands.

Jim: Yes, I used red ribbons of tape a lot.

Irene: Shall we go downstairs where we would be more comfortable? [The group begins to file back down the narrow stairs to the apartment below.] Was there a young man who left this house not long ago, who really seemed to be out of it? I also have the feeling that there was a woman who used to walk by this house a lot and stop in front and just look in. It was as though this woman was a friend of someone here. She was interested in psychology—maybe even a psychologist.

Jim: Yes, I know the woman.

Brad: What about the man who left here whom Irene described as being "out of it"?

Irene: He used to come up here and play a drum. . .a weird little drum.

Jim: That sounds like my brother.

Irene: Is his name Henry?

Jim: Yes.

Irene: Did you drink some wine not long ago? I see you mixing something that looks like wine.

Jim: Yes, it was my birthday on the thirteenth, and we had a little party.

Irene: You made the wine?

Jim: We didn't make it, but we mixed it.

Irene: I also saw half a watermelon that something peculiar seemed to have happened to.

Young man: [Laughing] Sue dropped one on the floor!

Irene: I see a knife and fork stuck in the watermelon, and I feel that some argument occurred and some relationship broke up while the watermelon was being eaten.

Jim: Yes, we had a big argument with the downstairs neighbors during my party.

Irene: I feel that you have been looking for a lamp, but you have not found it yet. I see that you want to hang it high. I see it falling, and it not only causes trouble here, but it causes an injury. I urge you not to buy it, but you will anyway.

Jim: I think it's symbolic of what I'm doing now.

Irene: No, this is real. It's all cut out, like a globe.

Jim: This is materialistic? And there is nothing that I can do to stop myself from hanging it?

Irene: I hope you can, and I'm warning you not to; but this is one of those situations where I can see beyond and know that it will be done.

I want to make a comment about your painting. [A large painting of a golden incense burner covered most of one wall in the bedroom of the apartment.] I had the psychic impression when I walked into the room that you felt that you were a part of all humanity. You caught everything in the world and now you are in the process of eliminating it.

Jim: [Pointing to the young man] Ask him about that! I told him that I just turned down a scholarship.

Irene: You are trying to find yourself.

Jim: That's exactly what's happening.

Irene: There was a Dorothy who was very meaningful in your life.

Jim: That was my mother.

Irene: May I go back to November about three years ago? I feel that on the inside of your left arm that you either thought about slitting your wrist or that you actually did it.

Jim: Not unless my memory has erased it.

Irene: Please go back a little. I see you sitting on a stool. I see you thinking about it strongly or actually doing it.

Jim: I don't think I ever did, but maybe my memory erased it.

Irene: May I take you back again? This seems important to uncover so that I may take you forward and on to the problems in this house. I saw you tearing up what looked like an arithmetic book which you said you hated because it was symbolic of something.

Wait!—Now I see that this is not you, but a young man to whom you are very close. It was he who did these things. His name is Pat.

Jim: That's a very important name. Pat, He's just been reborn spiritually. He is very important to me, perhaps he has dominated my thinking to a large degree. He was one of those who was leaving just as you came in. He's been one of the very few I've been communicating to about this thing that I'm into.

Irene: [A bit apologetically] It seems like I'm tuning into him [Jim] more than I am the house.

Brad: It may be that the manifestation in this house is related more to him than to any others, past or present.

Jim: I think it is.

Irene: I saw a winding road that looked to me like it was gravel, and it seemed to me that you were walking along the road. You were thinking about some kind of berries, and all I can think of in my mind is blackberries, but it seemed to me that there were berries on your mind. It seemed to me at first that you were alone, but then I could see a figure in front of you and a figure behind you.

Jim: Yes, I can visualize the scene. It happened in Canada.

Irene: I can see a lake higher than the road.

Jim: Yes, there was a lake up there.

Irene: I also see what looks to me like the beginning of a little cave. I see you walking into it, then bending over and sitting down in there.

Jim: I could see how that'd be symbolic, but not anything else.

Irene: No, this happened in reality. You had one can of beans with you. And you said: "Okay, let's get the beans ready!"

[Jim and his two friends begin to laugh at the same time as they recognize the scene that Jim had temporarily forgotten.]

Girl: All we had was one can of beans!

Irene: [To the girl] When you spoke just now, I heard you calling, "Fred, Fred, Fred," as if you were really concerned.

Girl: Oh, wow. Fred is my cat. She had her kittens yesterday and we couldn't find them outside.

Jim: That's really cool. She's been worried about Fred all morning.

Irene: Paulson, I hear the name Paulson. He is a man who wears clothes like a minister or a priest. You had a talk with him on a rainy night outside a church. I can see you standing there. He's taller than you.

Jim: This is really weird. I was best man at a wedding and it was rainy that night, and I was talking to a minister named Paulson outside the church.

Irene: Did you go to England, stay about a month, then come back?

Jim: No, we went to Canada for about ten days.

Irene: This could be a future thing, then, because I see England for a month, then on to Mexico.

Jim: We were talking about going to Mexico before you came. It's a long story, but we would like to try the Sacred Mushroom.

Irene: But the Sacred Mushroom is nothing to fool with. I've held it in my hand. When I worked as an editor for the *International Journal of*

Psychiatry, a psychiatrist told me of the mushrooms, and I said, "Gee, that's what I need with my psychic ability."

Well, he lectured me for half an hour, saying these things are extremely poisonous. He said if you take just one bit too much, you can be gone. Nobody knows exactly how much a person should take, not even a doctor.

[Irene elicits a promise from the young people that they will curtail their plans to drive to Mexico to sample the Sacred Mushrooms.]

Did you just pack your bags and your bedroll, tie it up with strings and all, then change your mind about leaving for somewhere?

Jim: That's exactly right. Yesterday I was talking to my wife about driving about in a big bus, helping people, helping the Indians in the Southwest. Today I decided to unpack and stay in Moline for a year.

Irene: There are people right here in Moline who need your help. You don't have to leave.

Jim: I realize that.

Irene: Did you just have a baby sleeping on this mattress?

Jim: Yeah, the lady downstairs brought her baby to take a nap on it.

Irene: This is meant only in a psychic way. I'm not criticizing your housekeeping: did you just buy a broom?

Girl: [Laughing] I just tore one up!

Jim: There was one in here before you came in. There was a discussion about a broom just six minutes before you came.

Irene: Were you and your wife discussing a purchase of an unusual looking rosewood couch?

Jim: Yes, we were. This was a couple of months ago.

Irene: Sometime ago, did you have a very violent argument with a rabbi or minister or priest? It was a very disagreeable argument.

Jim: I got into a very disagreeable word exchange with the priest who married my wife and me.

Irene: Your wife has very dark hair.

Jim: Yes, she does.

Irene: I feel about this house that there was once a person who lived in it who had something to do with the society of this area. In other words, they were one of the important families. I can see that they would be entertaining in one particular room downstairs.

Jim: That's really good.

Irene: It seemed to me that it was a very dignified, high class family. All of a sudden I have an impression of a man who is a traveling accountant.

Jim: You're talking about a friend of mine who is a traveling accountant. He has been on my mind recently.

Irene: Well, back to the house: I see a woman who is very lonely.

She is very attractive. She seems to be alone, now, but she first came to feel very lonely when she was thirty-five.

Jim: There was a woman who used to live here, Miss Wood, a music teacher. That could tie in.

Girl: Just a couple of days ago, we were downstairs talking about the ghost and everything, when the mailman came and delivered a letter to this address for Miss Wood. And, really, *the postmark on the envelope was July 6, 1930!* The post office usually doesn't make those kinds of mistakes. I mean, letters can get delayed and all, but . . . .

The envelope was marked personal, and we opened it. There was no date on the letter. It was just about someone who retired from this Chicago department store, who wanted to contact Miss Wood. There was a calling card in it, too.

Brad: Would you show us the letter?

[Irene held the strangely tardy letter, but could receive no impressions from it directly related to the house. It certainly seemed to all of us to be a most peculiar coincidence that such a letter would be delivered just a few days before our arrival and forty years too late, almost to the day.]

Irene: [To Jim] One thing that bothers me—when I look at you, I see a policeman's star above you.

Jim: That's a very bad sign. Could it be symbolic?

Irene: It doesn't feel that way. It really doesn't.

[A few months later, Tom Holloway informed us that Jim had been arrested after creating a minor disturbance in a draft office. The offense was not terribly serious—just a case of an injudicious choice of words at the wrong time—but Irene had seemed definitely to pick up impressions of a future difficulty with a policeman's badge.]

Irene: Could I touch the lamp behind me? [She is handed the lamp.] I feel that the manifestation—or a manifestation—has been seen in connection with this lamp. I feel also that there is a voice that talks. It is as though a man comes up in the corner, and it is as if he speaks of the here and the hereafter.

Jim: That is exactly right!

Irene: I would say that December 19, 1969, was a tremendous turning point in your life.

Jim: Yes, it was! It really was!

Irene: It was as though you jumped across the Grand Canyon.

Jim: You're exactly right. That's the day Christmas vacation started when I was still attending college and that's the day I got out of my power-materialistic trip and got into a spiritual trip. It was that very day—December 19, 1969. You're really blowing my mind!

Irene: Well, I don't mean to "blow your mind." I'm hoping that this experience will give you some guidance in your life. I feel that once more you're going to have a tremendous turning point in your life.

Jim: I've had two recently. No, they weren't really turning points; they were elevation points.

Irene: Are you gaining from these elevations, so that you may plant yourself more solidly in the plane on which you now live, as well as expand yourself to reach other dimensions?

Jim: That sounds exactly right.

Irene: To change the subject for just a moment . . . you have very pretty teeth, but I see you in a dentist's chair. Does it hurt on your left side?

Jim: Yes, my wisdom teeth are coming in on that side, and it hurts.

Irene: It looks as though there may be a little oral surgery, but you will not have to worry about it.

Did you have a connection with this house before you and your wife moved in last year?

Jim: I used to live in this house with my father. When my wife and I moved in, he moved out.

Irene: I really feel that at times there is an apparition that comes to this house, but, I must be honest, it is not this true apparition that haunts you, but a fragment of your own psyche. I see it running up and out, like a symbol of frustration.

There is a period of time coming in your life in which you will meet a young couple who will give you strength and help to guide you. This will be a very meaningful time for you, and it will really get you going straight. I don't mean that you are now going wrong, but you will gain greater strength and a more definite sense of direction. Spiritually, I feel that you will gain a greater balance. You will realize that once you have learned how to fit properly into the spiritual, the material side of life will make more sense. As long as you balance the material and the spiritual, you will find a place for everyone and everything in the world.

Jim: I've already reached the point of the material making more sense to me.

Irene: I can see the transformation coming soon.

Suddenly I feel as if water is spilling over me and throughout this house, washing away the apparitions. They are gone. No longer after you.

Jim: That's really good news. Those things scared the hell out of me. All of my life I have been conditioned to this world, then I find that everything I once believed has been completely reversed. It scared me.

Tom Holloway: Irene, you believe that the apparitions that he and his friends have been seeing were more or less manufactured by his subconscious and projected into the environment, rather than being visitors from the spirit world?

Irene: No, as I said, there is a *true* ghost that comes to this house from time to time, but the apparition that haunts this young man comes from his mind.

I see a Sunday afternoon back in May or June. I feel that he was on what drug users call a "trip." It was at this time that this false apparition came from a lower part of his mind and freed itself as a projection.

Young man: Tell her a little about that Sunday afternoon in May.

Jim: Well, I went out of my mind while tripping. I was on a bum trip after I saw that ghost appear.

Young man: He was standing outside the house by himself when he saw a gray figure go past the window of his workroom.

Jim: I lost my composure when I saw that. This was a good acid; I was really moving. My mind was really in another state, but when the ghost appeared, it scared me.

Young man: Yes, you were pretty happy before that.

Jim: Not happy, really, but I had wanted a ghost to appear; I had wanted to get into the ghost thing. But after it appeared, I didn't want to hang around here.

Irene: You say ghost like we say Father, Son, and Holy Ghost, but long ago we changed it to Holy Spirit, because it is eternal, the part that lives forever. The spirit within us all is not a spook, but something holy and real. It is life eternal, and it is not to be played around with—through alcohol or sacred mushrooms or hallucinogenic drugs.

Prayer and meditation offer one a different kind of ecstasy, but it is the real ecstasy. Try it once, and you'll see.

"Well, Glenn, what did you think of Irene's explanation of the haunted commune?" I asked him as we relaxed in our motel room with our traditional glasses of Dr. Pepper and Royal Crown Cola. "The young artist's own fragmented psyche was haunting the place, and according to Irene, maybe stirring up a real ghost that had been held to the house for several years."

Glenn ground a cigarette out in the ash tray at his side before he answered. "I really don't know what to think," he said. "Is it possible?"

I reached for my cigar case, removed my after-dinner Brazilian Caballero.

"Let's take it from the angle of astral projection, or out-of-body experience first," I suggested. "Remember what W.H. Myers termed astral projection? 'The one definite act which it seems as though a man might perform equally well before and after bodily death.' Other researchers, such a Eugene E. Bernard, have observed that out-of-body experiences occur most often during time of stress; during natural childbirth; during minor surgery; and at times of extreme fear.' Surely our young artist had been going through a series of psychological stresses, which coupled with the LSD, may have caused a projection of his essential self."

"But in out-of-body experience," Glenn reminded me, "the essential self, the soul, returns to the body. It doesn't remain separate to haunt somebody."

"Quite true," I agreed, "but I am saying that the mechanism involved in getting a portion of Jim's psyche to dissociate, to fragmentize, may have been similar to the more familiar phenomenon of astral projection. In a sense, the ghost that haunted the commune was more like a quiet poltergeist than a real ghost."

Glenn snapped his cigarette lighter and drew the flame to a fresh cigarette. "You are using the definition of poltergeist that sees it as a fragmented psyche that has been given temporary independence to go racketing about the house, using an adolescent or someone under emotional stress as an energy center."

"Correct," I nodded, accepting his lighter for my still unlighted Caballero. "Only this particular projected fragment was not a noisy one," I said around the cigar. "This fragmented bit of psyche lingered to disturb the young man and to add to his confusion about the path in life that he should take.

"The role of the hallucinogenic drug in all this is, of course, difficult to assess," I went on. "I certainly do not feel competent to judge whether or not the LSD might have prompted the appearance of the ghost. I don't think anyone knows enough about the drug to make any kind of proper evaluation at this time."

"It seems to me, though," Glenn remarked, "that I have read and heard of certain drug users reporting a *doppleganger* effect from the hallucinogenic drugs. By that I mean that they have said they have seen their doubles across the room from them or even seated next to them."

I slipped off my boots, propped my stockinged feet up on the edge of a bed. "Yes, well, the *doppleganger* phenomenon is a most interesting one."

We discussed the phenomena of psychic projection and fragmentation of psyche late into the night. Although we knew at the outset that neither of us could provide any final answers, such an airing of various views and theories enabled both of us to keep mentally alert and as analytical as possible.

Before we leave our young artist, who, from all subsequent reports, appeared, with Irene's guidance, to have got himself "all together" again, I would like to present a case study of the appearance of mysterious blood spots and an astral double for purposes of comparison and contrast.

It was a Monday morning in June 1961, when Mrs. Edwin King, who was happily doing her household chores, noticed two dark wet spots on the floor of the dining room of their Houston, Texas home. The spots came up readily on her dust cloth and rinsed right out, so Mrs. King did not think any more about them.

The next morning, however, she found two new wet spots in exactly the same place. This time she took a few moments to carefully examine the stains on the cloth. She suddenly knew that the spots were drops of blood, and she received impressions of something else trying to force its way up from her subconscious, but the images were too rapid to form clear pictures. Perhaps some alert part of her brain was censoring the impressions, not permitting them to register with her conscious thought-mechanism.

Her husband listened somewhat solemnly to her report of the blood spots which she had discovered on two consecutive mornings. He became a bit wary that someone may have been playing a rather bizarre practical joke on them.

The next morning both of the Kings got up at 4:00 A.M. and went directly to the dining room in order to inspect the particular tiles that had been soiled on the previous two mornings. Husband and wife felt a sense of great relief, the floor was as clean and unsoiled as they had left it the night before.

Mrs. King began preparing breakfast. They thought they might as well get an early start as long as they were up so early. A bit later, though, some perverse attraction led her to re-examine the dining room floor. This time she found two dark red spots on a section of tile. All the doors in the house remained locked, and neither she nor her husband had re-entered the dining room.

When they awakened on the following morning, the red spots were once again on the dining room floor.

King was determined to discover the origin of the blood-like drops and to find out just exactly what they were. On Thursday night before retiring, he covered the two mysterious tiles with a sheet of plastic. About 1:30 A.M., he got out of bed and went to inspect the squares. There were red spots on the plastic.

King hurried back to the bedroom to report his discovery to his wife, but he stopped short in the doorway when he saw that there were similar dark red spots on the face of his sleeping wife. When he awakened her and wiped off the spots with a washcloth, they left what appeared to be bloodstains.

Later that morning, King took the spots on the plastic down to the police station. The mystery had become more than a domestic intrigue, and he felt that he must consult professional mystery crackers. The police lab confirmed the suspicions of the Kings: The stains were human blood.

Edwin King was determined that he should apprehend the culprit responsible for perpetrating such a weird practical joke upon them. It did not occur to the practical Texan that something paranormal might be at work in their home. That night, with a neighbor and a shotgun, King resolved to maintain an all night vigil in an effort to call a fast halt to the nocturnal invasion of their home.

It was about 4:00 A.M. Saturday morning when the two watchmen were startled to hear terrible moaning and sounds of agony echoing through the house. Quickly tracing the disturbance to the master bedroom, they found Mrs. King thrashing about on her bed, obviously in the throes of a nightmare. As they switched on the light, they were astonished to see splotches of blood on Mrs. King's face.

As rapidly as her husband could wipe the drops from her face, more appeared to take their place. The men at first assumed the blood to be seeping from the pores of her skin, but even a superficial examination made it apparent that Mrs. King did not have a scratch or a break in her skin anywhere on her face.

That afternoon, a skin specialist examined Mrs. King and discovered that she did have one broken blood vessel, but it was by her ear. When her husband and their neighbor had observed the strange stigmata, the blood spots seemed to be coming from the center of her cheek and, occasionally, from her forehead. Her pulse was normal, and her blood pressure was a bit below normal. Laboratory analysis of a blood sample showed no irregularities, and the specialist could ascertain no physical reason why Mrs. King should bleed without cause.

Unfortunately, word of the eerie manifestations at the Edwin King home reached the ears of a reporter, and the Kings and their children were subjected to the curiosity of friends, neighbors, crackpots, self-styled psychic investigators and evangelists seeking devils to exorcise. Since the Kings were basically very quiet, unassuming people, they soon grew weary of the publicity and the gossip which had suddenly intruded upon the serenity of their home, and they shut themselves off from all outsiders, including serious and sincere researchers of the strange and unusual.

Eventually, David Wuliger, a member of the faculty of Houston University, was able to gain their confidence, and he learned through extensive interviews with Mrs. King that, almost without exception, Mrs. King would have a particular dream before the blood-spots appeared. In this peculiar dream, Mrs. King would speak with her double, which always appeared before her clothed in a loose-fitting white robe. The double had a face exactly like Mrs. King's, and she would talk to her in a voice similar to hers. Mrs. King and her double addressed one another by their first name, Doris. In each conversation, the mysterious double would assure Mrs. King that "all will be well." Mrs. King would always awaken feeling very puzzled, since the only problem she had in the world was the bizarre appearance of the blood spots.

Edwin King told Professor Wuliger that his wife made whimpering noises and muttered unintelligibly when she was undergoing one of her disturbing dreams. Although he would attempt to awaken her whenever she would begin to toss about, he said that she would not respond to his attentions. He eventually got the impression that she was in what appeared to him to be some kind of deep trance.

When Doris King awakened from one of her strange dreams in which she conversed with her double, she would always complain of being cold, a condition which puzzled her husband, since June nights in Houston range from 75 to 85 degrees—and the Kings had no air conditioner.

After each dream the Kings and Professor Wuliger determined that the blood spots appeared either on the tile or upon Mrs. King's face. On one occasion the phenomenon also occurred in the home of Mrs. King's mother, and it seemed to happen most often when one or the other of the King's children were gone for the evening. Perhaps her motherly concern for the absentee child so disturbed her sleep that the double appeared to tell her that "all will be well" in order that she receive enough necessary sleep time and the even more necessary dream time.

Professor Wuliger learned that the appearance of Doris King's double was not confined to her dreaming hours. Twice she claimed to have seen her double while awake. In one instance, the double had told her that the blood spots were left so that she would have proof that she had really been talking with her duplicate image and not just dreaming.

Although our young artist in Moline had not seen his double, he had seen the image of a man appear; and he had heard the sound of a voice reminding him of the eternal truths and cautioning him to emphasize the spiritual, rather than the material in his life. In a sense, the projection of his fragmented psyche had been telling him that "all will be well," if he only chose with care the path in life that could be more richly trod.

12

Ghostly Scenes of the Past

The late psychoanalyst Dr. Nandor Fodor theorized that genuinely haunted houses were those that had soaked up emotional unpleasantness from former occupants. Years, or even centuries, later, the emotional energy may become reactivated when later occupants of the house undergo a similar emotional disturbance.

The "haunting"—mysterious knocks and rappings, opening and slamming doors, cold drafts, appearance of ghostly figures—is produced, in Dr. Fodor's hypothesis, by the merging of the two energies, one from the past, the other from the present.

In Dr. Fodor's theory, the reservoir of absorbed emotions, which lie dormant in a haunted house, can only be activated when emotional instability is present. Those homes which have a history of happy occupants, the psychoanalyst believed, are in little danger of becoming haunted.

There is another kind of paranormal phenomenon in which an entire section of landscape seems to be haunted. In most cases of this particular type of haunting, a tragic scene from the past is recreated in precise detail, as if some cosmic photographer had committed the vast panorama to ethereal film footage. Battles are waged, trains are wrecked, ships are sunk, the screams of earthquake victims echo through the night—all as it actually took place months or years before.

Thomas A. Edison, the electrical wizard, theorized that energy, like matter, is indestructible. He became intrigued by the idea of developing a radio that would be sensitive enough to pick up the sounds of times past— sounds which were no longer audible to any ears but those of the physically sensitive.

Edison hypothesized that the vibrations of every word ever uttered still echoed in the ether. If this theory ever should be established, it would explain such phenomena as the restoration of scenes from the past. Just as the emotions of certain individuals permeate a certain room and cause a ghost to be seen by those possessing similar telepathic affinity, so might it be that emotionally charged scenes of the past may become imprinted upon the psychic ether of an entire landscape.

An alternate theory maintains that surviving minds, emotionally held to the area, may telepathically invade the mind of a sensitive person and enable him to see the scene as "they" once saw it.

It cannot be denied that some locales definitely have built up their own "atmospheres" over the years and that such auras often give sensitive people feelings of uneasiness—often of fear and discomfort. Whether this may be caused by surviving minds, a psychic residue or an impression of the actual event in the psychic ether is a question that remains unsolved at the present stage of parapsychological research.

Restored battle scenes offer excellent examples of what seem to be impressions caused by the collective emotions and memories of large groups of people.

Perhaps the most well-known, most extensively documented, and most substantially witnessed was the Phantom Battle of Edge Hill which was "refought" on several consecutive weekends during the Christmas season of 1642. The actual battle was waged near the village of Keinton, England, on October 23 between the Royalist Army of King Charles and the Parliamentary Army under the Earl of Essex.

It was on Christmas Eve that several countryfolk were awakened by the noises of violent battle. Fearing that it could only be another clash between soldiers of the flesh who had come to desecrate the sanctity of the holy evening and the peace of their countryside, the villagers fled from their homes to confront two armies of phantoms. One side bore the king's colors; the other, Parliament's banners. Until three o'clock in the morning, the phantom soldiers restaged the terrible fighting of two months before.

The battle had resulted in defeat for King Charles, and the monarch grew greatly disturbed when he heard that two armies of ghosts were determined to remind the populace that the Parliamentary forces had triumphed at Edge Hill. The king suspected that certain Parliamentary sympathizers had fabricated the tale to cause him embarrassment. The king sent three of his most trusted officers to squelch the matter. When the emissaries returned to court, they swore oaths that they themselves had witnessed the clash of the phantom armies. On two consecutive nights, they had watched the ghostly reconstruction and had even recognized several of their comrades who had fallen that day.

On August 4, 1951, two young Englishwomen vacationing in Dieppe were awakened just before dawn by the violent sounds of guns and shell fire, dive bombing planes, shouts and the scraping of landing craft hitting the beach. Cautiously peering out of their windows, the two young women saw only the peaceful pre-dawn city. They knew, however, that just nine years previously, nearly one thousand young Canadians had lost their lives in the ill-fated Dieppe raid. Being possessed of unusual presence of mind, the young Englishwomen kept a record of the frightening cacophony of sound, noting the exact times of the ebb and flow of the invisible battle. They presented their report to the Society for Psychical Research, whose investigators checked it against detailed accounts of the event in the war office. The times recorded by the women were, in most cases, identical to the minute of the raid that had taken place nine years before.

Another area which seems to be drenched with the powerful emotions of fighting and dying men is that of the small island of Corregidor, where in the early days of World War II, a handful of American and Filipino troops tried desperately to halt the Japanese advance against the city of Manila and the whole Philippine Islands.

Defense Secretary Alego S. Santos has said that the valiant defenders of the Philippines "fought almost beyond human endurance."

According to several witnesses, their ghosts have gone on fighting.

Today, the only living inhabitants of the island are a small detachment of Filipino marines, a few firewood cutters and a caretaker and his family. And then there are the non-living inhabitants.

Terrified wood cutters have returned to the base to tell of bleeding and wounded men who stumble about in the jungle. Always, they describe the men as grim-faced and carrying rifles at the ready.

Marines on jungle maneuvers have reported coming face to face with silently stalking phantom scouts of that desperate last-stand conflict of a quarter of a century ago. Many have claimed to have seen a beautiful red-headed woman moving silently among rows of ghostly wounded, ministering to their injuries.

Most often seen is the ghost of a nurse in a Red Cross uniform. Soldiers on night duty who have spotted the phantom have reported that, shortly after she fades into the jungle moonlight, they find themselves surrounded by rows and rows of groaning and dying men in attitudes of extreme suffering.

According to the caretaker and his family, the sounds that come with evening are the most disconcerting part of living on an island full of ghosts. Every night the air is filled with horrible moans of pain and the sounds of invisible soldiers rallying to defend themselves against the phantom invaders.

The supervisor of tourism for Luzon, Florentino R. Das, said that he and his wife have visited the island and have heard the terrible sounds of men in pain. Das stated that the sounds go far away toward Malinta Tunnel. Upon his investigation, he was unable to find any physical cause for the eerie disturbance.

How long might the violent emotions of warfare saturate the psychic ether of a terrain? The Phantom Marchers of Crete have been parading for centuries and seem to be armored men right out of the pages of Homer's *Iliad.*

People come from all over the island to observe the ghostly army, which usually puts in an appearance during the last weeks of May and the first week of June. No trained observer has been able to put the spectral army into any precise historical context. The ghostly ranks are filled with the images of tall, proud men, who wear metal helmets of classic design and carry short, flat swords.

The native islanders call them the "shadow men" or the "dew men," because they always appear just before dawn or just after sunset. They seem to form out of the sea, march directly for the ruins of an old Venetian castle, then disappear with the growing darkness of the night or the light of day. Historians have discarded any theory of a connection between the ghostly army and the Medieval castle because of the design of the phantoms' breast-plates and weapons.

For almost a century, feature stories on the spectral army have been carried in the major newspapers of Greece. In addition to the local peasants, Greek businessmen, archaeologists, and journalists have reported seeing the phenomenon. German and English archaeologists and observers have also been on hand for the parade of phantoms. During the Turkish administration of the island in the 1870s, an entire garrison of Turkish soldiers sighted the ghostly marauders and were frightened into readying themselves for combat.

Most theorists have discarded the possibility that the phantom marchers are only a mirage. Mirages have maximum ranges of about forty miles and only occur in direct sunlight. The army, as has been noted, appears only in the half-light of dawn or dusk. Then, too, a mirage is a reflection of reality. This would mean that somewhere, within a range of forty miles, such an army would truly be marching. It would seem beyond all range of imagination to suppose that an entire army of men, who enjoyed conducting annual secret maneuvers in ancient armor, could exist on the island of Crete without being detected by the populace.

Sir Earnest Bennett, a graduate of Hertford College, Oxford University, collected all available reports of the phenomenon and stated his conclusion that the marchers were a psychic manifestation of a bygone army of men who belonged to an ancient culture that had once inhabited the island.

The sea has provided many classic cases of ghostly scenes from the past. Every culture that has ever sent men to sea, has its share of ghost ships.

One such vessel puts in sporadic appearances at Cape d'Espoir in Gaspe Bay, Canada. The ship is said to be the ghost image of a British gunboat that was sent to harass the French forts along the Eastern seaboard of Canada. Observers of the phenomenon state that ghostly crewmen line its decks, and at the wheel stands a man with a woman at his side. As the vessel approaches the shore, its lights gradually go out and it appears to sink at exactly the same spot where the British gunboat sank two hundred years before.

In 1647, a ship was seen to vanish in full view of a crowd of people who had been awaiting its arrival at New Haven, Connecticut. This incident has become something of a classic case, and it is of great interest in our study of such phenomena, because in one sense, the phantom vessel seems very much like a massive crisis-apparition that had been directed toward those waiting on the docks. Five months earlier, the ship had put out from New Haven and had been feared lost. When her sails and rigging were spotted coming into the harbor, the word quickly spread, and a crowd of eager friends and relatives gathered to welcome the ship home. Then, before their startled eyes, the vessel became transparent and began to slowly fade from view. Within a few moments, the astonished crowd was left staring at the harbor.

Dozens of reputable witnesses claimed to have heard the terrible screams which issued forth from the ghost ship *Palatine* just five miles off the coast of Rhode Island. John Greenleaf Whittier committed the legend to poetry, and the story of the ghostly ship has found its way into several formal histories of New England. Although the ghostly recreation of the disaster was last officially reported in the 1820s, there are several old-timers in the Block Island area who can relate the details of the phantom ship.

The story of the tragic ship *Palatine* and her final voyage goes back to November 1752. With a full passenger list of immigrants, all bound for the prospering districts around Philadelphia, the vessel set sail from a Dutch port. The immigrants carried everything they possessed with them, for none planned to return to the Old World.

The voyage was uneventful until the *Palatine* reached the vicinity of the Gulf Stream, then it seemed as if all the fury of the North Atlantic was hurled upon them. Storm after storm smashed the ill-fated ship, driving her far off course into uncharted seas.

The captain had become ill shortly after the *Palatine* had set out and the turbulence of the storm soon drove him to his bed. With her master in quarters, the ship's crew began to slack off. For weeks the little vessel was mauled by the vicious sea while the crew did little to get her on course. Without their captain to drive them, the seamen stayed below and let the sea rule the *Palatine.*

When the captain died, all hope was lost for the ship's passengers. Ambitious young officers, backed by the crew, seized control of the provisions. To those passengers who could pay their exorbitant prices, the greedy officers doled out meager rations of food and water. Those without money starved to death and were cast overboard.

The supplies gave out around Christmas time. The crew took to the lifeboats and abandoned the *Palatine* and its surviving passengers to the whims of the sea. The vessel drifted for several more days, until it finally ran aground on the sand shoals off Block Island. Most of the surviving passengers left on board had suffered mental breakdowns.

Residents of Block Island removed the survivors to the safety of the village homes. One woman had become so crazed by her suffering and by the death of her loved ones that she refused to leave the ship. She maintained that she had to stay aboard to await the return of her family so they could all disembark together.

The islanders decided to allow the woman to remain on board and selected a committee that would be responsible for providing her with food and water. The *Palatine* was towed into a cove, and the villagers planned to salvage any usable cargo and to dismantle the ship at their convenience. Perhaps by that time, they reasoned, the poor woman might have regained her senses.

One day while the islanders were working on the *Palatine*, the ship was blown adrift by a sudden storm. In his haste to leave the ship, one of the workmen accidentally tipped a brazier of coals. Flames began leaping upward from the dry timbers, and the work crew scrambled for their boats.

As they rowed toward the shore, the islanders looked back at the *Palatine*, its deck enveloped in flames.

"That one was jinxed by Old Nick himsellf," one of the men said solemnly.

Then the men heard the agonizing screams lifting from the flaming vessel.

"Mercy'pon us! We've left the daft woman behind!"

The workmen were filled with shock and pity. They knew the flames were too intense to risk going back to the *Palatine*; there was nothing they could do for the trapped victim except to offer a prayer for her soul. They watched, horrified, as the rising wind slowly pushed the blazing vessel out to sea.

In flames, the *Palatine* sailed into legend. There are observers who claim that the ship returns every year on the anniversary of her destruction. Others contend that the *Palatine* came back only as long as any member of her original crew remained alive. Historians found dozens of witnesses who claimed to have seen the image of the burning ship and to have heard the terrible screams of the dying woman.

Dr. Aaron Willey reported having viewed the *Palatine* light on several occasions. In spite of the doctor's attempts at maintaining an enforced objectivity, his story exactly paralleled other reports: a blazing fire the size of a ship appears near shore, then slowly recedes until it is only a tiny light on the horizon.

There are scores of ghost ships that appear and disappear on the high seas. Much rarer are ghost trains, but these, too, have been reported. John Quirk and several of his customers in the Bridge Lunch saw the phantom train of Pittsfield, Massachusetts, go by one afternoon in February 1958.

"We saw it regardless of what anyone else tries to tell us," Quirk told newsmen. "It consisted of a baggage car and five or six coaches. I can describe that locomotive down to the last bolt. It was so clear and plain that I was even able to see the coal in the tender. And my customers saw it just as plainly as I did."

Several other Pittsfield residents, who are convinced of the existence of a phantom train, swear they have seen the specter on a stretch of track between the North Street Bridge and the Junction, and passing the Union Depot.

Railroad officials reply in the same formalized statement whenever such reports reach the home office: "We have operated no steam engine on that line for years. There has definitely not been a train which has passed Union Depot or the Junction at the times when certain witnesses claim to have seen a locomotive in that area."

At 6:30 A.M. one frosty March morning, Bridge Lunch employees and customers caught another glimpse of the ghost train.

"The place was full of customers and every one of them saw the ghost train," said the luncheonette employee Steve Strauss. "Just like every time before, the steam engine pulled a baggage car, five or six coaches, and was highballing east toward Boston."

A number of truck drivers piloting their powerful engines on all-night runs across the still Dakota and Nebraska plains, have reported catching images of wagon trains or pony express riders in their headlights. One man said that he slowed down, shut off his motor, and was able to hear the creaking of the ancient wooden axles and the banging of pots and pans against the sides of the ghostly wagons.

In 1956 the St. Louis *Post-Dispatch* carried a story by Leonard Hall, who witnessed a restored scene of the past while he was camping on the upper Current River in the Ozarks in the early autumn of 1941.

Hall remembered being awakened by the sound of voices. About one hundred yards from his tent, he saw several figures moving about a roaring fire. As he crawled from his blankets to investigate further, he was amazed to see that the clearing was ringed by a dozen campfires.

Hall readily identified many of the shadowy figures as tall, bronzed Indians, naked except for breech clouts. He could hear the occasional stamp of a horse's hoof, the contented nicker of a grazing animal, the murmur of voices. Although Hall was astonished at having awakened to a scene from the past, he was even more surprised to observe that some of the figures seated about the fires wore the armor of the Spanish conquistadores.

Hall crawled back into his bedroll, convinced that he was dreaming. When he woke the next morning, he found no trace of the phantom visitors and did not bother to relate the incident to his traveling companions. Many years later, when his research disclosed that bands of conquistadores under DeSoto and Coronado had been in the Ozark area of the Current River in August 1541, Hall began to put stock in the amazing "dream" he had experienced in August 1941. Exactly four hundred years earlier, a party of gold-seeking Spaniards, with their Indian guides, could well have camped on that very meadow where Hall had seen the flames reflecting off tarnished armor.

Veterans of the Korean conflict returned with tales of a ghost town that came to life on cold, still nights.

By day, Kumsong, Korea was nothing but piles of battered rubble. The population had long since given up residence of their war-washed village to the rats. The American troops, who looked down on the charred ruins from their positions in the frontline bunkers, called Kumsong, "The Capital of No Man's Land."

But, then, on some nights, soldiers would come back from their frozen bunkers with stories of music, singing, and the laughter of women that had drifted up from the ghost town. So many Allied troops heard the ghostly music that "Ching and his violin" became a reality to the frontline soldiers.

One morning the GIs awakened to find that some wit had nailed a poster to the side of a long bunker: "Come to the gala dance this Saturday night—located in lovely, convenient Kumsong. Dancing partners and delicious drinks without cost."

Soldiers who scoffed at the tales of the weird phenomena were invited to put on their long-johns and join the sentries on the hill that overlooked the battered city.

An issue of *Search* ran an item on the haunted village of Kumsong and reprinted a poem Sergeant Joe Schwaller of Monterey Park, California, had written to celebrate Kumsong's ghostly dance:

There's a place to dance in your combat pants
And a place to forget the fight;
There's gals galore and no sign of war,
In Kumsong, Saturday night.
It's down the line, don't step on a mine,
Far from the battle's din,
Where you can jig to the phantom music
Of Ching—and his violin.

Although both haunted landscapes and haunted houses seem most liable to receive their emotional energy from the psychic charges generated by scenes of violence and tragedy, there have been reports of pleasant restorations of the past.

On a rainy evening in October 1916, Miss Edith Olivier was driving from Devizes to Swindon in Wiltshire, England. The evening was so dreary that Miss Olivier wished earnestly for a nice, warm inn in which to spend the night. Leaving the main road, she found herself passing along a strange avenue lined by huge gray megaliths. She concluded that she must be approaching Avebury. Although Edith Olivier had never been to Avebury before, she was familiar with pictures of the area and knew that the place had originally been a circular megalithic temple which had been reached by long stone avenues.

When she reached the end of an avenue, she got out of her automobile so that she might better view the irregularly falling megaliths. As she stood on the bank of a large earthwork, she could see a number of cottages, which had been built among the megaliths, and she was surprised to see that, in spite of the rain, there seemed to be a village fair in progress. The laughing villagers were walking merrily about with flares and torches, trying their skill at various booths and applauding lustily for the talented performers of various shows.

Miss Olivier became greatly amused at the carefree manner in which the villagers enjoyed themselves, completely oblivious to the rain. Men, women and children walked about without any protective outer garments and not a single umbrella could be seen. Miss Olivier would have joined the happy villagers at their fair if she had not been growing increasingly uncomfortable in the rain, which was becoming steadily heavy. She decided that she was not made of such hardy stock as the sturdy villagers and got back into her automobile to resume her trip.

Miss Olivier did not visit Avebury again until nine years had passed. At that time, she was perplexed to read in the guidebook that, although a village fair had once been an annual occurrence in Avebury, the custom had been abolished in 1850!

When she protested that she had personally witnessed a village fair in Avebury in 1916, Miss Olivier was offered a sound and convincing rebuttal by the guide. Even more astounding, perhaps, was the information she acquired concerning the megaliths. The particular avenue on which she had driven on that rainy night of her first visit had disappeared before 1800.

Just how substantial is a phantom? Can a scene from the past return and assume temporary physical reality once again? Did Miss Olivier drive her automobile on an avenue which was no longer there, or did she drive on a solid surface which had once been there and had temporarily returned?

In the January 1967 issue of *Fate,* Francis J. Sibolski wrote that he had witnessed a phantom street fight take place outside of his home thirteen times in twenty years.

From his front window, Sibolski claimed that he had seen a 1937 Plymouth taxicab pull up and disgorge two angry men in their mid-twenties. The punching and mauling lasted about three minutes, then the smaller of the two men jumped into the waiting taxicab and sped off. The larger man rummaged for a cigarette, shook the last one out of the pack, crumpled the package to the sidewalk, and began to walk for the corner. Before the taxi reached the corner or before the big man had taken more than a few steps, the tableau faded away.

Sibolski has had his wife witness the phantom fighters, and he has researched the incident to the extent that he has identified the two men (now both deceased, though one was still alive when Sibolski began witnessing the restored scene from the past) and has obtained testimonials from those who can remember the original altercation. Sibolski claims that the cigarette package exists for several minutes, sometimes even hours, *after* the tableau has vanished.

Once Sibolski approached the phantom scene and attempted literally to become a part of the past.

"When I came within six or seven feet of the fighters," he writes, "my nostrils and throat suddenly became congested with a taste and smell that recalled my childhood colds. While I was capable of moving, I had no desire to. I retreated to the bottom of my porch steps watching the act finish off, feeling very odd—as if I were looking at old, old clothing in a forgotten attic."

The conventional idea of time existing as some sort of stream flowing along in one dimension is obviously an inadequate one. In this view, the past does not exist; it is gone forever. Neither does the future exist, because it has not yet happened. The only thing that one can rely upon is the nebulous present.

If the past completely ceased to exist, we should have no memory of it. Yet each of us has a large and varied memory bank. The past, therefore, must exist in some sense. Perhaps not as a physical or material reality, but in some sphere or dimension of its own. It may be, some researchers have theorized, that our subconscious minds—our transcendental selves—do not differentiate between past, present, and future. To the subconscious mind, all the spheres or dimensions of time may exist as part of the "Eternal Now."

When Eleanor Jourdain and Anne Moberly took the train from Paris to Versailles in August 1901, they did not expect to meet Marie Antoinette. Neither did they expect to find people dressed in the costume of that tragic queen's period, speaking in a French dialect that dated from the late eighteenth century. These and other mysterious circumstances transformed a tourist's visit of the palace grounds, and especially those of the *Petit Trianon*, the "little chateau" that Louis XVI of France built for his Mistress Marie, into a journey into the past.

Like all proper tourists, the two teachers began their promenade with a visit to the long rooms and galleries of the palace. Afterward they stopped to rest in the *Salles des Glaces.*

It was a pleasant afternoon. The French late summer had been hot, but on this day a protective curtain of grey cloud had been drawn across the sun's brassy face and from the open windows a cool, spritely breeze enticed the travelers to come out-of-doors.

"Suppose we visit the *Petit Trianon,*" Miss Moberly suggested to her companion.

Eleanor Jourdain quickly agreed. The two friends started out on the path that would take them to the pavilion where Marie Antoinette and her friends diverted themselves by living as peasants, a pastime that enjoyed great vogue in France at that time.

They made their way down the great steps of the palace and past the fountains, quickened by a foretaste of autumn which was afforded by a cool breeze that deepened the mood of sweet, nostalgic memory of happiness past.

Along the central avenue they walked, their steps growing brisker with impatience. They reached the fountainhead of the pond and turned right, as indicated in their guide book. The mood of the day seemed to change as they passed the *Grand Trianon* and turned off the paved walkway onto a broad, grassy drive.

In their haste they missed the path that would have taken them directly to the *Petit Trianon*. Instead, they crossed it and walked up a lane leading in the other direction.

As they proceeded along this route Miss Moberley saw a woman lean out of the window of a nearby building to shake a dust cloth.

"Eleanor..." the name barely escaped her lips. "She knows the way, silly," she said to herself. "Otherwise she would have asked that woman in the window."

What would Anne Moberley have thought if she knew that her traveling companion had seen no woman?

"What did you say, Anne?"

"Nothing really. I was wondering out loud what Professor Oliver would think of all this. It's such a shame that he gets seasick before he gets to the dock."

"So right," she laughed. "Should we tell him we saw Marie Antoinette?"

Anne Moberley's lips tightened as she remembered the woman in the window. Had Eleanor seen her after all?

The travelers found that the path they were following had suddenly become three. Without a word Miss Jourdain marched straight ahead in the middle one.

"Are you sure this is the way?" hesitated Miss Moberley.

"No. We must have gotten off the path somewhere. Look! Let's ask one of those gardeners."

"Strange looking gardeners," observed Anne Moberley.

Gardeners or not, the two men in the path ahead were strange indeed. True, there was a wheelbarrow and spade nearby, but there the role ended. They were dressed in long, grayish green of the finest cloth, and wore three-cornered hats of black velvet. In answer to Miss Jourdain's question, they directed the two women to walk straight ahead.

"Anne . . ." For the first time Eleanor Jourdain started to lose her self-assurance. For that matter, the two were not to realize until later that somewhere along the way they had lost much of their holiday gaiety.

"What is it? Are we lost agin?" Anne tried to mask the anxiety that had risen in her since the moment they had left the main path.

"Not if the directions we got are right. I don't know—suddenly everything seems so unreal."

"Unreal?"

"That woman and girl back there. Did you see them?"

"Yes. At the time I thought it was quite strange. They looked more like—well, they looked more like . . . but that's ridiculous."

"What's ridiculous?" Eleanor sounded as if she wanted to be told that everything was as it should be. "They looked like what?"

"They looked as if they were figures in a tableau." Anne Moberley almost ran her words together, trying to get them said before her nerve failed again.

"Let's go on."

The mood of the day had changed. The sky seemed covered with grey dust and the spritely breeze that had once danced across the palace grounds, lending wings to the feet of the women, now clawed at their spirits like the cold fingers of an old crone that held the two back at each step. Neither of the women spoke, both trying to conceal the foreboding that had walked like a ghost with them down the narrow path.

The path that they were traveling ended abruptly in another, which ran across the other at an angle, like a ribbon across the edge of a package. Beyond this rose a woodland. As though the new path were a dividing line between sections of a patchwork dream, it chopped off the blue-green lawn from a stretch of ground with tufts of wild grass and dead leaves for a covering. The eerie, unnatural look deepened, and though it was still afternoon, the light was diminished.

"Eleanor, look at those trees over there," said Anne, pointing to a spot beyond the somber buildings, "they look like they're woven into the sky."

Miss Jourdain had already noticed. She had realized, with a mounting sense of dread, that although the wind still breathed around her face that no branches waved, no leaves stirred, in the forest of "woven" trees.

Even with the weak sunlight that filtered through the clouds, the trees should have cast some shadow, but although both women strained their eyes, they could not see a single one. The scene throbbed with stillness.

Beside the bandstand with his back turned to them sat a man dressed in the same manner as the others. As Anne and Eleanor approached, he turned and the women almost gasped for the sight of his face. His countenance was dark, and his pock-marked face, with its mouth that drooped like a Greek mask of tragedy, revealed an appearance of decay and evil that could not be concealed by staring, sightless eyes.

So stricken were Anne and Eleanor by this sight that they did not see the other man until he called to them.

"Mesdames, mesdames," he shouted at them.

Two frightened women spun around to face the newcomer.

He gave them directions, pointing the way as he spoke in an accent which neither of the two teachers grasped. They thanked him, nevertheless. At once the man ran off and disappeared into the woods. But still the pair heard the sound of his running footsteps.

Eleanor and Anne started off in the direction their mysterious guide had indicated. Hurrying along a narrow path nearly roofed by overgrown trees, the women soon found themselves at last before the *Petit Trianon*.

Rough grass, such as one might expect to find growing happenstance around the cottage of a French peasant in the days of Louis XVI, covered the terrace around the north and west sides of the house.

"Anne! Look there on the grass. What's that woman doing?" Eleanor Jourdain took hold of her friend's arm as she spoke, as though looking for something real to grasp.

"She appears to be sketching. See, now she's holding the paper at arm's length."

"Yes, of course, but look at her clothing. She's dressed like a picture I remember of Marie Antoinette."

"Don't be silly." [Miss Moberley, too, had noticed the full skirt and fichu, and the wide white hat, but had told herself that there must be some kind of pageant in progress. Otherwise, why should anyone dress so to go sketching?]

In spite of her attempt to explain away the events and sights of the afternoon, Anne Moberley felt herself to be dreaming as she and Miss Jourdain walked up the steps to the top of the terrace. The dreary atmosphere hung over the scene like a musty blanket. When they reached the top, Anne looked back. The woman with the sketching pad was still there. She looked up at them, her face old and ugly.

A door slammed. Fearful for what they might see, the two sightseers turned in the direction of the sound. A young man, dressed for kitchen work stood before them on the terrace. He carried a broom and seemed to have stepped out to shake the dust from it. He seemed as surprised as they.

"*Salut*, mesdames. If you seek the way into the house, it is that way [pointing], through the *cour d'honneur*. Would mesdames be pleased to have me show them the way?"

"Anne, I believe he's making sport of us," said Eleanor Jourdain. "Let's go on around to the front entrance."

Once inside the *Petit Trianon*, the two found their spirits improving. A wedding was in progress, not one from the time of Marie Antoinette, but one which was unmistakably an event of 1901. Eleanor Jourdain and Anne Moberley felt the cloud of depression that had followed them to the *Petit Trianon* lift. Leaving the house of Marie Antoinette, the two took a carriage back to Versailles. The ride back was passed in silence.

A week passed and still the two friends did not speak of the afternoon in Versailles. Then one day Anne Moberley sat writing a letter to another friend about the strange, unaccountable happenings. As she wrote, the same dreamy depression settled over her thoughts.

"Eleanor," she said, "do you think that the *Petit Trianon* is haunted?"

Her friend looked up. "Yes," said Miss Jourdain, "I do!"

"I do!" though a simple statement of conviction, spoke volumes when uttered by Miss Eleanor Jourdain. Neither she nor Anne Moberley were the sort to be making brash statements containing more emotion and drama than reason. Miss Jourdain held the post of Taylorian lecturer in French at Oxford University, and Miss Moberley taught in an Oxford girl's school. Both were daughters of Anglican clergymen. They were both interested in music, not only in the areas of listening or playing, but in the theory of harmony itself.

It stands to reason that if one of these ladies said that she believed a thing, that she was convinced both emotionally and intellectually.

In addition, both women were psychically sensitive. But knowing that emotion often rushes in where reason fears to tread, each was reluctant to speak of her endowment. Not only did they avoid the exercise of this gift, but spoke of their "horror of many forms of occultism."

It is not likely, then, that the two dignified, conscientious teachers were trying to establish themselves as channels of psychic phenomena. (When they later published a book describing their strange afternoon at Versailles, both wrote under pseudonyms.)

As if they were not yet satisfied with their conclusions, Eleanor Jourdain and Anne Moberley returned to Versailles, separately and together.

Miss Jourdain's second visit to the haunted grounds was on January 2, 1902. In contrast to the brisk, forerunner-of-autumn day on which the two had made their first visit to Versailles, the day of Miss Jourdain's return was cold, and rain collected into little pools that would freeze as hard as mirrors when night drew its dark skirts across the gardens of Marie Antoinette.

Eleanor Jourdain did not walk to the *Petit Trianon* this time. As she moved along the drive, she tried to mark each incident as it occurred when she and Anne Moberley made their memorable trip on foot. Things looked the same. But wait! What building was that? Where had it been last August?

Eleanor dismounted from the carriage and approached the bridge leading to the Queen's Village. Once again she saw the darkness deepen. The same depression she had felt the first time across the bridge descended upon her with the cold rain that ran in tiny rivulets down the back of her neck. Miss Jourdain almost turned back.

"What on earth," said apprehensive Miss Jourdain to herself, "are those men doing out there in the rain, filling a cart with sticks?"

Eleanor looked away for an instant. When she looked back the laborers and their cart were gone, and the landscape was barren as far as she could see. She hastened out of the village and found herself lost in a maze of crisscrossing, diagonal paths that all seemed to end in other paths.

Slipping through the dripping woods was a man in the same costume as the one who had given her directions the time before. Suddenly, Miss Jourdain felt herself being jostled, as if by a passing crowd, and heard the whispers of silks brushing the tall grass. She heard voices speaking French, with "*Monsieur*" and "*Madame*" spoken close to her ears. From the distance eerie music drifted in from an unseen band.

Miss Jourdain looked at her map. She selected a path, thinking only to get out of this otherworldly place as quickly as possible. She started out only to find herself drawn to another path by a sense of urgency she could not understand.

She bolted onto the path she had first chosen and was immediately lost. The clouds seemed to lower, and the rain thicken. Grayness was everywhere, even the raindrops had the look of wet clay; the ground itself appeared to dissolve the grayness and ooze over the edges of the paved walk. Fear all but drew the breath from Eleanor Jourdain's throat as she desperately sought her way back to the present.

In her haste, she almost ran into a bearded giant of a man who suddenly appeared on the path in front of her.

Miss Jourdain was too tired to be frightened. Catching her breath, she simply asked for directions.

"Just follow the path you are presently on, Madame."

Eleanor heard herself say *"Merci,"* as she hurried on. The man's directions proved accurate, and soon a badly shaken Eleanor Jourdain was on her way back to Versailles.

Although Miss Jourdain made several trips to Versailles with her class of girls, it was not until July of 1904 that Miss Moberley was able to accompany her.

As Eleanor had told her incredulous friend, things had changed since their first visit.

Gates that had been open when the two had first visited the grounds were closed and locked, and the passing years had placed a seal of cobwebs upon them, as they had upon the kitchen door which the jovial youth with the broom had slammed. Only the ghosts that remained at *Petit Trianon* knew when that door had last been opened. The tapestry of trees which could not open their leafy arms to the sun or welcome the passing wind were gone, faded from view and memory. The bandstand and its sightless watchman were no more, and the old woman who shook out her dustcloth as Anne and Eleanor passed was gone, as was the window from which she had leaned.

Marie Antoinette had gone to sketch other scenes, and in her place, rose a well-rooted shrub of a size that gave mute testimony to the decades of growth which it had seen come and go.

The grounds were devoid of people in strange dress; only the sight of conventional tourists met the eyes of Eleanor and Anne as they negotiated the complex system of paths and wondered if the whole weird business were not a dream. Although the two friends could think this in their minds, they could not dismiss so easily the events of that first day in August.

Had the great wheel of time somehow turned back, bringing the past into the present? Or had the two psychically-sensitive teachers become as harps whose strings had vibrated to notes played in a past moment of time, and recorded forever upon the infinite ether? Or is it enough to say, with

Anne Moberley, an answer in passing to the question, "Do you believe the *Petit Trianon* is haunted," a simple "I do."

The wind still dances across the lawns of *Petit Trianon*, not noticing the missing terraces, and strokes with fleeting fingers trees not woven. If one listens there is sometimes the whisper of silks as they brush the tall grass in haste.

In his article "Time Marched Backward" (*Fate*, October 1962), William P. Schramm recounts two interesting incidents of ghostly reconstructions of the past.

The first related experience occurred to Paul Smiles, a friend of Schramm's. Smiles was on duty with the British Army in Nairobi, East Africa, in 1942, when he had his adventure into the unknown. He had taken advantage of a furlough to head for the lion country below Mount Kilimanjaro. Once there, he learned that a pride of lions had put themselves outside the protective laws by hunting native stock. A guide led Smiles to a shooting platform, and the hunter was directed to await the lions, which, according to the guide, would come down to the pool to drink.

Smiles was about to drift off to sleep when he was brought fully to his senses by the roar of a lion. Just as he was bringing a large male with full, dark mane into his sights, a rifle shot split the night's silence and sent the pride of lions scattering.

The shot had come from the direction of the tree in which Smiles' guide sat perched. The two men had agreed that "Bwana Smiles" should have the first shot. The Englishman was about to castigate his guide when ". . . a bedlam of rifle fire broke loose, as if hundreds of troopers had gone into action. Amidst this din sharp commands rang out in both English and German. The fusillades ensued time after time, interposed with excited commands. Then came silence."

Startled and shaky, Smiles came down from the shooting platform. His guide stood at the foot of his tree, waiting for him. He had not expected Smiles to be able to shoot a lion on that night, the anniversary of the "War Fight" that had been waged on that ground between the English and Germans twenty-five years before. On the first night that he had heard the sounds of phantom warfare the guide had thought that he had experienced some kind of nightmare. He had never told anyone what he had witnessed for fear that they would say he was bewitched. That was why he had brought Smiles to that particular shooting platform on that night. The guide had wanted corroboration of his story.

The native led Smiles through the brambles until they came to the open veldt. There under the African moon, Smiles saw rows of crosses marking the graves of both British and German infantry.

Outnumbered two to one, and maybe taken by surprise, the British regiment had been annihilated. Since then every year on the fight's anniversary night, Simbia explained, the souls of the troopers came back and fought the battle over again.

On August 10, 1957, author Schramm claims to have had a "Panoramic phantasm" of his own when he and his family were living on a farm near Russell, Minnesota.

One night, while walking his dog near the lake, the animal seemed to sense someone down by the water. When Schramm investigated, he was amazed to see an Indian family ". . .a middle-aged man, his squaw, and three or four youngsters. . .dressed as Indians in the early days when the Sioux roamed the virgin, unsettled territory."

Schramm sensed that the mysterious family group was no longer composed of flesh and blood individuals. By its low growling and nervous behavior, the dog, too, seemed to sense something unusual about the "Indians." Schramm writes that ". . .the wraiths made no sound, nor showed any sign of being aware of our presence."

In 1948, Charles Ingersoll of Cloquet, Minnesota, found that the trip he had planned with his parents to the Grand Canyon had to be postponed due to business reasons. It was not until 1955, seven years later, that the long awaited trip was realized.

Upon returning to Minnesota, Ingersoll purchased a five-hundred-foot, 8 mm print of Grand Canyon scenes from a local photographic supply store. That night when he ran the film for his parents, they were amazed to see Charles in a sequence of the footage.

The mystery deepened when they read the 1948 copyright of the film. The footage had been shot the year in which the Ingersolls had so very much wanted to visit the Grand Canyon but had been unable to make the trip. Automobiles of 1948 vintage are seen in the background, and tourists are dressed in the fashions of that same year. Yet, somehow, there is Charles Ingersoll walking up to the rim of the canyon to take a picture with his 35 mm camera. For a man who did not make the trip until 1955, Ingersoll is very much in evidence in film that was shot of the Grand Canyon in 1948.

Skeptics accuse Ingersoll of having had the film made up after his return from the Grand Canyon. The Minnesotan points out that not even a week had passed from the time he left the park with his parents to the day he bought the film. Ingersoll also offers as evidence in behalf of the experience the fact that every inch of the film footage is of the same quality and is subject to the closest scrutiny. To further substantiate the strange episode, the film dealer will testify that he had that particular reel of film on his shelf for well over a year before the Ingersolls made their trip to the Grand Canyon.

In additional correspondence with Ingersoll, I have learned that he has had a number of paranormal experiences which may have prepared him for such a dramatic trip on the Time track. For example, he has told me that, as a child, he often seemed to be able to foretell events before they occurred. When he was about twelve years of age, Ingersoll began to have a recurring dream which seems illustrative of the manner in which the subconscious mind may occasionally pluck from the "Eternal Now" an event which lies in the future for the conscious and calendar-time oriented organism.

"In the dream," Ingersoll writes, "I would be walking along a dusty road . . . and I would approach a large three-story brick building. As I would near the building, a small, shaggy brown dog, a cocker spaniel, would come to meet me. I would reach down and pat the friendly dog, and at this point in the dream, a woman would start to scream. The scream would increase in pitch until I would awaken."

Ingersoll had this dream, perhaps three or four times a year, until 1950, when he was thirty-six years old. At that time he had experienced a business failure and was having a difficult time finding a job. Finally he answered an ad in a Duluth, Minnesota, newspaper that asked for men to work as orderlies in a county home in Superior, Wisconsin.

"I arrived in Superior and was informed the bus only went within a mile of the hospital," Ingersoll recalls. "As I walked the mile from the highway, I recognized the large building as the one that I had seen in my dreams for so many years. When I left the dirt road to enter the grounds of the hospital, the shaggy, brown dog, a cocker spaniel, came running up to me. Just as I reached down to pat him, the shrill scream of a woman emanated from the hospital."

Ingersoll secured work at the hospital, an institution for the insane who were also afflicted with tuberculosis.

"I worked there for nearly a year," he told me, "and after I experienced this incident, I never had the dream again. By the way! The shaggy, brown dog became my constant companion all the time I worked there."

13

The Secretary Who Stepped Back in Time

"I think I have discovered the secret of Irene's psychic abilities," Glenn McWane announced one evening at dinner.

All table talk ceased at once, and Glenn could not have seized our attention more completely if he had announced that he had found the secret of eternal youth.

Irene, especially, was understandably curious to receive the full impact of Glenn's revelation.

"Well, would you please tell us, Glenn?" she smiled. "I really would like to know *how* I do it. I mean, I've theorized about it, but I've never found the 'secret.' "

Glenn grinned expansively. "It's simple, my friends. Look at what she is eating right now."

Irene's fork hovered over her plate, and she squirmed a bit uncomfortably, like a child caught with her hand in the cookie jar.

"She's eating a plate of raw onions," Joan Hurling said, crinkling her nose distastefully.

"Right," Glenn said, as if Joan were teacher's pet who had supplied the correct answer to a classroom question while all the other students sat silent as dolts.

"And what does she order along with every meal?" Glenn prompted his captive audience.

"A side order of raw onions!" we chorused.

By now Irene was laughing in unrestrained amusement. "So that's my secret, is it?"

"Well, Irene," I said, siding with Glenn's theory, "what ordinary mortal could regularly devour whole, heaping plates of raw onions? They must provide you with some ingredient that produces a chemical reaction somewhere within your system that sparks your psychism!"

"Hah!" Joan Hurling snorted. "Then, I, too, must be superhuman. I'm the one who has to room with Irene, and I'm the one who usually rides next to her in the backseat of the station wagon!"

We fed Irene an extra large helping of onions on the night that we visited the campus of Nebraska Wesleyan in Lincoln. We wanted her to have all the extra psychic energy that she could muster for this challenge to her paranormal abilities.

Of all the haunted places that we visited on our psychic safari in July 1970, the office on the Nebraska Wesleyan campus was the only place that had received previous investigation to any degree whatsoever. And even though the incident that took place within a particular office on that particular campus has become a contemporary classic in the annals of psychical research, we made it a special point to keep Irene Hughes ignorant of exactly where we were and what we would be seeing that night.

Any reasonably intelligent person could, of course, determine that we were on a college campus, but only a psychic person could divine *why* we had come there. And we followed these precautions even though I had gained (through cautious, casual conversation with Irene several days prior to our arrival on campus) complete certainty that she had no knowledge of the case wherein a secretary stepped into a scene from the past.

On October 23, 1963, Mrs. Coleen Buterbaugh, secretary to Dr. Sam Dahl, dean of the college, was walking across the campus on an errand for her boss. At exactly 8:50 A.M., she entered the old C.C. White Building, which is used primarily as a music hall.

Her heels clicked softly as she walked down a long corridor to an office at the end. Mrs. Buterbaugh could hear the sound of a marimba being coaxed into a semblance of melody by a practicing student.

Yawning, whispering students were changing their first-hour classes for either another classroom session or a welcome cup of morning coffee. Mrs. Buterbaugh paused to let a group of students pass in front of her, and she mused to herself that it was a typical early morning at Nebraska Wesleyan.

Then she entered the office of Dr. Tom McCourt, a visiting lecturer from Scotland, and found that she had stepped into a scene that was far from typical.

She was struck at once by an almost overwhelming odor of musty air. When she had opened the door to the office, she had observed that both rooms were empty and that the windows were open. But now...

"I had the strange feeling that I was not in the office alone," she later told Rose Sipe of the Lincoln *Evening Journal.* "I looked up, and for what must have been just a few seconds saw the figure of a woman, standing with her back to me, at a cabinet in the second office. She was reaching up into one of the drawers."

The secretary then noticed that she could no longer hear the noisy babble of the students in the outer hall as they passed from their classes. She had the eerie, other-worldly feeling that she had suddenly become isolated from present-tense reality.

The woman, who seemed to be filing cards so industriously, was tall, slender, and dark-haired. Her clothing was of another period—a long-sleeved white shirt-waist, an ankle-length brown skirt.

Then Mrs. Buterbaugh felt yet another presence in the office.

"I felt the presence of a man sitting at the desk to my left," she told the newswoman, "but as I turned around there was no one there.

"I gazed out the large window behind the desk and the scenery seemed to be that of many years ago. There were no streets. The new Willard Sorority House that now stands across the lawn was not there; nothing outside was modern.

"By then I was frightened, so I turned and left the room!"

The startled and confused secretary hurried back to her desk in Dean Dahl's office. She sat down at her typewriter, fitted the dictaphone plug to her ear and tried to work on the letters that the Dean had dictated.

But it was just no good. Mrs. Buterbaugh's nervous and shaky fingers simply refused to obey the recorded voice of her boss. She decided that she must relate her experience to someone. The whole, jumbled business was too much for her to keep to herself.

When she entered her employer's office, Dean Dahl got at once to his feet and helped the pale and shaken woman to a chair. He listened courteously and without comment to her story, then asked her to accompany him to the office of Dr. Glenn Callan, chairman of the division of social sciences, who had been on the Wesleyan faculty since 1900. Once again, the secretary was fortunate to have a listener who heard her out and treated her account with respect.

After a careful quizzing of Mrs. Buterbaugh, together with the aid of a number of old college yearbooks, Dr. Callan theorized that she had somehow "walked" into the office as it had been some time circa 1920. Cautiously piecing together a number of clues from her strange tale and utilizing the yearbooks in the manner of police "mugbooks," Dr. Callan and

Mrs. Buterbaugh determined that she had seen the ghost of Miss Clara Mills, whose office it had been during that time. Miss Mills had come to Wesleyan as head of the theory department and as instructor in piano and music appreciation. She had been found dead in her office in the late 1930s.

Psychical researchers Gardner Murphy and H.L. Klemme employed hypnotic time regression as a means of eliciting further details of Mrs. Buterbaugh's remarkable paranormal experience. After they had placed the secretary in the hypnotic trance state, they instructed her to relive and to describe the events of that most extraordinary morning.

Once again, the secretary heard the sound of students practicing music, specifically noting the marimba. She dodged the students moving from their first-period classes, then entered the first room of the professor's suite.

While in the state of hypnotic regression, she was again stopped short by a very musty, disagreeable odor. Raising her eyes, she saw a very tall, black-haired woman extending her right arm to the upper righthand shelves of an old music cabinet.

Mrs. Buterbaugh told the researchers that when she had first walked into the room, everything had seemed quite normal. But after about four steps into the room, the strong odor had hit her.

"When I say strong odor," she emphasized, "I mean the kind that simply stops you in your tracks and almost chokes you."

As soon as Mrs. Buterbaugh was stopped by the odor, she felt as though there was someone in the room with her. It was then that she became aware that there were no noises out in the hall. "Everything was deathly quiet."

She looked up and something seemed to draw her eyes to the cabinet along the wall in the next room. "And there she was. She had her back to me, reaching up into one of the shelves of the cabinet with her right hand, standing perfectly still.... While I was watching her, she never moved."

Mrs. Buterbaugh explained that while the woman was not transparent, she knew somehow that "she wasn't real." Then, while the startled secretary was looking at her, "she just faded away—not parts of her body at a time, but her whole body all at once."

Mrs. Buterbaugh said that up until the time that the woman faded away, she was not aware of anyone else being in the office suite. "But just about the time of her fading out, I felt as though I still was not alone," she recalled.

"To my left was a desk, and I had a feeling that there was a man sitting at the desk," Mrs. Buterbaugh went on. "I turned around and saw no one, but I still felt his presence. When that feeling of his presence left I have no idea, because it was then, when I looked out the window behind that desk, that I got frightened and left the room."

Although she had weathered a fading lady and the sensed presence of an invisible man quite well, Mrs. Buterbaugh fled the room after she looked out the window and saw ". . .there wasn't one modern thing out there. The street was not even there and neither was the new Willard House. That was when I realized that these people were not in my time, but that I was back in their time."

It soon becomes apparent to the collector of psychical mysteries and to the reader of such collections and theorizations that man really knows very little about that mystery he calls "time." Perhaps it is impossible to ever place firm lines of demarcation around Past, Present and Future when, for some level of consciousness, everything in an Eternal Now.

As we noted earlier, Thomas A. Edison speculated that since no form of energy was ever lost, scenes of the past may have become imprinted somewhere in the psychic ether, just as images are registered on motion picture film. If Edison was correct, a person of the proper sensitivity might be able to pick up the etheric images imprinted all about him and literally see scenes of the past being replaced on the "screen" of his brain. Mrs. Coleen Buterbaugh may have been on the precisely proper psychic "wave length" to tune in on some past scene "broadcast" by the old office.

When psychic researcher Gardner Murphy pressed Mrs. Buterbaugh for additional details of the scene that she had glimpsed out of the office window, she replied that she seemed to be seeing a very warm, summer afternoon rather than an early October morning.

"It was very still," she remembered while in hypnotic trance regression. "There were a few scattered trees.... The rest was open field. The new Willard Sorority House and Madison Street were not there.

"I remember seeing a very vague outline of some sort of building to my right and that is about all. Nothing else but open field."

The secretary went on to say that she had fled to the hallway and had felt instantly reassured when she heard the familiar campus noises and the notes of the marimba, still being tapped into melody by a conscientious student.

Researchers Murphy and Klemme received permission to conduct a thorough search of the university files, and they at last uncovered a photograph dated 1915 that depicted a campus scene similar to the one which Mrs. Buterbaugh had glimpsed out of the window into the past. The two investigators thought it highly unlikely that the secretary could ever have come across the picture or even one like it prior to the time of her most unusual experience. They also agreed that the picture of Miss Clara Mills found in old yearbooks fit the description of the tall, dark-haired woman whom Mrs. Buterbaugh had seen in the office, and they established the fact that Miss Mills had died shortly before 9:00 A.M. in the same building in which the secretary had begun her trip into the past at about 8:50 A.M.

In a brief summation of the case in his paper, "The Hypnotic Trance, the Psychedelic Experience, the Psi Induction: A Review of the Clinical and Experimental Literature," Dr. Stanley Krippner notes that a psychological examination of Mrs. Buterbaugh uncovered no evidence of serious mental illness.

"In an interview," Dr. Krippner writes, "the 41-year-old secretary recalled having had a number of *deja vu* experiences during her lifetime, in which she recalled being in a new situation before, even though, apparently, the situation was completely new to her. Mrs. Buterbaugh also reported occasional 'predormital sleep paralysis' in which she felt unable to move just before falling asleep.

"Murphy and Klemme concluded that Mrs. Buterbaugh's psychological and physiological condition (a history of *deja vu* experiences and predormital sleep paralysis) may have made her susceptible to an episode in which she left the 'here-and-now' and 'plunged into the past.' The transition from one state of consciousness to another is often favorable to the occurrence of paranormal phenomena, as this case demonstrates. Furthermore, the case illustrates the value of hypnotically induced time regression in eliciting the recall of psychic experience."

And now we awaited a nightwatchman's key to provide us access to that same office wherein Mrs. Buterbaugh had "plunged into the past," seeking to test whether or not a gifted sensitive might elicit the recall of a psychic experience.

Irene Hughes still did not know where we were, other than being on a college campus and seated on, strangely enough, an old church pew in the corridor of a very old classroom building.

"Oh, the impressions that are coming to me, Brad!" she said, her eyes closed, viewing some private psychic scene. "Oh, boy, am I tuned in!"

But now circumstances were to foul us up just a bit.

Dick Mezzy's friend Doug, through whose intervention we were able to gain access to the C.C.White Building on Nebraska Wesleyan's campus, had gone in search of the night custodian, who obviously had not quite understood Dick's directions as to where to leave the key to the office.

"Has he shown up here?" Doug said, upon a return from a quick search of the immediate buildings in the vicinity.

At the slow, sad shaking of our heads, Doug smiled apologetically and said that he would look in another section of the campus. "He has to be around here," he told us over his shoulder, as he walked back down the stairs. Somehow the declarative statement sounded more like a prayer.

In the meantime, our eager medium was becoming a bit restless. Impressions were bombarding her from every corner of the old, well-used classroom building, but no one had given her the "go" sign yet, so she simply sat, as serenely as possible, awaiting whatever assignment she hoped that we would soon give her for that evening.

Irene Hughes is an elegant lady, who constantly retains control of the situation about her. But that evening, I could sense that the unaccountable delay was beginning to chip away a bit at her patience.

"I know that you don't want to tell me anything about the experiment tonight, Brad," she said, "But I am receiving psychically that it has to do with something that happened in one of these classrooms. Perhaps if I could just stand outside the room...."

"Doug will have the key in just a bit," I smiled, trying to reassure her.

But the day had been long, and like nearly all of the others on our psychic safari, very hot. I could see that Irene was becoming physically tired as well as impatient. We had been on the road for several days, keeping late hours, driving long miles. Since we were all becoming a bit sluggish with the heat and the strain of maintaining our schedule, it could come as no surprise that the usually energetic seeress was also beginning to give evidence of her mortality.

Finally Dick Mezzy and Doug returned triumphant from one of their key-hunting expeditions. They had found the night watchman, borrowed the key to the office, and we were soon crowding into the suite that had served as a portal to the past one morning in October 1963. Irene walked directly to the back office of the suite.

"I have the feeling that the desk was further over this way," she said, "because I feel like I want my back right to the window. You know," she added, "I am just getting so many different impressions. People...people...so many people have been walking through here."

Then the seeress began to receive an impression that made us instantly more attentive: "She came as a young lady. I see her in a long skirt that seems to open in the back. It's folded over in the back and seems to open...down to her ankles. Her hair is bouffant...pompadour...rolled over. I feel her around in here very much. She seems to be a very pleasant and pretty woman. Involved with teaching."

It seemed as though Irene was indeed providing us with a description of Miss Clara Mills.

"When we were sitting out there in the hall," she continued, "I kept looking down the hallway toward this office, and I kept seeing a man going in and out. He looked—how do I describe him? He looked like a typical college president-type. I know it is pretty difficult to have a 'typical college president-type' in this day and age, but let's go back a few years.

"This man's face was neither heavy nor thin. And I had a feeling of him walking across campus. But now when I look outside this window, it does not look the way it did when I was seeing it through his eyes. Those buildings weren't there. There was only a road or a sidewalk.

"And I feel as though this building should be turned around. I feel the main entrance was in another place."

Doug spoke up: "The desk that she mentioned used to be in another room, facing another direction, so that its back would have been toward the window."

"What about the description of the man she was giving us?" I asked Doug.

"The description of the man who most likely would have been sharing the office with the woman (Miss Mills) at the time of the reported scene would fit that description," he said. "He was not the college president, but he looked like a college president of that time would have looked."

Irene: I have the feeling that maybe about twenty years ago some situation happened that created major changes here at the college.

Doug: Twenty years ago the college was turned over to a new administration.

Irene: I see that the man who would have been president then looked a little bit like J. Edgar Hoover.

Doug: That's a good description.

Irene: I get the psychic impression that there was a specific incident which occurred in this office which you want me to pick up. I feel it had to do with a woman. I get that she was a secretary. [After a moment's pause] She saw a man who was in spirit walk into this office, and then she saw him sitting at that desk.

Doug: In this incident that was not the primary point, but a female secretary did see, or sense, a male figure at that desk.

Irene: I feel that there must have been a table or couch along this wall.

Doug: There was a couch.

Irene: Was is somewhat like a green velvet one in the hall?

Doug: More Victorian in style.

Irene: But not as long as this one. It was shorter.

Doug: Yes.

Irene: I see the secretary more clearly. Ah, she saw a woman, too. She came into this office and.... Now I feel more like I'm seeing the woman I saw in that back office. I feel as though I am that tall and pretty woman and I am standing here, and the man is resting on the couch. Do you know if the furniture has been changed around?

Doug: Yes, it has.

Irene: Because it seems to me that I want my back to the window again in here.

Doug: How old is this man you keep picking up?

Irene: I remember seeing him on the couch, and he seemed to be forty-eight, maybe fifty.

I keep hearing the song, "All Hail the Power of Jesus' Name." I hear it being beautifully conducted. The first thing I heard when I entered this building was that song.

Doug: The benches you sat on in the hall were originally used in the choir.

Irene: I see a man conducting the choir. He looks a little different to me from the man I described a moment ago. He looks like a very vigorous man. But with him I also feel a deep sadness, because I feel he became totally blind.

Doug: You've got two people now. And both of them are still alive. You know, the way you were acting when you were directing the choir was very much like the mannerisms of this one man. You did a very good job of imitating him. He was very affected. And "All Hail the Power of Jesus' Name" was one of his favorite choral pieces.

Irene: But I saw a huge choir, and there was light streaming through a stained glass window. Everybody was standing on a stage, which didn't really seem to be there at all, and I was standing in a hall looking up at a high room with beautiful stained glass windows.

Doug: There's a church across the street with such windows.

Irene: Is there a stage there that feels out of place? The choir seems to be there, and it might have been a rehearsal, and there might have been an old piano down a little bit below him—yet I felt it should be on his right.

Doug: You might be describing the stage that existed in this building. But without the stained glass windows.

Irene: This conductor looked like he was in his early thirties or forties.

Doug: You've got mixed images of two men. One was the mentor of the other. Sort of like the big bear and the little bear. One was a student of the other, and he came back here to teach. He more or less worshipped the older man.

Irene: Was the older man a bit heavier than the younger one?

Doug: Yes.

Irene: And the younger man was smaller, more emotional?

Doug: Yes.

Irene: I would say that people probably liked the older man very much and got along with him very well. But I would say the younger man...I see turmoil and a storm around him. I see that he did not get along well with his students.

Doug: The older man was head of the deparment. Students called him "Pop," and he got along well with everyone. The second man was eventually fired after everyone stuck it out for twenty stormy years.

Irene: I feel both the lady and the presence of the older man about whom we were speaking. I feel that she must have been in love with the man, or at least felt very close to him. She was in this building because she taught here...and she was in love with him.

Doug: I don't know about that. Do you feel things better when you touch them. I mean psychically?

Irene: It all depends. I'm starting to get very physically tired, and I think most of my impressions came while I was sitting on the bench out there.

I can see the man in this office come in and sit down at the desk.

Then I see the secretary walking down the hall and entering the office. She walked in and wanted...tried to see him at the desk. I saw him straight, like this, rather than from the side or anything.

Then I see the woman in the office—not the secretary, now, but the woman who belongs in there. I can see her hair, and it is very pretty.

Brad: Can you tell us more about the woman's physical description, Irene?

Irene: I think she was very tall for a woman, and that her hair was dark, but not really black. It was worn in a roll and pushed over. I could see her skirt dark and long. And she had on a white blouse. She had a very pretty smile, and she busied herself around the office.

[In the 1915 yearbook, a picture of Miss Clara Mills bore the caption: "A daughter of the gods thou art, divinely tall and most divinely fair." The picture and the description, according to Mrs. Buterbaugh, matched the appearance of the tall, dark-haired woman she had seen in the office. It also seemed to match the description which Irene Hughes had divined through her psychism.]

Doug: The woman we were interested in having you pick up did dress like that, did wear her hair up like that, and was tall as women go.

Irene: I see the secretary walking in and seeing the woman over there [pointing toward the wall where the filing cabinet had been]. Then she looked and saw the man sitting at the desk. Then...then she looked out the window. I think maybe she saw him looking out the window and turned to see what he was looking at. And...and things weren't the way they are now. I'd say she definitely saw him sitting there.

Brad: It is very interesting to me that although the secretary who came into the office saw the woman rather than the man, Irene seems to be saying that it may possibly have been the man who was the strong entity or vibratory force. We may have a reverse of what seemed to be obvious to the percipient. Irene has continually picked up and focused on the man rather than the woman in this paranormal experience.

Irene: Oh, I feel the woman, too, but I feel the man very, very powerfully. I feel that the woman was very kind and may have loved this man very much.

Brad: From what I have read of the case, it seems to me that Irene has described the woman (Miss Clara Mills) exactly as Mrs. Buterbaugh described her.

Doug: Yes, and she (Miss Mills) wore that style of dress all of her life, even after the styles had changed, which made it difficult to determine the date of the paranormal scene which Mrs. Buterbaugh witnessed. She (Miss Mills) began work in 1913, I believe. [Doug was only off by one year. Miss Mills joined the faculty in 1912. And, so it would seem, her spirit has not yet retired!]

An Afterword: Ghosts, Spirits, and Reporting the Unknown

The famous psychoanalyst Dr. Carl G. Jung once described a personal encounter with a ghost that took place in 1920 during a weekend visit in a friend's rented country house.

Although the home had been temporarily acquired as a haven of peace and quiet, the nights in the old manse afforded no rest for its inhabitants. The after-dark hours were afflicted with an extensive repertoire of a full-scale haunting, complete with raps on the walls, noxious odors, and the mysterious dripping of a liquid.

Dr. Jung's recollections of the ghostly weekend included his observation that he would experience a sensation of incapacity whenever the phenomena would begin, and cold perspiration would bead his forehead.

From the psychoanalyst's point of view, the climax of the haunting occurred one night when the head of a woman materialized on the pillow of his bed, about sixteen inches from his startled gaze. The phantom had one eye open that seemed to be staring at the astonished Dr. Jung.

He managed at last to light a candle, and the ghostly head disappeared. Dr. Jung later learned from the villagers that all previous tenants of the country house had terminated their occupancy in short order after they had spent a night or two within its haunted walls.

Again, it seems to this author, that even in such a dramatic instance as turning over in bed to behold the one-eyed stare of a phantom woman next to one's own head on the pillow, the actual nature of the haunting in the country place was an impersonal one.

In my opinion, the only true interaction between ghost and percipient lay in the physical fact that someone of the proper psychic affinity had to be present in order to activate the dormant memory patterns that had in some way charged the house with some as yet unnamed and unknown psychic impulses.

But I promised at the outset of the book not to be dogmatic.

The materialized head on the pillow might have been the transient return and appearance of the spirit of one who had once lived in the country home and whose essential self was still bound to the earthly plane as the result of some kind of spiritual confusion.

Twentieth century science no longer regards solids as solids at all, but rather as congealed wave patterns. Psychical researcher James Crenshaw notes that the whole imposing array of subatomic particles—electrons, protons, positrons, neutrinos, mesons—achieve "particle-like characteristics" in a manner similar to the way that "wave patterns" in tones and overtones produce characteristic sounds.

Crenshaw theorizes that ghosts may be made up of transitory, emergent matter that "... appears and disappears, can sometimes be seen and felt before disappearing ... behaves like ordinary matter but still has no permanent existence in the framework of our conception of space and time. In fact, after its transitory manifestations, it seems to be absorbed back into another dimension or dimensions. . . . "

Throughout this book, we have seen the eerie results that may occur when someone of the proper telepathic affinity moves into a place where powerful emotions have permeated the very heart of a house.

We have observed that, generally, the ghost is nothing more than a "psychological marionette," an image somehow retained on the psychic ether of a place, no more aware of its percipient than the celluloid image of an actor on film is aware of his audience.

In the case of the crisis or postmortem apparition, however, we have noted that the ghost has a mission, a communication to complete to a percipient who had a strong emotional link with the agent of the apparition.

In the chapters wherein we dealt with the "haunted mind," we noted the ability of some individuals to send forth "living ghosts" via astral projection (out-of-body experience), or to set loose the psychokinetic fury of the poltergeist.

Finally, we have seen that powerful emotions might seem to saturate a landscape, causing vast, panoramic scenes to be restored from the past.

During the past several years, I have interviewed, corresponded with and visited dozens of mediums, ministers of Spiritualist churches, psychical researchers, professional seers and clairvoyants, and ordinary men and women who have undergone experiences that defy, perhaps even denounce, the tenets of our orthodox scientific and religious views. I am restating, then, that although I may favor the theory that *most* ghostly manifestations are the result of a memory pattern that has left a psychic residue powerful enough to make itself known to certain individuals when certain stimuli are present in the environment, I certainly will not deny that the spiritistic hypothesis may be totally applicable in many instances.

Then, of course, for either hypothesis there is the matter of "scientific proof."

I must admit that I am much more concerned with the philosophical, the spiritual, implications of psychical research than I am with proving anything to the scientific satisfaction of anybody.

I realize that with our twentieth century technology, parapsychologists feel compelled to prove the validity of psychical phenomena, and I understand why that must be so. But the parapsychologist has a different role to play than do I as a reporter, a communicator.

Because of the efforts of certain dedicated parapsychologists, many of the generally elusive psychic phenomena are able to satisfy the "scientific" requirement of repeated performance, and this statistical "proof" was gained through thousands of hours of laboratory tests in telepathy and clairvoyance. For those who continue to scoff at the statistics of psychical research and suggest that the parapsychologists have misinterpreted their data or cheated by deliberate misinterpretations, I feel it should be pointed out that there are several phenomena under the aegis of orthodox science that do not lend themselves to the demand for experimental replication. There is the whole area of natural phenomena, which must be observed at the moment of occurrence and cannot be controlled by any laboratory in the world. Meteors, eclipses, lightning flashes and the Northern Lights are transitory, sporadic phenomena incapable of being reproduced at the will of an investigating scientist, yet it would seem foolish should someone maintain that they not be recognized by orthodox science.

I rather doubt if the parapsychologist shall ever be able to offer his skeptical colleagues the kind of proof that is obtainable in such material sciences as chemistry and physics.

It would seem to this observer of the psychic scene that the proof which the psychical researcher can best offer would more nearly resemble the legal proof acceptable in the courtroom. In other words, they may present evidence in an open and objective manner so that any reasonable person who chooses to examine the evidence will conclude that the cons balanced by the pros indicate the probability of the psychic thesis.

I can already hear the objections that will be raised to the above opinion by the laboratory and academic parapsychologists.

I do understand the pressures placed upon them by their colleagues, but I must confess that I feel that our one truly human factor, our spirituality, cannot be distilled, dissected, or defined by any scientific elucidation.

Since all thought is subjective, I wonder if there can ever really be such a thing as objective knowledge or absolute proof. It has been said that proof is an idol before which the pure mathematician tortures himself. The physicist, so it would seem, is generally satisfied to pay homage to the more accessible shrine of plausibility.

Do the criteria which we have formed into artificial worlds and given the collective name "science" have any greater reality than dreams, visitations, or inspirations?

As a reporter of the psychic world, I have often been asked if I believe that the essence of the human personality may lie in an invisible spirit or entity.

I believe that man and his mind are more than physical things.

I believe that man is more than biochemical compounds, a mere cousin of the laboratory guinea pig.

I do not accept the mechanistic doctrine that tells us that we are trapped in the same cycle that imprisons the atoms of hydrogen and oxygen.

I believe that contained within each of us is the Divine Spark that is necessary to unlock all of life's mysteries.

In an admittedly simple analogy, when we speak with a person, we are looking at his or her exterior—clothing, skin, hair—but the actual "person" to whom we are speaking remains invisible to us. In my opinion, that invisible, essential stuff of personality can survive without a physical brain, without a physical body.

Another query that is frequently put to me is whether or not I am concerned with the dangers inherent in psychical research. It is apparent, of course, that these well-meaning, or deliberately disparaging, individuals are referring to the psychological dangers of probing the strange, the unusual, and the unknown.

I agree that if a would-be reporter of the paranormal is an extremely nervous sort, he would do well to leave the field alone. Nor is there a place for the emotional or overly credulous investigator in psychical research. I maintain, however, that if one is able to keep intact common sense, objectivity and a sense of humor, there is no reason why this field should be any more fraught with psychological dangers than any other area of intellectual pursuit.

So now we have come to the point in this volume where we must bid *adieu* to one another. The reader shall return to other pursuits, while I shall continue my spiritual quest. I do hope that the reader might care to rejoin me in the future volumes of investigations which will be published by Para Research.

If the reader should elect to come along on some future psychic safari, the same conditions shall be presented to him or her. I shall not force any dogmatic assertions on anybody, and I shall not provide any neatly packaged proof of the paranormal beyond that which accrues from faithful and objective reportage.

KAHUNA MAGIC

Brad Steiger

Based on the life work of Max Freedom Long, *Kahuna Magic* lays open the secrets of the Kahuna, the ancient Hawaiian priests. Long used the secrets of the Hawaiian language to unlock the secrets of this powerful and mystical discipline.

Long was a much-respected psychic researcher. His student Brad Steiger chronicles Long's adventures on the way to understanding the magic of the Kahuna. By following Long's trek, the reader will learn how the Kahunas used their magic for both the benefit of their friends and the destruction of their enemies.

Central to the Huna beliefs was the thesis that each person has three selves. The Low Self is the emotive spirit, dealing in basic wants and needs. The Middle Self is the self operating at the everyday level. The High Self is the spiritual being that is in contact with every other High Self.

The subject matter of *Kahuna Magic* is contemporary and compelling. The book incorporates many of the concepts and concerns of the modern Western psychological tradition of Jung and Freud while bringing in subjects as diverse as Eastern philosophies and yoga in a manner that will help the readers understand themselves and those around them.

ISBN 0-914918-34-6
127 pages, 6½" × 9¼", paper $10.95

ASTRAL PROJECTION
Out-of-Body Experiences
in Other Worlds and Times
Brad Steiger

Parapsychological researchers have established that one of every one hundred persons has experienced out-of-body projection (OBE). These experiences are not limited to any single type of person, but rather they cross all typical boundaries.

In *Astral Projection,* Brad Steiger investigates the phenomena of OBE and correlates those events into broad categories for analysis and explanation. In his clear and non-sensational style, Steiger relates how these spontaneous experiences occur and when they are likely to re-occur. In addition to the standard and well-documented categories of spontaneous astral projection at times of stress, sleep, death and near death, Steiger devotes considerable time to the growing evidence for conscious out-of-body experiences, where the subject deliberately seeks to cast his or her spirit out of the physical shell.

Along with his study of astral projection, Steiger sets guidelines for astral travellers, tells them the dangers they may face and how this type of psychic experience might be used for medical diagnosis, therapy and self-knowledge.

ISBN 0-914918-36-2
250 pages, 6½" x 9¼", paper

$19.95